...nt
...it
seemed to take form from the shadow of the dense trees, like something in a dream, the leaves framing it.

It was a man, red-haired and laughing, or a horse, or a huge, red-eyed stag – or it was all three and yet none of those things at once; something out of nightmare, out of legend . . .

Rowan felt as though every part of her being had ceased to function. Her heart did not beat, her mind was locked, her muscles were immobilised . . . Her only emotion was undiluted, primeval terror . . .

CROWN OF HORN

Louise Cooper

Hamlyn Paperbacks

CROWN OF HORN
ISBN 0 600 202380

First published in Great Britain 1981
by Hamlyn Paperbacks

Hamlyn Paperbacks are published by
The Hamlyn Publishing Group Ltd,
Astronaut House, Hounslow Road,
Feltham, Middlesex
(Paperback Division: Hamlyn Paperbacks,
Banda House, Cambridge Grove,
Hammersmith, London W6 OLE)

Printed and bound in Great Britain by
Cox & Wyman Ltd, Reading

For Gary
from the Hawthorn to the Vine . . .
With all my love.

I would like to give grateful thanks and acknowledgement to Martin Carthy, musician and story-singer, for the inspiration of the title.

1

There was a faint, soft haze like woodsmoke over the land on the day old Maud Fairfax was laid to rest; the first hint that autumn was beginning to take its hold on Exmoor. In the little churchyard at Barton Tavey the mourners gathered under the slanting, mellow rays of the sun that picked out deepening tints of crimson and gold in the trees behind the squat Norman church.

It was a quiet, serene occasion, with perhaps some forty people at most filing into the creaking pews. Maud had had few close friends; she had kept herself to herself, living her unremarkable life and dying at a noble age, and most of the congregation were present simply because, in a small country village, a funeral was a funeral and something to be attended as a matter of course.

But Agnes Teale, who sat in the third row on the chancel side with her black hat, black coat and gloves and small, bird-bright eyes in an elderly face, perhaps more than anyone, had good cause to be here today; Maud had been her next-door neighbour and over the years the two women had struck up a friendship that Maud, at least, had found invaluable. In her last, declining months, when she had been barely able to do more than raise herself from a supine position in her bed, Agnes had been in almost constant attendance, preparing her meals, washing her frail body, listening patiently while Maud's vague conversation meandered through the patterns of her past. It had been a tedious time in many ways, but now that Maud was gone, Agnes would miss her. A widow herself, she had derived a surprising pleasure from what she considered her neighbourly duty. It had given her life a purpose, made her feel wanted and needed. Now she would return to her old anonymity, with little to occupy her beyond jam-making and the simple if uninspiring pleasures of village gossip.

Gossip was Agnes's forte. She was rarely malicious, but little ever happened in Barton Tavey that escaped her sharp eyes and ears. And now, as she sang the words of "Oh God Our Help" – Maud's favourite – that she knew by heart, she was surreptitiously glancing across the aisle to the front pew and the small, slight young woman who sat there alone.

A stranger. Agnes knew every local inhabitant, and this girl was new to her. She could not see her face now, but the glimpses she had had earlier had told her that there was a marked resemblance between the newcomer and old Maud. The girl had the same almost fragile cast of bone that had been the most distinguishing feature of Maud in her youth. Recalling the faded photographs that her neighbour had so often shown her, Agnes surmised that with a change of hairstyle this girl could almost be Maud's twin.

A relative, then. Probably her grand-daughter, although Maud had never mentioned her family; in fact they had been conspicuous by their absence from her life. Agnes's lips pursed with disapproval. All very well for the relations to start showing an interest when it was too late. No doubt the girl had come – or had been sent – to see what was going in the way of a legacy. She herself had tried to give Maud some useful advice about her will, but the old lady had been intractably secretive, saying that she would do what she would do and it was none of Agnes's business. Of course, she hadn't been quite right in the head during her last weeks, and gloomily Agnes faced the thought that she had probably left her possessions, lock, stock and barrel, to the family who had not even troubled to come near her while she lived.

The hymn ended with a last asthmatic chord from the ancient organ, and Agnes, along with the rest of the congregation, lowered herself to her knees for the final prayer. The girl knelt too, hurriedly and a little late, as if she was not familiar with church procedure, and as she bent her head over her folded arms Agnes saw her shoulders quiver slightly, suggesting that she was crying. Crocodile tears.

With a sudden warm feeling of self-righteousness, Agnes closed her eyes and gave her concentration to the service.

Agnes was not the only person in the church to take notice of the stranger. From his position in the pulpit, the Reverend Tom Rushford had the best possible view of the young woman. He too guessed that she was a relative, and wished that he had had the chance to speak to her before the service, to offer his condolences and make her feel at least a little at home. It must have been hard for her to arrive here alone and knowing no one, and to be thrown straight into the painful necessities of this occasion. He could see from the tense, strained lines of her pale face that she was not finding the experience easy. Perhaps afterwards something could be done.

The prayer concluded, he made a small motion towards the four pall-bearers who stood waiting. Solemnly they bent and lifted the oak coffin – Maud had insisted on oak – from its place before the altar, and as they straightened, the vicar stepped down from the pulpit and made his way to the aisle to lead the procession to the graveyard. This was always the most harrowing part for the relatives; it had that sense of irrevocable finality that could crack the hardest of hearts. Rushford saw the girl glance towards him uneasily, as if uncertain what she should do, and with a reassuring and sympathetic smile he signed to her to follow directly behind the pall-bearers. She moved awkwardly from her pew, looking small and lost as the only chief mourner, and slowly the procession began its march to the church door as a single bell in the tower started to toll on a deep, poignant note.

Tom Rushford felt a familiar sense of relief as he stepped back from the grave on which the first shovelfuls of rich, red earth were falling with a hollow thud. He had long ago reached the stage where he could remain unaffected by funerals – though he remembered, as a young and green curate, having to fight on many an occasion to keep back embarrassing tears – but he could not help the feeling that they were unnecessarily dismal. Still, his duty was done now, and he could look forward to getting home and spending a relaxing evening in front of the television.

There was just one more matter to resolve. The girl had stood by the grave throughout the "ashes to ashes" ceremony, her face immobile, the hair that was nearly as black as her coat blowing in a capricious breeze, apart from all the other mourners. And now, as people began to drift away from the grave, she still stood staring at the sexton with an odd, faraway look.

Rushford moved quietly towards her. 'Excuse me...'

She looked up, and immediately he saw that her eyes were a quite brilliant green, wide and unmade-up. Her lips parted, then she hesitated, as if wanting to speak but unable to think what to say.

'Miss – Fairfax, is it?' Rushford asked.

A slight smile. 'No, Vosper. Rowan Vosper. She was my maternal grandmother.' Her accent was well-schooled Home Counties.

'Ah, yes. May I offer my sympathies, Miss Vosper? I'm sorry I didn't have the opportunity to speak to you before the service.' He glanced over his shoulder at the grave. 'Mrs Fairfax was a charming and delightful lady. Her passing has been a very great loss to the whole village.' The usual words, and he hoped they sounded sincere.

Rowan Vosper nodded, lowering her head, he thought, to hide sudden tears. 'Yes, I – thank you.' She hesitated, then, 'I feel terrible about it all. I haven't seen her since I was seven, and now . . . I didn't even know it had happened, until her solicitor contacted me two days ago. My parents are both dead, and so I was the only one who could possibly represent the family. But,' she looked up again with a glance of startling frankness, 'I almost wish I hadn't come. I feel like an intruder, as though I have no right at all to be here.'

Rushford felt suddenly sorrier than ever for her. Certainly, for someone from up country, Barton Tavey was not the most welcoming of places. She must have seen the oblique looks, the nodding heads, the clandestine whisperings. Impulsively, hoping he was not being overly familiar, he reached out and laid a hand on her shoulder.

'My dear, I understand. It can't be easy for you. But I think Mrs Fairfax would be glad to know you came. Now,' he added, as the practical side of his pleasant nature took over, 'did you know that Agnes Teale, one of our parishioners, has prepared a small tea for those of us who were close to Mrs Fairfax?' He could have kicked himself; the statement might have been more tactfully phrased. Hurriedly he went on, 'I'm sure she will want you to go along. She and your grandmother were neighbours.'

The girl looked unhappy. 'Will you be going?' she asked.

'Certainly. So if you feel you need any moral support, you can count on me, Miss Vosper.'

For the first time, a real smile brightened her features. 'Thank you, Reverend—'

'Rushford, but everyone calls me either Tom or vicar.'

She nodded, 'Then if I can call you vicar, you must call me Rowan.'

Rushford began to feel that he was making progress. 'Rowan it is, then. Come along; I'll take you to Agnes's house. And when that particular ordeal's over, I insist that you come back to the vicarage for dinner with my wife and me.'

She smiled and said nothing. Together they walked towards the lych-gate.

For Rowan, the afternoon passed like a vague nightmare. She knew she would wake eventually, but Tom Rushford's joke about the ordeal was not so far from the truth. Agnes Teale made her welcome, but under the smiling surface she was aware of a current of resentment and none too charitable curiosity. She was made to walk the usual gauntlet of describing the flat she lived in in London, talking about her job as a furniture buyer with a department store – though there were aspects of that she carefully avoided – and to suffer in silence the subtle digs about her grandmother's loneliness in her last years. And when the tea and sherry had been drunk and the cakes eaten, there was the solicitor to contend with.

She had been forewarned that the will was to be read immediately after the funeral, but she was not prepared for that particular ritual to take place in Agnes's parlour, where a gaggle of village worthies drew up their chairs in a semi-circle to listen to the list of Maud's bequests. Rushford offered to stay for the reading, and she was grateful to him. And as the will was read out, she could feel the discomfort of a dozen pairs of eyes boring into her neck.

Maud's will was simple. To Agnes, her friend and companion, she left five hundred pounds, a bone china tea service and a pearl and amethyst brooch which Agnes had admired for years. To the church she left two hundred and fifty pounds, which, the lawyer said apologetically, about took care of her monetary assets. Everyone looked at Rowan then to see how she would react, and she knew that some at least were disappointed when she showed not the slightest sign of annoyance or chagrin. And then came the major bequest. The remainder of Maud's assets, namely her house and all the furnishings it contained, were to go to her only grandchild, Rowan Catherine Vosper, with the hope that she would use them well. That last phrase seemed to carry a sting in its tail; from what her mother had said about Maud, Rowan knew that the old lady had always resented the fact that her daughter had moved away from Somerset shortly after her marriage to Derek Vosper, and the implicit hint that Rowan should restore the balance by returning to the village to live in her grandmother's house was obvious.

Rowan took the news of the bequest with no outward reaction. Inwardly, she felt numbed. She could remember nothing of Maud's home – it was nearly twenty years since she had so much as set foot in Barton Tavey – and the glimpse she had had of it as she walked with Tom Rushford to Agnes's house had done nothing to revive her memory. To her, the house was nothing, an unfamiliar asset which had been thrust willy-nilly on her, and she could not decide whether she was glad, sorry or indifferent about it. Perhaps if other things had not been preying on her mind like a slow poison – but no, she mustn't wander down that pathway again, not until today was over.

The lawyer concluded the reading and stood up. Immediately, Agnes was on her feet offering him a glass of

Bristol Cream, and by degrees everyone began to relax a little. Rowan sat on her chair, hardly aware of the rising buzz of talk around her, until a hand on her shoulder made her look up.

'How are you feeling?' It was Tom Rushford.

She gave him an apologetic smile. 'I'm all right, thank you. Just a bit tired.'

'Then you'll come back with me and we'll make you comfortable. You have an appointment for dinner, remember?'

She knew he was doing his best to help, and that knowledge made her feel guilty. But she couldn't accept the invitation. Not tonight. Embarrassed, she shook her head. 'I'm sorry, vicar, but will you forgive me if I cry off this time? It's all been very exhausting, and I feel the need to be alone for a while.'

Rushford's face creased. 'Well, of course I won't try to press you if you'd rather not, but are you sure you'll be all right? Where are you staying?'

'I hadn't fixed anything up, but I thought – the house – if I'm allowed to go there yet.'

'Agnes has the keys, so I'm sure there'll be no problem there. But do you really feel . . .'

She interrupted him, knowing what he was going to say. 'Yes. I'd rather stay there than anywhere else. Hotels are so impersonal, and I think I'd be happier in Gran's home.'

A multitude of practical objections ran through Rushford's mind then – there would be no food in the house, no heating, perhaps no clean bedlinen – but with an effort he forced himself not to voice them. Rowan was obviously determined not to be persuaded away from her intention, and that had to be respected. Defeated, he sought out Agnes and had a quiet word with her about the keys.

Agnes's whole attitude towards Rowan had undergone a transformation. At first she had been suspicious and terse, resenting the arrival of this interloper who, she felt sure, would deprive her of what she saw as her fair share of Maud's legacy, a just reward for the care and attention she had lavished on the old lady. Now, five hundred pounds and some beautiful china and jewellery richer, she felt that justice had been done, and she could afford to take pity on Rowan. That house was a liability, and as for the furniture – it was old and battered stuff that should have gone to a junk shop long ago. She handed the keys over to the vicar and told him to let the poor girl know that if there was anything she needed, she only had to ask. Rushford passed the message on with secret amusement. Now that Agnes had discovered that she was not to be deprived of anything she wanted, she would probably prove as good a neighbour to Rowan as she had been to Maud.

And so Rowan left Agnes's house with the keys in her hand. The first signs of dusk were beginning to show. The air outside had a faint grey bloom to it, and as she walked back to the church where she had left her Mini she could hear the racket of starlings squabbling over roosting-places in the trees at the back of the graveyard. The leaves were turning, changing their colour, and she knew that within a few weeks the full glory of autumn would have replaced the green of summer. The thought sent a stab of pain through her. There was always something inescapably sad about autumn with its mist and its smoky colours and its sharpness that hinted of the more bitter cold to come. And this autumn would be the most terrible of her life; one which she did not know if she could find the strength to face. This autumn would be a season of might-have-beens.

The image of the church, now almost in silhouette as the dusk gathered, blurred before her eyes, and she felt a dampness on her cheeks. *Don't cry now*, she pleaded with herself, *not now*. It would have been better if these tears could have been for her grandmother, but she could not pretend that, even to herself. These were tears for a different kind of loss; in its way far more agonising than bereavement, because bereavement was final and irreversible, and this other loss might so easily have been averted. And because she might have been able to avert it, it had a terrible power to haunt her every moment. These were selfish tears, self-indulgent and pointless.

She almost blundered into the squat shape of her car. Fumbling awkwardly with the key, she unlocked it and slid into the driver's seat. A moment to collect herself and wipe her face dry with the back of her hand, then she shut the door, enclosing herself in the familiar cocoon of the Mini. This car was like a faithful friend to her; it was her passport, she sometimes felt, to sanity, her one way of escaping from herself and her surroundings by the simple act of driving.

The engine started with an irritable cough, as though the car were annoyed at being disturbed, and Rowan swung the wheels out on to the road and back towards her grandmother's house.

She had barely noticed the house before, but now, stopping the car at the gate and climbing out, it confronted her in all its reality.

It was larger than she had expected. Her grandmother, in her infrequent letters, had always referred to it as a cottage, but the term was far too modest. Stone built and detached, it stood in its own quite considerable plot of land, separated from Agnes Teale's home by a high stone wall and a fair distance, so that the usual idea of a next-door neighbour was at least misleading. And it was old, a good two hundred years old, Rowan guessed, if not more. The dusk, now fast turning to darkness, had bled all depth of colour from the surroundings, so that the stone walls appeared a ghostly moth-grey, the garden an indistinct and untended dark tangle.

Feeling an odd coldness settling on her, Rowan heaved her one suitcase out of the car and opened the front gate. It creaked back on its hinges and clicked hollowly behind her as she walked up the path and felt in her bag for the key to the front door. The door was heavy oak, set with two diamond-shaped panels of leaded glass, and was sheltered by a porch over which climbed a dense creeper, brittle and woody and in need of severe pruning. The door opened; a silent emptiness waited beyond it.

A switch on the right, Agnes Teale had said. Groping, Rowan found it and pressed it, and the hall sprang into startling brilliance as an overhead light came on. Oak panelling on the walls; a short passage with two doors leading off that led to what looked like the kitchen; and a flight of dark, uneven stairs curving round into the darkness of the upper floor. The hall was cluttered with bits and pieces of furniture that looked as though they had been intended to give it a welcoming touch. But even their untidy cheerfulness did nothing to lift the sense of empty loneliness that hung still and chilly in the air.

Rowan shivered, closing the front door behind her, and, setting down her case, went in search of the living-room. There were two reception rooms, and neither showed much sign of having been occupied for some time. Her grandmother had been bedridden for months before the end and no doubt the rooms were as she had left them – neat, tidy and filled with that same emptiness. The front room she disliked immediately: it felt stiff and unwelcoming. After a moment's glance she went quickly to the second room, which looked out over the walled garden at the back.

This room had the same uneasy air, but as soon as she switched on the light Rowan knew that this had at least better possibilities than the other. A vast stone fireplace dominated the room, but the log-basket was empty and a small electric fire stood incongruously on the hearth. Beams criss-crossed the low ceiling, and the single long window gaped on to the now charcoal blankness of the garden. Beside the fireplace a second door with a loose latch provided another way through to the kitchen and a savage draught was blowing in underneath it.

Rowan stood in the middle of the room, surveying it with mixed feelings. She remembered nothing of it from her childhood, but in a sense she was glad of that, as its newness captured her attention and took her mind off other things. If she could hold that mood for a while, it would be so much easier.

Then she shivered again, suddenly and violently, as a cold breath that was half real and half imaginary blew softly past her with a tiny whisper. The draught from the kitchen – but it had seemed like a premonition of something. Quickly she glanced round the room once more. Make it look a little more homely, she thought, then she could see about the rest of the house.

She closed the curtains – beige and pink with a pattern of roses – then switched on the electric fire and looked about for a way to change the harsh overhead lighting. There were two lamps at the far side of the room, both with rose-pink shades, and their soft glow did a lot to lift the forbidding atmosphere. It was still cold, but the fire would soon take the edge off that. She did not view the prospect of going upstairs, to the floor and the room where her grandmother had so recently died, with any pleasure, but it had to be done, and the sooner the better.

Reluctantly she left the comparative cosiness of the living-room and looked for a switch that would light the stairs. She found it, but the bulb had gone. With a sigh, Rowan lifted her case and began to carry it up the stairs. It was an effort; the stairs were steep and narrow and the edge of the case caught on each riser with a dull thud, but at last she gained the landing and stopped for breath.

The landing was as narrow as the stairs. At the far end an uncurtained window showed as a grey rectangle against the blackness, and there were four doors set at unequal intervals in the walls. Which bedroom had been the one?

She had set down her case, and now half-turned to pick it up once more. And in that split second when the light from the stairwell below caught her, she let out a cry of shock and fright as a shape leaped out of the shadows at her.

Her back slammed against the wall and she heard a loud thump as the suitcase fell on to its side. And then, as every inch of her flesh crawled with cold terror, she realised what it was that had menaced her.

A heavy, full-length mirror had been fixed to the wall in a small cranny of the landing. It was invisible from below – the small space where it hung was probably originally intended for a linen chest – but when she turned, the dim light from downstairs had shown her an unexpected and unprepared-for glimpse of her own reflection.

For a moment she stayed still, looking at the figure which stared back at her out of the glass. Her face was half in shadow, but the reflection was clear enough to show it was unhealthily thin and pale, the eyes looking over-large with their smudges of blue-grey exhaustion, the frame of near-black hair hanging loose and heavy over her shoulders, her body half-bent towards the fallen case. *God, what a mess*. In her black coat, which she hadn't yet taken off, she looked like some kind of Dickensian waif.

Rowan sighed, half in anger and half in resignation. One of the first things she would do would be to take down that mirror. Already it had made her feel uncomfortable and uneasy. She walked the length of the passage, opening all the doors and turning on all the lights inside the rooms, telling herself that she wasn't really nervous; it was simply a sensible precaution against tripping over anything on the gloomy landing. Shafts of brilliance streamed out into the corridor, and Rowan relaxed.

The first room she looked into was obviously her grandmother's. The bed was clinically neat, and a selection of bottles and other medical-looking items was arrayed neatly on a table. A portable television had been positioned so that anyone in the bed could see the screen, and the curtains were closed. Rowan shut the door on that room, feeling that as yet she would rather not face it, and went next to the door that was farthest away from it.

This was a guest room at the back of the house. It contained a largish bed, and the ceiling sloped down at one side to an incredibly small, low window at which she had to kneel if she wanted to look out. The furnishings reminded her of those small country hotels that are the backbone of the English tourist trade: a rickety wardrobe, a small kidney-shaped dressing table, one cane chair. All that was missing was a washbasin.

But for tonight at least, it would do. Heaving her case on to the counterpane of the bed, she clicked it open.

The photograph in its leather frame stared at her from the top of a hastily-packed pile of jumpers. A young man, his straight dark hair tousled and his eyes and mouth laughing, looking into the camera with an expression that could only be interpreted as love. And in the spring, when that picture had been taken, it *was* love.

'Oh, Neil!' The sound of her own voice broke the silence

and seemed also to break something inside her, something she had been fighting to hold back. Her body hunched suddenly and she put both hands over her face as the old, ugly pain with all its full power came flooding through her. The sense of loss, of helplessness, of frustration – of something which had seemed so perfect, yet which had been snatched away from her without any warning, leaving her clutching at air and asking over and again, *Why?*

A loss worse than bereavement; yes, when the thing lost was not beyond recall, when the loss had been not through fate or circumstance, but caprice. That was the worst loss of all, because it left room for hope. And that was something that worried and tore at the mind, dogged every footstep like a ghost and let the imagination make terrifying promises that would never be fulfilled. Even now, after three months, she couldn't give up, couldn't allow logic to take control over imagination. All she was left with were some photographs and a devastating list of 'if onlys'.

If only ... in three weeks from now she would have become Mrs Neil Grant. She would have left her single flat for a larger flat for two. She would have had a purpose, someone to live for, someone to accept all the love that was now locked up and shuttered inside her. If only. But Neil had written to her in June, and it was over. No reason. Just over.

The memory of those first few days was like a savage scar on her mind. Two years had been tossed aside, thrown out on the rubbish heap, and Neil had not even had the humanity or the courage to tell her why. Oh, she had tried – Rowan was a fighter, and did not lightly give up what she had gained. She had telephoned him, finally getting an answer on the third day. And Neil had treated her like a stranger, sounding as cold and distant as an Arctic winter, and when she had forgotten the last vestige of her pride and begged him to tell her what had gone wrong, he would not respond. Was it someone else, she had asked him, or was he simply afraid of marriage, of being tied? And he had been evasive. I can't talk to you. I don't want to talk to you. It's over, Rowan, that's all there is to it. *What have I done?* she had screamed at him. Oh, she hadn't done anything. Don't blame yourself, he had said. *For God's sake, let me see you, talk to you!* No. It wouldn't do any good. It would be better for her, he had said, to cut the links now, completely. And even as she cried out, '*You patronising bastard!*' as her self-control broke altogether, he had said goodbye and hung up. And when she tried to call back – fifteen times in an hour – the phone just kept on ringing.

After that, it had been worse. She had sat by the phone day in and day out, waiting for a call that never came. And at last she had called him again.

He answered this time, but as soon as he heard her voice that polar iciness returned to his tone. No, he didn't want to talk to her. No, he wouldn't see her. It was over. He didn't want to hear from her again, and if she rang back he would hang up.

In her blackest despair she had thought of suicide, but rejected the idea, not because there was anything else worth living for, but because there might be a small chance that Neil would come back. She went on hoping while her life fell to pieces around her. And then one morning one of her colleagues had found her sitting in the little cubicle that was her office, crying hysterically. They had called her doctor, who, being progressive, had made pronouncements about trauma and emotional strain, and prescribed tranquillisers and a sabbatical. Not really a nervous breakdown, and certainly nothing to suggest that she was mentally unbalanced – this sort of thing happened all the time. And when she had tearfully cleared out her desk and cried over the present her workmates had given her, Rowan knew that she would not be going back to the store. This was the end of another road.

And so she had spent the summer in a chemically-induced daze, still waiting for a call, never receiving one. She had sat alone for hours, with the one unanswerable question gnawing at her mind. *Why?* If Neil had had the decency to explain, she might have been able to accept it in the long run. But to be left bewildered, only knowing that she would never know, was the ultimate cruelty. She tried to hate Neil for that, but she couldn't manage it.

Sometimes she felt she really was going mad, as if the

swinging balance of hope and despair would finally tip her over the edge when she couldn't stand it any more. She desperately needed an escape, but could not find one. She still had her share of all the money she and Neil had saved towards their wedding, though now it felt like thirty pieces of silver, and so there was no incentive to find another job. And every man she met she found herself comparing to him, and they all fell short of perfection. All they did was make her more aware of what she had lost.

In a perverse way it had almost been a relief when Maud Fairfax's solicitors had contacted her and told her about the old lady's death. At least she had not only a reason but a duty to get out of London with its painful memories. And today, for a few hours, she had been able to put her thoughts of Neil aside, and for a while had felt stronger for it. It was like an incessant physical pain at last relieved by a dose of morphine. Driving down the M4 towards Somerset she had felt as if a constriction had been eased. Now, in a few seconds, it had all come back, as she had known it must. Maybe that was why she had packed the photograph. She could not escape from Neil, and some self-destructive instinct had made her take this reminder of him, as if to tell her that she had no right even to try.

She felt her body relaxing, growing calm as it had done so often after a bout of crying. But this time there were no tears; her throat and her eyes were dry, and there was only a dull, formless ache.

Her hand closed again over the photograph. She stood up and crossed to the dressing table, where she set the picture down so that it faced the bed. She couldn't escape him because she still didn't want to. And as long as she felt that way, as long as she refused to face and accept the truth, then life, however painful, seemed worth continuing.

2

Strangely, although she had dreaded spending a night alone in her grandmother's house, Rowan found that when it came to bedtime she had no qualms at all – in fact, the opposite. She had spent the evening in a slightly disturbing blend of restlessness and lethargy, alternating between curling herself up in an armchair in the living-room and prowling about the silent house when sitting and thinking grew dangerously uncomfortable. But in the space of those few hours it seemed that the house had in its own way reached out to her, enveloping her with the quiet, subtle atmosphere which was uniquely its own, and which, without realising it consciously, she found comforting. As the hands of her watch crept round towards eleven she slipped into a kind of melancholy peacefulness and exhaustion. London and all that London implied were a hundred and fifty miles away and had no place here. This was another world, and she had the feeling that this world was trying to be her friend. She was grateful for the respite.

By eleven-fifteen she was climbing in between the fresh, cold sheets of the bed in the little back room. Probably she should have aired the linen, but she was too tired to worry about it.

Now and again, during the evening, it had crossed her mind that she would have to start making some decisions before long. The house and all it contained were hers – but did she want to settle here, as her grandmother's will had implied she should, or would she sell up and put the money to some other use? She wasn't sure if she wanted to return to London, and yet, despite all that had happened, London was home. Could she resign herself to life in this small, isolated community where time seemed to have slowed to a crawl and she would have little to do but spend her days gardening and brooding?

It wasn't a subject she wanted to dwell on as yet. Perhaps, she thought, she would spend a few days here getting acclimatised, get the feel of the area, see how strongly it appealed. And in the meantime she would write to Neil, just a brief, polite note to let him know that she was in Somerset for a while.

She bit her lip. That would be a futile exercise; he wouldn't want to get in touch. But she would write anyway.

Realising that she was on the dangerous edge of tears, she turned over, away from the photograph that stood on the dressing table, and switched off the bedside light. The room plunged into a depth of blackness that startled her momentarily; total darkness was something she had only rarely known, but of course here there were no bright streetlamps, no headlights of cars going by at all hours, no all-pervading city glow. And the intensity of the night was very far from unpleasant.

She was asleep within five minutes.

Rowan's new-found sense of well-being was too good to last. In the small hours the nightmares began.

She dreamed about Neil, a Neil who laughed at her and mocked her distress when she tried to reason with him. Neil running away from her, so that when she tried to catch up with him her legs turned to lead and every step was an agonising effort. Neil with another woman, seducing her before Rowan's eyes, and always laughing, laughing. And then abruptly the dream changed. She had been pursuing Neil, aware only of the pain that throbbed through every muscle of her body, unable to draw any closer to his distant, fleeting figure, until with a shock she rounded a corner that had not been there a moment before, and saw him clearly.

He was standing in the middle of a wide, windswept field (yet surely, her confused mind protested, she had been running through a city?) under the bare, bone-white branches of a dead tree that rose up from the field's ploughed red earth. Rowan stopped running, but still she seemed to move, almost swimming through the air as though propelled by an invisible force she couldn't control. Neil watched her, expressionless. She was moving closer to him, closer –

Suddenly he vanished, and Rowan was alone in the field.

The sky turned from indeterminate grey to blue-black, and the branches of the dead tree were thrown into chillingly stark relief against the darkness. There was something threatening and yet compelling about that great, motionless shape; she didn't want to approach it, but she had to. Slowly she began to move again, this time under her own motive power. The tree filled her vision, towering over her. And then with a violence that made her scream aloud, a single bolt of white lightning split the sky directly overhead, and the tree gave voice to a terrible groan as it slewed over and began to fall inexorably towards her –

She woke with a violent spasm, the echoes of her scream still reverberating in the room. Suffocating darkness filled her nostrils and mouth; the blankets were tangled round her like a strait-jacket, and in the first few seconds of near-panic she only succeeded in enmeshing herself further in their folds. With a vast effort she took a grip on herself and reached out a shaking hand to grope for the lamp. It came on, soft and comfortingly bright, and Rowan lay back, attempting to quell the painful pounding of her heart. *God, what a hideous dream! Whatever would a psychiatrist have made of that?* She was trying to laugh at that thought, trying to bring back some semblance of normality and reason, when she thought she heard a sound outside, in the far distance. Instantly she raised her head from the pillow. The wind had heightened and was prowling fitfully and gustily around the house, rattling the window-pane and sneaking in through a crack in the frame to set the curtains shivering. There was something primeval about the sound of that wind, and Rowan shuddered under her blankets. But it wasn't the wind that had disturbed her.

The sound came again, from far off, seemingly over the hills. It was the eerie baying of dogs, carried on the wind like the cries of a pack of banshees.

Something in Rowan's Celtic ancestry stirred then, stabbing her with a primitive fear that centuries of civilisation couldn't wipe out. Fighting with herself, she argued that she was being stupid – baying dogs were baying dogs, and this was hunting country – the local pack was probably stabled, or whatever one did with foxhounds, somewhere in the area, and their noise was as much a part of country life as a cockerel crowing. But however rational the explanation might be, that unearthly noise was disconcerting, and if it was something that happened every night, she knew that she would have a lot of trouble getting used to it.

For a few more minutes she lay tensely listening, but whatever had disturbed the dogs seemed to have passed, for there was no more baying. Eventually she judged it safe to go back to sleep without fear of further disturbance. But for the rest of that night, the bedside lamp stayed on.

Rowan woke at eight. It was her normal time, but to her surprise she found that she had none of her usual unwillingness to get up once her eyes had opened. In London that had been a matter of necessity if she were to be on time for work, though all her instincts had urged her to stay in bed longer, to go back to sleep. But now she climbed out of bed as if there were something worth getting up for. It must be the invigorating country air, she thought while she dressed – hastily, as the room was very cold – and went downstairs.

Was she imagining things, or had a subtle change taken place in the house since her arrival yesterday? Reaching the foot of the stairs, she paused, certain that something was different, although she could not pinpoint it. After the funeral, the house had discomfited her. On the surface it had seemed welcoming enough, but she had felt that the welcome was merely a veneer, a false mask that had only barely hidden a sense of wariness. The house had been suspicious of her. Now it was as if the house, or perhaps the spirit of the house (she laughed at herself for the fancy, but the laughter was tinged with uncertainty), had accepted her and made her a part of itself.

As if in answer, she thought she felt a brief and incredibly faint breath of cool air brush past her face. Her skin tingled; it had been like the breath that had passed her last night in the living-room, something almost tangible yet too vague and formless to be truly real. But this time there was something else; a scent that lingered when the breath had gone, subtle, sweet and a little heady.

Roses. Their perfume was always unmistakable. But how . . . ?

She thought perhaps it was best not to attempt to answer that question. The chances were she had imagined it; certainly it had faded now, although the memory of it was still strong, like an after-image.

Quickly Rowan went into the living-room.

The room was gloomy and filled with a chill that carried more than a hint of damp. She switched on the electric fire and, as the bar began to glow, opened the curtains to see what kind of a day she had awoken to.

The window looked out on to the rear garden, which was a tangle of overgrown grass, shrubs and dying flowers, untended now for months. Huge hollyhocks were going to seed alongside rioting honeysuckle and fading, overblown roses, and in places the grass was almost as tall as the bushes. It looked depressing and a little eerie. Beyond the wall that marked the garden boundary, she could see the rising hump of distant, golden-brown hills as the land lifted itself out of the valley in which Barton Tavey nestled, towards the wild and windswept reaches of Exmoor.

Rowan had been surprised yesterday by her first view of Exmoor as she had driven towards the village. Childhood memories deserting her, she had envisaged a flat, bleak landscape broken only by the occasional tor or marshy pool, and instead had encountered a breathtaking vista of vast, rolling hills that plunged with dizzying suddenness into deep, narrow valleys, the steep slopes thick with great tracts of forest. A proud land, untameable and uncompromising, a land that seemed to say, *respect me or perish*. There was something menacing about the hills that enshrouded Barton Tavey, closing in the skyline and dominating the village like protective but demanding overlords. Looking at them now, their lower reaches still half-hidden in white mist that the sun had not yet melted away, Rowan began to realise that for the people who lived in its embrace Exmoor was a hard if beautiful taskmaster.

Turning from the window, she went through the latched connecting door to the kitchen. It was a peculiar but not altogether unpleasant blend of the old and the new. A gleaming electric cooker stood incongruously side by side with a far older and very imposing black range, and she guessed that in her latter years her grandmother had found the upkeep of the range too much for her failing energy. The sink was old enamel with a stainless steel draining board, and under that was a fridge which had seen better days. No washing machine. The rest of the space was taken up by cupboards, topped with a huge slab of marble which served as a working top and which now, Rowan knew, was worth a small fortune, and by a vast walk-in pantry lined with shelves.

The sight of the pantry reminded Rowan that she was hungry. She had not felt like eating last night, and now the pangs were gnawing insistently at her. But the pantry was virtually empty, containing only a large stone jar of flour, several packets of dried fruit, some tea, a jar of instant coffee and a packet of brown sugar. Well, coffee would be better than nothing. She checked the fridge, and found it still switched on. No milk though, and not so much as a single egg. So, black coffee it would have to be, until she could go shopping. A pity she hadn't thought to bring a few things with her when she left London, but then she had been in such a state that it was a miracle she had remembered to pack a case at all.

She filled the electric kettle which she found on the worktop, and plugged it in. As it began to hiss contentedly to itself, the front doorbell rang.

Visitors, at eight-thirty? Curious, Rowan left the kitchen and hurried down the hall to open the door. A gust of cool and incredibly fresh air blew in, bringing with it the smell of damp leaves and mist, and she saw Agnes Teale standing on the doorstep.

Agnes was holding a basket before her ample middle (which was swathed in the folds of a brightly-printed overall) and, seeing that Rowan was dressed, she gave a little nod of approval.

'I thought you'd likely be up,' she said.

'Yes, please come in.' Rowan stood back to let her pass, and closed the door again. 'I was just making some coffee. Can I offer you some?'

Agnes looked round the hall as though seeking for any changes that might have taken place in the last twenty-four hours. Then her small, bright eyes came back to Rowan. 'I'll have tea, if it's all the same. A bag'll do; no need to make a pot special.'

'Ah yes, of course, but I'm afraid there isn't any milk. I haven't had time yet to – '

Agnes interrupted her with the kind of smile that suggested some private theory had been vindicated. 'No, you must have been in a proper flurry what with the funeral and the will and all. I thought likely as not you'd not have anything in, so I took the liberty of ordering you a couple of pints from George this morning. And a loaf of bread and some eggs.' She brandished the basket.

Rowan's face broke into a warm smile. 'Oh Agnes, how kind of you!'

'And I brought a pot of my own jam. Blackcurrant. There was a glut of them this summer, so I'd got plenty left over.'

'You shouldn't, really – '

Agnes huffed. 'No point being neighbours if you can't be neighbourly, is there?'

'Well, thank you. Thank you very much. What do I owe you?'

Agnes was not a believer in unnecessary social graces; with her there was none of the polite *no-really-don't-mention-it* that often accompanies a favour done. She said immediately, 'Ninety-three pence, that came to.'

'My purse is in the living-room. If you'd like to . . . ' She led the way and Agnes followed eagerly. Her eyes missed nothing, and as soon as she saw the electric fire glowing at full power she shook her head.

'Terrible expensive things they are, if you leave them on. Eat the money right out of your pocket before you know where you are. If I was you, I'd see about getting that fire going now winter's coming on.'

Rowan reminded herself that Agnes wasn't being rude; it

was simply her way to be direct, albeit that it was none of her business how Rowan chose to heat her own house. And anyway, she had a point.

'There's logs outside the back door what Ben Wright brought over from Oare way last month,' Agnes went on, without any attempt to explain who Ben Wright might be or where Oare was. 'All chopped up and ready. Providing they haven't got too damp, you only need to set them and light them. Apple wood, too – best for burning, if you're not used to it.' She paused, looking at Rowan sideways. 'Suppose you don't have fires like these any more up London.'

'No.' Rowan smiled at the implicit disapproval. 'No, we don't.' She headed towards the door. 'Would you like to come through to the kitchen? The kettle must be boiling by now.'

It was; clouds of steam were billowing from the spout and turning the kitchen into a sauna. Waving a hand to clear the fog, Rowan set about making tea, and as she worked she realised suddenly that she was almost enjoying herself. This bucolic domesticity, making breakfast and chatting idly to a neighbour, was a side of life that was new to her, and though she foresaw that the novelty would soon wear off, it had a certain mind-calming appeal. She decided to break with her habit of long years and have tea herself.

Agnes produced the purchases she had brought from her basket. If Rowan had expected wholesome brown bread still warm from the oven, she was disappointed; some of the habits from 'up London' had clearly filtered down here, for Agnes's idea of a proper loaf was sliced, bleached white and wrapped in plastic. But the jam was all she could have hoped for, and she spread it generously on two slices of bread.

Agnes was appraising the kitchen now, although it was difficult to tell quite what the mind behind the comfortable face and over-bright eyes was thinking. At last she said, 'Maud couldn't manage the range, of course, not in the last couple of years. I kept telling her, why don't you get the thing taken out and have all that extra space, but she wouldn't listen. Still, at least she got a nice clean electric.' Her glance darted from the cooker to Rowan. 'I expect you'll be having that old thing taken away now, though? Make the house all modern?'

Not quite sure what she was implying, Rowan said hesitantly, 'I haven't really thought about it yet. But I'll probably leave the range, if I can work out how to use it, at least while I'm here.'

Agnes sniffed. 'More trouble than it's worth, if you want my opinion. Dirty, messy thing. But then that was Maud all over – she never could bring herself to throw anything away. Look at the furniture she filled the house with – all old and worn out, and full of woodworm. I kept telling her, why didn't she get in some new bits and pieces the way I did after my Charlie died? But no, not her. It wasn't as if she couldn't afford it, but no, she wouldn't change a stick.'

Rowan poured tea from the big china pot, aware of a sudden quickening of interest. 'Do you think much of the furniture's old, then?' she asked. Last night she had not been in the mood to look too closely, and this morning it had not crossed her mind.

'Old?' said Agnes. 'Most of it was old before Maud was even born!'

'You see, I'm in that line of business myself,' Rowan told her, 'Or rather, I was. Maybe I should look it over.'

The birdlike eyes glinted sharply. 'Do you think it might be valuable?' Agnes demanded.

'I don't know. Probably not, but you never can tell.' She picked up the tray on which she had set cups, milk, sugar and the teapot. 'Shall we go back to the living-room? It's probably warmer, and I can give you the money for the supplies.'

Agnes trailed after her, and as soon as Rowan set the tray down, she pointedly picked up the teapot and placed it carefully near the electric fire to keep warm. Then, settling herself into the nearest armchair, she seemed suddenly to remember that the social graces which *were* necessary had been neglected.

'Well,' she said, 'and how was your first night here? Did you sleep well?'

'Yes,' Rowan said. 'That is, quite well.'

Agnes watched her over the rim of her cup. 'Nothing to disturb you?'

What was she getting at? Rowan frowned. 'What sort of thing?'

A thin chuckle escaped Agnes's lips. 'Oh, you wouldn't be bothered by superstitious notions, would you? But I don't suppose you slept in old Maud's bedroom?'

'No, I didn't.' Rowan allowed herself to smile as she realised that Agnes was attempting to make a little joke. 'I had enough on my mind, to be honest, without worrying about ghosts too.'

'Of course you did. And anyway, if you want my opinion, people who believe in ghosts want their heads looking at. But it does make some uncomfortable, I know, sleeping alone in a place where there's just recently been a death. I remember when my Charlie died – '

'Agnes,' Rowan interrupted her almost without realising it. 'Agnes, there was one thing – '

'What was that, dear?' Instantly Agnes was all ears and Charlie was forgotten.

'I woke during the night – I'd been dreaming – and I heard dogs baying.'

'Dogs . . . ? ' The brisk tone of Agnes's voice dropped suddenly and she frowned, but quickly forced her expression to clear. 'In the middle of the night?'

'Yes. It sounded like a whole pack of them. It really scared me when I first heard it.'

'You must have dreamed it, dear. Dogs don't bark in the middle of the night.' But despite her comfortable words, Rowan could tell that Agnes had lost some of her composure. The old woman was uneasy.

She pressed her point. 'I wasn't dreaming, I was wide awake. And they weren't barking, they were *baying*. I thought – are there foxhounds kept anywhere in the village?'

Agnes shook her head. 'The nearest hunt pack belongs to the Major over towards Brendon, and that's a good two mile.' Her eyes met Rowan's again, and the girl thought she detected a trace of fear in their expression. 'Mind, the wind was very strong last night. Could be that they were barking over something and the wind carried it here. Yes, that must have been what you heard. The Major's hounds.' Relaxing, she folded her hands on her lap and added in a tone of voice that closed the matter, 'Couldn't have been anything else, could it now?'

Rowan murmured agreement. But she was not convinced. She had been quite happy with her foxhounds theory until now, but Agnes had unwittingly set doubts in her mind. Something in what she said had upset the old woman and frightened her. Still, there was no point in pressing Agnes further. Rowan knew she would cling to the idea that the noise had been nothing more sinister than the Major's dogs, whatever she might privately believe.

The morning had suddenly turned sour. Reaching for the teapot, Rowan refilled the two cups.

Within an hour, however, Rowan's unease had been eclipsed by a new discovery. Encouraged by Agnes, who was in no hurry to leave and whose curiosity had been thoroughly aroused by the hints about possible value, she decided to take a cursory look at some of the furniture in the house.

The room in which they were sitting yielded nothing of real worth, barring a couple of late Victorian pieces which, had they been in better condition, might have been minor collectors' items. That was not surprising – with her trained eye Rowan would have recognised anything of value when she had first set foot in the room. But when, with Agnes at her heels, she went into the large, cold front room, which she had only glanced at on her arrival, she had a surprise that stunned her.

It was incredible. How her grandmother had come by them she could not begin to guess; perhaps they had been in her family for generations. But the four dining chairs which had been casually pushed into a corner were undoubtedly Regency, the huge, forbidding bookcase of dark mahogony could not be later than 1830 and, though her knowledge of that period was a little hazy, she knew that the vast, heavily carved oak chest that stood to one side of the room dated from the seventeenth century – probably Cromwellian.

But it was the small *escritoire*, pushed sadly and unobtrusively into a dusty corner, that provided the most breathtaking surprise of all. It was in such a bad state that for a few moments Rowan did not recognise it for what it was. The wood was scratched and battered, the leather covering the hinged lid of the writing table badly worn, and at one time someone had made a ham-fisted attempt to varnish it, resulting in unsightly discolouration. But there was no mistaking it. This was a genuine writing desk of the Queen Anne period.

Rowan stood staring at the *escritoire*, much as a Crusader might have viewed his first glimpse of Jerusalem. Behind her, Agnes's head bobbed as she looked from the desk to the girl and back to the desk again.

'Is it valuable?'

That varnishing – it was little short of an act of sacrilege, but it could surely be remedied. A lot of renovation would be needed, but –

'Yes,' Rowan said, her voice sounding a little bemused. 'It's valuable.'

'Well, now!' Agnes moved round her to get a better look, and her mouth pursed. 'You'd never think so, would you, what with the state it's in and all. All those scratches. But then I suppose you know what you're talking about, being in the business. Seems funny to me, what people'll put value on these days. It's very old, then?'

'Oh, yes. About two hundred and fifty years.'

'Well! Who'd have thought it? If I'd had my way, it would have gone for firewood long ago. Not that it would have burned very well, by the look of it.'

Rowan winced inwardly at the idea of such vandalism, then turned her attention to the *escritoire* again. 'It needs a lot of work done on it,' she said. 'That's going to be the problem. I'll need to find a good renovator.'

'Someone who puts old antiques to rights, you mean?' Agnes asked.

'Yes. Why, do you – '

She was interrupted. 'In that case, you'd better pay a call on young Mal Lyndon.'

'Mal Lyndon?'

'That's right. Young fellow, lives at the other end of the village. He does that sort of thing for a living. Got a proper workshop and all, though goodness knows how he manages to keep body and soul together. I wouldn't have thought there's much call for that kind of work round here.'

Rowan could hardly believe what she had heard. It was just too much of a coincidence that a restorer should be working here, in Barton Tavey, and she felt the stirrings of a professional excitement within her.

'Agnes, that's marvellous! Where exactly can I find him?'

Agnes looked pleased; she was rapidly making herself indispensable, she believed, and that was how she liked it.

'Like I said, he's at the other end of the village. Take the right fork past the post office, towards the coast road. It's called Coombe Cottage.' She sniffed. 'Used to be a pretty little place, but he's turned it all upside down till you can't tell house from workshop, and don't ask me where he does his cooking and sleeping in all that mess. But that's men for you. A woman's touch, that's what Coombe Cottage needs.'

If that was an unsubtle hint that Rowan might have other reasons than business for making Mal Lyndon's acquaintance, it cut no ice. For a moment a painful anger flared in Rowan's eyes, then it quieted as she realised that Agnes had meant no spite. How could she? She knew nothing of Rowan's recent past, and could not be blamed for her tactless but doubtlessly well-intentioned remark.

'Well, I'll certainly go and talk to him. Thank you, Agnes. Thank you very much.'

It soon became clear to Agnes that in the wake of the morning's discoveries Rowan was in no mood to spend any more time over chit-chat, and when the debt of the milk and bread had been settled she took her leave.

Rowan saw her out with mixed feelings. There was no doubting the fact that Agnes would prove to be a very good neighbour in the traditional sense, but she was already beginning to find her comfortable, gossiping curiosity a little overbearing. She would have to handle the old woman with kid gloves, keeping her at a distance without antagonising her, if that was possible.

But Agnes's visit had been a blessing in one sense, as she realised when she had closed the front door and retreated to the living-room. It had got her through what could otherwise have been the most difficult hour of the day – the time when, having just got up and finding nothing yet to do, she would have been at her most vulnerable had she been alone.

She emptied the teapot and put the cups in the sink. Despite Agnes's thoughtfulness, there were still a lot of basic things she needed, if she were to stay here even for a few days. She could not recall having seen a grocery or general store in the village, but there must be one. Perhaps she should go now, while the thought was still fresh in her mind. And on the way, she could find Mal Lyndon's workshop.

The morning air was like a draught of some magnificent wine as she stepped out of the front door and closed it behind her. There was an autumnal sharpness to the atmosphere that was far more noticeable in the country than in the enclosed and heated air of London, but it was a pleasant, invigorating sharpness, not truly cold. Rowan decided to walk on her errand; Barton Tavey was so small that she doubted if Coombe Cottage could be more than half a mile away, and her car tended to be troublesome if she used it for very short journeys. She turned out of the front gate and started to walk briskly in the direction of the high street.

There were a number of people about in the village, all strangers, but most nodded to her and murmured a 'good morning'. As she passed she could almost physically feel the eyes watching her back, speculating. The chances were most of them already knew who she was and why she had come; even without Agnes to do her part Rowan guessed that the Barton Tavey grapevine was extremely efficient. She was an object of curiosity. But the greetings were all pleasant enough in a reserved way.

There *was* a grocery shop, and the blurred voices of gossiping women filtered out through the open door.

Rowan walked on, making a mental note to buy what she needed on her way home, and, remembering Agnes's directions, headed for Coombe Cottage. She passed the turning that led to the church, and could see the little spire rising out of a clump of trees. The sight of it brought a pang of remembrance, but she realised with more than a trace of guilt that the pang was dutiful rather than genuinely emotional. Still, it could make little difference to her grandmother now.

A little further on there was the village green, looking as though it had remained unchanged for five centuries or more. It even boasted a pond, bounded on one side by a low rail, and Rowan stopped for a few moments to watch two pairs of ducks which sailed on the water's surface in lazy circles.

Opposite the green, as she had known there must be, was a pub. It was built from the same stone as her grandmother's house, and probably dated from the same period. The sign that hung outside, swinging slightly in the gusty breeze, proclaimed its name as the 'Oak and Ash'. The name intrigued her; it was one she had not come across before. In a place like this, its heritage divided between farming and the sea, she might have expected Ships, Anchors, Ploughs and Harrows and suchlike. But the Oak and Ash – it was unusual; possibly even unique. She wondered idly how it had come by the name, then, with a shrug, dismissed her curiosity and walked on.

Beyond the pub the road forked and as instructed Rowan turned right. An RAC signpost at the junction read 'COAST ROAD – UNSUITABLE FOR HEAVY VEHICLES', and as she walked in that direction she fancied that she caught the distinctive smell of brine mingled with the woodier scents of the country.

The road began to climb, buildings giving way almost immediately to a high stone hedge topped with a tangle of bushes and small trees. Towards the north-west, where the land gave way to the sea, the sky was washed and almost colourless, with that slightly unnerving openness peculiar to the coast and Rowan felt a sudden urge to take her car and drive to the nearest accessible beach, simply for the pleasure of savouring that openness. Despite her urban upbringing, she loved the country and the sea, but at the same time it always made her feel a little uncomfortable. So much raw nature played on her sense of vulnerability, recalling some deep-rooted racial memory from the world of her distant ancestors, when life must have been a constant battle against often hostile elements. But perhaps, she told herself, that was what she needed right now - a total contrast to the safe, cosy and self-indulgent environment she was used to.

She was wondering just how long it would take her to acclimatise to these new surroundings with their unfamiliar demands, when she came on Coombe Cottage. It was suddenly visible as she came round a sharp curve in the road, standing out against its background of trees and isolated among them.

Rowan stopped, forgetting her other considerations as she appraised the house. It stood at the far side of a small piece of rough ground that most people would have turned into an attractive garden, and flanking it were a couple of low stone outhouses which had probably originally been byres. A large ginger cat with a tail like a fox's brush was walking slowly across the yard on some laconic errand, and from inside the house came the sound of a radio playing.

Rowan crossed the yard, smiling at the cat, which turned briefly to regard her with unfathomable amber eyes. Finding no bell at the front door, she raised the black knocker and rapped loudly. After a few seconds the noise from the radio died abruptly, and she heard footsteps on the other side of the door.

Mal Lyndon was not dressed for visitors, and there were smudges of woodstain on his hands, crumpled shirt and old jeans, but apart from that his appearance was a more than pleasant surprise. Rowan had half-expected some unprepossessing country yokel with a potato face and a thoroughly bucolic air. Instead, she was confronted by a man of around thirty, of medium height and a little under average weight, with untidy light brown hair that was tinged with Celtic redness and eyes that were startlingly and incongruously dark. Despite her present antipathy to men in general, Rowan had to allow that he was good-looking.

He gave her a quick but quite brilliant smile. 'Good morning.'

'Good morning; I – ' Rowan sought for the right words; his unexpected appearance and manner had put her off her stride. Swiftly she collected herself. 'I hope I've come to the right place – are you Mal Lyndon?'

'Certainly. And you're – ' he let the question hang unfinished.

She held out a hand, wanting to be formal and business-like. 'Rowan Vosper. You won't know of me, but I'm Maud Fairfax's grand-daughter.'

'Oh,' Mal's expression changed as he shook hands. 'Mrs Fairfax, of course. I was – sorry to hear about her death.'

'Thanks.' Rowan looked away, wishing that people didn't feel obliged to offer these awkward condolences. 'It seems I've inherited her house – I'm staying up there at the moment, and what I wanted to see you about was – '

He interrupted her at that point. 'And here am I being rude and keeping you on the doorstep! Come in – I can at least offer you a cup of tea if nothing else.' He stood back to let her pass, and she stepped into a large, light room. It was carelessly furnished, as if he had thrown together no more than the necessary basics without any thought for appearances, but it had an indisputably comfortable air. In the middle of the floor, standing on spread newspaper, was a large mahogany table which Rowan recognised as late Victorian.

'I'm sorry I forgot my manners,' Mal said with another smile, 'but I'm always a little bit cautious about strangers at first. They usually want to sell me something, or convert me to some cranky religion.'

Rowan was looking at the table, not really listening to him. 'That's about 1890, isn't it?' she asked.

His face became more animated. 'You know about antique furniture?'

'Well, yes – I was in that business for a few years, as a buyer for a London store. In fact that's why I'm here.' And she told him about the discoveries she had made in her grandmother's house: the Regency chairs, the bookcase and, in particular, the *escritoire*. Mal listened intently as she talked, and when she finished by asking him if he was interested in carrying out the renovation work, his face lit up.

'I'd relish it! Ye gods, I've been wanting to get my hands on something like that writing-desk for years! This really is incredible. I had no idea there was a secret treasure trove in Barton Tavey.'

'You didn't know my grandmother?' Rowan asked, surprised.

'I knew her to speak to in the street, but that was about all. I suppose living here I'm a little out of the centre of things, and I tend to be a solitary cuss anyway. Now look, are you quite sure that you want me to do this work? I don't want to talk myself out of a job, but if you've got London contacts you may want to find someone with more sophisticated facilities.' He hesitated, and Rowan smiled.

'No, I don't think so. I don't actually have any contacts in the renovation field and, anyway, by the look of that table you're more than professional enough for me.'

He looked relieved, and Rowan couldn't help being amused. London was still tarred with the brush of mystique to a lot of country people, and Mal was a countryman, she could tell, despite the fact that his voice had only the smallest trace of a West Country accent. It was a pity, she thought, that non-Londoners didn't have a more accurate impression. As far as she was concerned, the capital was overrated.

Mal moved towards a door through which Rowan could see the kitchen. 'I'll make some tea. And don't say "not if it's any trouble," because it isn't. Then we can – '

'No.' Rowan's voice was sharp; she forestalled him without knowing precisely why. All she knew was that at this moment she didn't want to stay, perhaps because she didn't want to get involved in anything beyond the strict run of business. Mal Lyndon was so confident, so self-possessed, so friendly – and that from a strange man was something she felt unable to cope with. It would be easier, and safer, to escape back to the solitude of her house.

'I can't stay, I'm afraid,' she told him. 'I've got a lot of things to do – this was only a sounding-out visit, you see, and, well, I must get back.'

'Of course, I understand.' His gentle smile suggested that he understood all too well. 'So, what shall we do about the furniture? If it's not too soon for you, I could come round this afternoon to take a look at it.'

She had no reason to veto that. 'Fine,' she said. 'Call in when you're ready. I'll be there for the rest of the day.' She was moving towards the front door as she spoke. 'Do you know the house?'

'I know it.' He crossed the room to open the door for her. 'Oh, by the way, just out of curiosity, who was it who put you in touch with me? Could I make an educated guess and say Agnes Teale?'

Rowan grinned suddenly. 'You could.'

He laughed. 'Our mobile information centre! I'll have to buy her a box of chocolates. Well, I'll see you this afternoon. Goodbye, Rowan.'

He watched her as she crossed the yard and turned into the lane. And Rowan only felt comfortable when Coombe Cottage was out of sight.

3

For Rowan, the day went by surprisingly quickly. Contrary to her expectations, she had found a lot to occupy her, from the shopping, which took longer than anticipated because of the grocer's eagerness to get to know this new face in the village, to generally familiarising herself with the house.

In an odd way the house was beginning to have quite a profound effect on her. After only twenty-four hours she was already looking on it as *hers*, not merely a capital asset but a home in the true sense. It was something she could hold to, something stable and secure and enduring that would not dissolve overnight and leave her wanting. She could rely on the house, on its permanency and loyalty. And, whether she was willing to admit it or not, that was something Rowan desperately needed.

She realised, when she unpacked her heavy carrier bags and stacked their contents away in the larder, that she had bought enough supplies to withstand a siege. She hadn't yet thought about how long she intended to stay in Barton Tavey, but it seemed her subconscious had made the decision for her. She would not be returning to London for some while yet. With the unpacking completed, she recalled Agnes's advice about the fire. The day was turning cold, and the idea of a log fire to replace the inadequate little electric appealed.

She unlocked the door that led to the back garden. There, neatly stacked, was a large pile of applewood logs, slightly darkened with damp but probably usable all the same. Rowan bent to gather an armful – and paused. Just for one brief moment she had had the distinct feeling that someone was watching her from the garden. Her spine tingled warningly, and slowly she raised her head.

Nothing. The untended ground with its sprouting grass and gone-to-seed flowers was innocent and still. The feeling passed – though for that fleeting second it had been as strong as a physical presence.

Imagination, Rowan decided. It happened often enough, like the voices that sometimes seemed to speak out of thin air when one was on the verge of sleep. That kind of phenomenon had always unnerved her, as it straddled the very thin dividing line between illusion and reality. But it was no more than a trick of the senses.

Nevertheless, as she picked up an armful of logs and turned back into the kitchen, she could not stop herself from glancing quickly over her shoulder, just to be certain. And when she closed the back door behind herself, she carefully bolted it again.

When Mal rang the front doorbell of the house a little after four o'clock, Rowan was on her knees, trying unsuccessfully to persuade the recalcitrant logs to catch light. Hearing the bell, she irritably left her seventh match to go out and went to the door.

Mal smiled. 'Hallo. Sorry I'm later than I planned.'

'That's all right. We didn't arrange any particular time, did we?' She stood back to let him enter, then followed him through to the living-room. 'I was just trying to get this fire to light, and I'm having trouble with it.'

Mal cast a practised eye over the arrangement of logs in the basket. 'If you don't mind my saying so, you're going about it the wrong way. Do you want me to try?'

Rowan smiled ruefully, not anxious to admit that she had never lit a log fire in her life before. 'Please do.'

He bent to the grate. 'These logs are a bit on the damp side. They will light, but they need more than a match to get them going. And you've got them packed too tightly here – no air space in between them, and a fire can't burn without oxygen. Have you got any newspaper?'

There were some old local papers in the rack. She handed one to him.

'Thanks. Now ... ' Mal crumpled several sheets and pushed them into strategic gaps between the logs. 'They'll burn for a minute or so, and with luck that should be enough to catch the wood.' He lit a match and touched it to the paper, which immediately flared. 'Keep your fingers crossed.'

Within minutes the logs were crackling. Rowan looked at Mal and said, 'Thank you, very much. I'd have been here all day trying to get it right.'

'Pleasure.' He gave a slightly embarrassed shrug. 'Now, what about this furniture?'

'It's in the other room.' She led the way, glad that he had turned the subject so quickly to the purpose of his visit. There was something about Mal Lyndon that made her feel uncomfortably vulnerable. He had a way of looking at her – maybe he used it with everyone, but somehow she doubted that – which put her immediately on the defensive. He was attracted to her, she was sure, and he was the kind of man who wouldn't go to great lengths to hide it. And why should he? He was unattached, and there was no reason why he shouldn't assume that she might return his interest. Rowan only hoped that once her attitude was made clear, he would have the good grace not to pursue it. She didn't want to get off to a bad start by making an enemy in Barton Tavey.

She opened the door of the front room, switched on the light and stood back to let him go in. He looked round the room quickly, then a sharp intake of breath told her that he had seen the desk and that his reaction was much the same as hers had been. He went straight to it, and while she watched from the doorway he ran his hands carefully over the wood, almost caressing it. Then he looked at her over his shoulder.

'It's incredible. Really incredible.'

Rowan smiled. 'You don't think it's too far gone?'

'No! I'll admit it's a bit of a challenge, and some of the things I'll have to do will make it worth less than one in prime condition, but – ' he shook his head slowly, looking rapt – 'it's fantastic!'

He came back to the door without even bothering to look at any of the other items Rowan had mentioned, but she didn't press it. She knew that Mal, like any true craftsman, was already so involved in his mind with the work to be done on the *escritoire* that there would be no point in trying to interest him in the rest of the furniture.

'Come on,' she said, turning the light out again. 'I'll make you some tea or something.' She herself was eager to hear what he had in mind for the desk. For a moment she reflected that she would like to watch him at work, to see exactly how the painstaking task of renovation was done, but dismissed the idea. If she suggested it, he could so easily take the suggestion the wrong way, and that must be avoided.

Over tea Mal explained precisely what he intended to do. Rowan listened, fascinated – she was familiar with a lot of the tricks of the trade, but to hear him talking about the work that would be involved was a true eye-opener. He obviously loved his work, speaking of it as if it were some kind of vocation, and she was forced to admit to herself that that was a rare and admirable quality in anyone.

At last the conversation grew more general, and Mal

asked her casually how long she intended to stay in the village.

Instantly Rowan felt herself tense inwardly. Mal had broken what had been a comfortable half-hour of shop talk, bringing her back to the harsher realities which she would have preferred to avoid. She shrugged.

'I don't know. I haven't really thought about it.'

'I suppose you have plenty of reasons for wanting to get back to London?' He was probing, trying to gauge her situation, and she resented it although in all fairness she had no justification. She gave him an oblique, cautious glance.

'Not at the moment. I resigned my job just before I came down here.' Another shrug. 'I'd been there a long time, and felt I was getting stale.' There was no need for that lie, she knew,but she had an irrational feeling that Mal suspected more than was apparent about her present predicament, and she wanted to allay any such suspicions. 'I haven't fixed up anything else yet, but as I can afford it for a while I thought I might as well take a sabbatical.'

He nodded. 'It must seem strange to you.'

'What must?' She spoke sharply, her head coming up, and he looked surprised.

'Barton Tavey – Exmoor. After London.'

'Oh. Yes, I suppose it is. A contrast, anyway.' *Damn!* She was getting jumpy. She wished he'd go.

'This area's got a lot to offer, though,' he added. 'I found that out when I came back after five years of city life.'

'You're local, then?' Rowan was curious, despite herself.

'Born and brought up in Porlock. I left when I was twenty-three – felt I was being stultified; most country-bred adolescents do. But after five years I realised that the city isn't all it's cracked up to be, and all I wanted to do was return and live the bucolic life.' He smiled self-deprecatingly. 'Or something like that.'

For a few moments a silence fell which Rowan found uncomfortable. She knew she should be more forthcoming, for the sake of politeness if nothing else, but she was not capable of it. All she wanted was for this young man with the disconcertingly dark eyes and the disconcertingly soothing voice to finish the business he had come for and leave her alone.

'About the *escritoire*,' she said suddenly, hardly aware that she had spoken before the words were out. 'How long do you think the renovation will take?'

Mal was no fool, and as she glanced at him she caught the expression on his face. He knew he was being elbowed out.

'Well,' he said, 'I've got a fair amount of work on at the moment, so – say a few weeks? I can't really be more specific.'

A few weeks. Would she still be here then, Rowan wondered? It was quite possible. London had nothing to offer her at the moment. She nodded. 'Fine.'

Taking the hint, Mal rose to his feet. 'I'll leave you in peace, then. Will it be all right if I come round tomorrow lunchtime to collect the desk? Then when I've had a chance to go over it properly, I'll be able to give you an accurate estimate of the cost and the time involved.'

'Yes, of course.'

'Well, thanks for the tea. And if there's anything else, any other pieces of furniture you want me to look at – '

'Nothing of real importance,' she told him. 'At least, not yet. I haven't had a chance to go through the house thoroughly.'

He smiled. 'It should be interesting when you do. I've never been in here before, but it seems to me that Mrs Fairfax was a very discerning lady with an eye for value. If you unearth anything else really exciting, let me know.'

'I'll do that.' Rowan was intrigued by the idea; certainly there were a lot of oddments in the house which she hadn't studied – for example, she had noticed a cardboard box which appeared to be full of ornaments and which had been shoved into a dusty corner of the front room. God alone knew what might be in there.

Mal was hovering, apparently reluctant to leave. 'Do you need any more wood bringing in before I go?' he asked.

She shook her head. 'No. Thanks, but I think I can just about manage to carry an armful from the back door.' The irony in her voice was gentle.

'All right. I'll see you tomorrow, then.'

'Lunchtime, yes.' She followed him into the hall and opened the door for him. 'Good bye, Mal. And thanks.'

When the door closed behind him, Rowan leaned her back heavily against it for a few moments, closing her eyes and releasing the powerful tension which had built up inside her in a long, thankfully-exhaled breath. The past hour had been an ordeal, and as she walked back to the living-room she realised just how ill-equipped she was, at the moment, for coping with the ordinary necessities of a social life. That was worrying – it showed how deeply the heartbreak of the past three months was affecting her.

She had been increasingly aware, as time went on, that she was withdrawing further and further into a shell of her own making, abandoning friends and activities for a dark, solitary and brooding existence. Her doctor had told her it was a hiatus, that as the weeks went by she would find herself coming out of it, but he had been wrong. If anything, it was getting worse, and the problem was compounded by the fact that she had no wish to do anything about it. To face the world now, to go back into the flow of it and fight as she had fought before, would be to re-open wounds that, though by no means healed, were at least veneered over to some degree. It was easier, safer, to stay in the shelter of her cocoon. That way, she could more often keep the pain at arm's length.

And now it had reached such a stage that she found contact with other people – at least on a superficial level – an almost intolerable strain. The Agnes Teales of this world weren't so bad; their company was so light and uncomplicated that she could switch on to a form of mental autopilot, needing to do no more than make the right response at the right moment. But others – and now Mal Lyndon in particular – were a different story. At this moment she wished that she could simply lock the door, barricade the windows and shut herself away in the house's comfortable gloom for the rest of her life.

The fire was dying down. She put more wood on it and watched as the new logs began to catch, staring into the flames and half-imagining pictures in their shifting brightness. Neil had been a creature of shifting brightness, quick, mercurial, unpredictable. In her fantasies Rowan saw the living-room door opening unexpectedly, saw him framed in the doorway, coming into the room. Savagely she shook her head to clear the unshed tears from her eyes. Her doctor had told her she was in no danger of a breakdown. She was young and resilient, a survivor. She'd survive this. But doctors weren't omniscient.

Maybe, she thought, she would have been better off without Mal Lyndon's sudden intrusion into her life. On a subliminal level she was aware that, had things been different, she could have found him very attractive, but as it was, she neither wanted to nor could get to know him better. Whenever she looked at him she thought of Neil, and anything he might do or say in friendship would be jaundiced by that. It wasn't that he reminded her of Neil in any way – they were as different as the proverbial chalk and cheese. But Mal was a man, a young man. And that was enough to make Rowan mistrust and resent him.

The fire was crackling cheerfully by this time, throwing splashes of soft, flickering light on the otherwise unlit room. Rowan rose a little stiffly to her feet, turned – and stopped.

It was the same feeling that had come to her as she stood by the back door earlier: that sense that someone was watching her. The shadows that dipped and bowed on the wall seemed suddenly more than shadows – and then her nostrils caught the unmistakable scent of roses.

She felt that time had slipped out of joint, as though she and the house were suspended, like a fly in amber, in a single unchanging and eternal moment. She should have been afraid. But there was no fear in her, only a dreamlike sense of wonder and fascination. *Roses* – it was as though the house were full of them with their heady perfume, and the shadows, not dark and menacing but soft and warm, seemed to reach out towards her like comforting arms.

The moment broke with an abruptness that was shocking. Rowan felt as if a bowl of ice-cold water had been thrown in her face, and she found herself swaying, gasping and blinking in the firelight, which was now nothing more than firelight. The shadows were quiescent, the scent of roses gone. And with it had gone that brief but magical aura of peace that had filled her entire being.

Without knowing why, Rowan burst into tears. It was a reaction to the shattering of that momentary mood. For a few seconds she had felt healed, all her fear and bitterness smoothed away by that extraordinary experience. But now that the moment was gone, she knew she could not recall it, and the knowledge was like a body-blow.

But the tears dried quickly. Once she was over the initial shock she felt calm again, though the familiar leaden ache inside her was back once more. Wiping her eyes, she stared at the room, half-expecting it to look different; but nothing had changed,

It was then that rationality came back and started to ask awkward questions. What had happened just then? The experience had been so real, so tangible, that she could not put it down merely to imagination. It had *happened* – whatever it was.

If she had glanced in a mirror then, Rowan would not have liked the haunted look that had crept into her eyes. Now, she *was* afraid, not of the experience itself, but of its implications. Any reasonable person, she told herself, would have only one answer. She had hallucinated. The whole thing had been an invention of her mind. And however real it had seemed to her, she had to try and accept that. There was no other sane explanation.

She shivered suddenly. This was serious – no, more than serious; it was dangerous. The one thing she feared above all else was the possibility of cracking mentally under the strain of the last few months and, being brutally honest, she knew that she had done nothing to help herself avoid it. But what could she have done? She simply wasn't strong enough – or so she had convinced herself – to fight against the odds.

The wind was rising again. She could hear it rustling leaves and grass in the garden, and the window-pane rattled as a particularly strong gust shook its old frame. The melancholy sound added to Rowan's disquiet, and quickly she drew the curtains and switched on a table lamp to add a little more light to the room. She needed something to occupy her mind, something practical. Perhaps, as she had promised Mal Lyndon, she could start going carefully through the furniture in the front room, to see what other treasures might be among the clutter. The prospect didn't particularly appeal, as she was tired, but she knew that if she did not keep busy she would be in a far worse state before the evening was out.

Once Rowan had made the decision to tackle the room, she found herself taking an unexpected interest in the task. The main problem was judging where to start, but as she picked her way carefully among the furniture crammed into the room, something caught her eye – the cardboard box which she had noticed before. She decided to manoeuvre it through to the living-room, so that she could examine its contents by the warmth of the fire.

The box was heavy, but by degrees Rowan managed to drag it down the hall and into the living-room. It had no lid, and already she could see that it contained a veritable Aladdin's cave of odds and ends, the sort of things that could well prove to be a bric-a-brac collector's dream.

She pulled the box on to the rug in front of the fire and sat down beside it, beginning to feel more cheerful. One by one she removed the top layer of objects from the box, blowing a thick accumulation of dust off each, then began to sort through them to see what she had unearthed.

She knew within five minutes that this was something that could keep her occupied for hours. The box yielded the most astonishing assortment of oddments and curios that she had ever encountered, and as she examined them Rowan mentally filed them into three categories – those that were possibly valuable, those she liked simply for their appearance, and those that were downright hideous. The pieces that fell into this third category were, she suspected, mostly gifts; it was unlikely that her grandmother would have owned them from choice.

At first she was somewhat disappointed by the individual items she found. There was nothing of any worth, and little that she found particularly attractive for its own sake. But eventually, when she was about half-way through the box, she came upon a small cut-glass bottle which interested her. It was a lady's scent bottle, the stopper miraculously intact, and she placed it immediately as early Victorian. Rowan pulled out the stopper, wondering idly if any traces of the bottle's contents still remained. Cautiously she sniffed – and almost dropped the bottle on to the stone hearth as a strong and familiar perfume struck her nostils.

Roses – exactly the same fragrance that had accompanied her hallucination no more than an hour and a half ago, and which, she now remembered, she had smelled shortly after getting up this morning. Rowan hastily replaced the stopper and stared at the bottle as though it were bewitched. This *couldn't* be coincidence – there had to be some connection. How could she have imagined the scent of roses, only to find the same perfume not two hours later, hidden in a box of junk?

Suddenly she didn't want to finish going through the box. She wanted to put it and its contents out of sight. And she didn't want to think about the roses, either. Quickly she shovelled everything haphazardly back inside, and, as she could not face dragging the heavy box back to the front room, she pushed it under a table in one corner of the living-room, where it would be unobtrusive. For the time being, that would have to do. But she carefully avoided even glancing at the box again.

The rest of the evening was soured for Rowan. Finding the Victorian bottle had reminded her all too sharply of her fears concerning her own state of mind, and as she sat down over a carefully prepared meal which, now that it was cooked, she didn't want to eat, she had to keep forcing her mind away from that subject.

She wished that there was someone she could talk to, someone to whom she could confide her terror that she was on the verge of a breakdown. But the only person in Barton Tavey whom she though of as a friend – albeit guardedly – was Agnes. And this was something way out of Agnes's league; Agnes wouldn't understand the subtleties of mental disturbance, and would therefore certainly dismiss them as nonsense. A very practical attitude, no doubt, but it wouldn't help Rowan at all.

She wondered if she might be best advised to return to London and see her doctor again. But the thought of going back to the city, with all the memories it held, turned her cold inside. Even after such a short time in this village she was becoming reluctant to leave. However dull life here might prove to be in the long run, for the moment it represented safety, security and a secluded hiding place. No, she wouldn't go back to London. All she could do was to stay put, keep a close watch on herself and hope that once she settled down a little things would improve.

With that thought in mind, she turned her attention once more to finding some way of keeping herself comfortably occupied. She decided that the best therapy of all was probably television. There had been that small set in her grandmother's bedroom . . .

Climbing the stairs and going into the room where Maud Fairfax had spent her last months, and in which she had died, was more than a little unnerving. Rowan had never considered herself superstitious, but there was something about the atmosphere of that room with its neatly made bed and too-tidy furniture that seemed to suggest it was only waiting for its occupant to return. Rowan snatched up the little portable TV set and left the room quickly, with a last careful glance as though to make sure it really was empty. She felt better when she was downstairs again.

The television succeeded in its objective, up to a point. Rowan spent the rest of the evening watching anything that happened to come on the screen, although her concentration was sporadic. But it kept the unease at bay, and by the time the announcer wished his audience a cheerful "good night", she was ready to sleep. West Country air, she decided, was having an effect on her. In London she would have been awake and restless until two or three in the morning, sometimes later; but here she felt healthily tired by midnight. So, bed. The fire was almost out, and she judged it safe to leave the last sluggish embers to die. She would have liked a bath, but felt that she would probably go to sleep in the water. It could wait until morning. Yawning, she switched off the television and the lights and made her way upstairs.

Rowan had no difficulty in getting to sleep. But once she *was* asleep, the nightmares started again.

It was the same dream that she had had the previous night. Neil figured strongly in it, and once more Rowan was pursuing him, trying desperately to reach him but failing. And, as before, the moment came when the entire scene abruptly changed and she came upon the eerily flat field with the great dead tree towering menacingly into the blue-black sky. Only now, instead of Neil, someone else was standing under the tree's leafless, clawing branches, waiting for her, silently drawing her towards him with a vast, cruel power.

The ground trembled under Rowan's feet as though shaken by an unheard peal of thunder, and the same force that had taken hold of her before started to propel her forward. She fought it, terrified of the figure who stood beneath the tree and waited, motionless. She could not see him clearly; it was as though a fine mist obscured any detail of his frame of feature, but she was desperately afraid of him and of the power she knew he possessed. And now, all around her, a sound was rising, increasing from a mere whisper in the dark and growing louder, louder and closer. Dogs – hounds – yipping and baying, a whole pack of them, as though they were streaking invisibly across the ploughed field towards her, in pursuit of some frantically racing quarry.

In her nightmare, Rowan clapped her hands to her ears, striving to shut out the baying that now filled her mind. The hounds were all around her, although she couldn't see them, and above their belling voices she heard another, more human voice – a man's wild and horrifyingly joyful laughter.

She woke with a physical jolt that shook every muscle. The noise of the hounds was still dinning in her ears, and only when she sat bolt upright in bed and shook her head violently till she was fully awake did the sounds diminish.

Even then, though the baying howls faded, they did not disappear altogether.

Rowan felt her skin begin to crawl as she realised that the faint noises, carried on the wind, were *real*, not a part of her dream. She was wide awake now, and still she could hear them. Somewhere out there among the hills, a pack of hounds was giving tongue.

The Major's hounds, that was what Agnes had said. Rowan neither knew nor cared who the Major might be. All that mattered to her was that he represented a rational explanation for that distant, eldritch howling. But then she remembered the look on Agnes's face when she had heard Rowan's story – that closed, guarded expression – and the way she had insisted so vehemently that it 'couldn't have been anything else, could it now?' Agnes had protested too much. Even as she had spoken, Rowan had known that the old woman didn't believe her own explanation.

Now, even above the distant baying, Rowan could hear the pounding of her own heart. Carefully she reached out and groped for the lamp, hastily quashing a childish fear of putting so much as her arm out of the bed. The room filled with light, and as it did so the faraway sounds seemed to diminish yet further, until she could no longer hear them at all.

She turned over, staring at the wall. This was ridiculous. Another few nights like this and she would be a nervous wreck without any help from her own disturbed mind. The worst thing of all was that, although she felt better now that the light was on and the baying had stopped, she had been close to the edge of panic. And if this happened again –

Maybe she could find out from Agnes exactly where the Major lived, and pay a call on him to satisfy herself that it was in fact his dogs which had disturbed her. It seemed a foolish idea, but if it put her mind at rest it would be well worth it.

She thought she would be able to sleep again now, providing she left the lamp on, and she slid down under the shelter of the blankets, pulling them up closely around her ears. It would all look different in the rational light of day.

4

Mal Lyndon had several things on his mind as he drove towards Rowan's house the next day. First and foremost was the desk. He couldn't remember ever having been so excited about an individual piece of furniture, and the more down-to-earth side of his nature wanted to laugh at the schoolboyish enthusiasm he felt. He had already planned how he would go about the renovation work, and had suffered one or two sharp pangs of conscience when he had had to remind himself not to get too carried away. It wasn't as if the desk were his, after all – it was someone else's property, and he had to remember that the customer's wishes came first.

And that was the second thing on his mind – the customer. As yet he couldn't quite be sure whether or not he actually liked her, but there was something about her that intrigued him and, if he was honest, that disturbed him too. She wasn't exactly the most forthcoming girl he had ever met – there had been moments yesterday when he could almost physically feel an undercurrent of hostility – and he had the distinct impression that she was either hiding something, or afraid of something. Mal had an instinct for judging people, although he had never thought of himself as particularly perceptive, and Rowan struck him as someone who had recently suffered a very severe blow, far more than a family bereavement, and was either unable or unwilling to recover from it. Normally that would have made him sympathetic but unwilling to get involved. He had his own life and his own preoccupations. But with Rowan, he had the feeling that it might be different.

He halted his old Ford van outside the front gate, and the engine stalled as he disengaged the gears. Some time he'd have to get around to doing some work on that engine, or it would let him down when he needed it most. He opened the door and swung himself lightly down, then pushed open the gate and walked up the path to the front door.

Rowan was almost glad to hear the bell. She had been restless and unhappy all morning, wandering aimlessly about the house and carrying out petty, unnecessary tasks, yet unable to concentrate on anything more taxing. She was still disturbed by last night's dream and the peculiar events that had preceded it. And at the back of her mind, worrying her like a cat with its prey, was the fear that perhaps this really was a sign that she was starting to crack up.

Yet, in a perverse way, Rowan almost took pleasure in that fear. In a clearer-headed mood she would have been disgusted with herself for such self-indulgence, but now the idea that there was something wrong with her gave her a bloody-minded justification for anything she might or might not do. She couldn't help herself, or so she reasoned – circumstances had conspired against her, and there seemed no point in even trying to fight them. She was, in effect, wallowing thoroughly in her own misery, with no inclination to pull herself out of it.

Nonetheless she went to the front door with a sense of relief, and smiled when she saw Mal standing on the step.

Mal looked at her. She gave the impression that she had not been out of bed very long, although in fact she had risen before nine. But she hadn't felt the incentive to take any trouble with her appearance, beyond the promised bath. She wore jeans and an old but beloved pullover, and her rich, dark hair had been treated to only cursory attention, so that it lacked its usual sheen. Yet even without a trace of makeup, to Mal she looked disconcertingly attractive in a waiflike way.

Mal himself had taken unusual pains with his appearance, though it hadn't occurred to him, consciously, at any rate, to consider his motives. Seeing him, Rowan felt suddenly guilty about her own state, and that made her nervous. Without any preamble she opened the door to the front room and said a little awkwardly. 'Do you think you'll be able to move it, or shall I help?'

She clearly wanted to get rid of him as fast as possible, Mal thought. And her unease showed in every gesture – the way she stood tensely in the doorway as though poised for flight, the way her fingers worked nervously through her hair in a self-conscious attempt to neaten it. She was in a bad state.

His steady eyes met hers, and she flicked her gaze away, downwards. 'I think it'll be easier with two,' he suggested.

'Okay.' Her voice was edgily resigned. She went into the room and started to pull over-energetically at the furniture which blocked the way to the desk. As she tried to drag a table aside Mal said, 'Here, let me – ' but she almost shook him off, and with a shrug he left her to it.

Between them they manoeuvred the *escritoire* out into the hall. The front door still stood wide open, and as they set the desk down and took a breather Mal had his first good look at it in full daylight.

For the next few minutes Rowan knew she might as well not have existed. Mal crouched down by the desk, his fingers running across the smooth wood, his narrowed eyes scanning the grain and his expression almost reverent. He touched it as a lover might touch his beloved's skin, with a strange blend of awe and possessiveness, and Rowan was fascinated by the abrupt change in him. From an ordinary man, he had become something else: a skilled, supremely confident craftsman, totally absorbed with the work he loved. It made her feel inadequate and, unreasonably, she resented that.

She turned away, suddenly embarrassed, and started to fuss with a print on the hall wall which she thought wasn't quite straight. When Mal looked up she had stepped back and was eyeing the picture, then, deciding that it still wasn't right, she moved forward to shift it again.

He said, 'Shall we get the second leg of the journey over and done with?'

Rowan stopped what she was doing with a little jump, and her cheeks coloured. 'Yes – yes, okay.' With one final glance at the picture she bent to the desk again, and they carried it slowly and carefully out of the door and down the path. The rear doors of the van stood open, and with Mal pulling from inside and Rowan pushing from outside, the *escritoire* was lifted and eased into position. Mal packed a pile of old rugs and foam-rubber pieces round it to keep it stable, then emerged from the van again.

'Now,' he said, 'about that estimate. We ought to talk about a rough price guideline, at least.'

Rowan pulled a faded flower head off a straggling marigold that grew by the low front wall, and twisted it in her fingers. 'It doesn't really matter – ' she began diffidently.

'Oh, but it does! It's not going to do much for my sense of professionalism if I don't sort that out right now.' He watched her face, saw it starting to close up, and knew that he would have to be careful if he wanted to avoid being politely thrown out. 'Look,' he added, 'I don't know about you, but I could do with a relaxing drink before I get down to my work this afternoon. I often drop into the Oak and Ash at lunchtimes. Come with me for a few minutes, and we can discuss it.'

'I don't think – '

'I'll admit I'm being a bit selfish, but it'll kill two birds with one stone, so to speak. My conscience won't let me take too much time off, and this way I can combine business with lunch and not give myself a black mark.'

It worked. Rowan visibly relaxed. By emphasising the business aspect of his invitation Mal had quelled her fears that this was the prelude to something else.

With only a few moments' hesitation she said, 'All right. I suppose it would do me good to get out of the house anyway.' Then her sense of self-esteem struggled back to the surface and she added, 'I'll just go and make myself presentable, if you'll hold on for a minute.'

Five minutes later they were walking towards the Oak and Ash. In a fit of shame prompted by Mal's comparatively elegant appearance, Rowan had changed her jeans for a pair of cord trousers, and a quick application of mascara had given her green eyes a little more life. As they approached the door, she realised how long it had been since she was last in a pub. In London, it wasn't usually advisable for any woman to go into one alone, and she and Neil –

No, don't think about Neil, she told herself. It was no use trying to imagine that it was him, and not Mal Lyndon, who was ushering her into the bar now; that was pointless and childish. She should at least try to get through the next half hour or so without becoming too maudlin.

The Oak and Ash had only one bar, and after the bright if watery daylight outside it took a few minutes for Rowan's eyes to adjust to the comparative gloom. At this time on a weekday it was quiet, and she could see that little had been done here to cater to the tourist trade. There were no advertisements on the walls, and no traces of the 'Olde Englande' cod-antique look that foreign visitors in particular were so fond of. All the furniture was wood, and old wood at that; battered and chipped and showing all the signs of long use. Most of the tables – and especially, she thought, the heavy oak settle by the big, empty fireplace – had probably been here almost as long as the building itself.

'Well? What do you think of our local?' Mal asked in an undertone as they approached the bar.

'Very authentic.' She noticed the line of pewter tankards hanging on nails behind the bar counter, and the polished horse brasses that seemed to be everywhere. 'I like it. It's so quiet.'

'It's more like hell on earth in the summer season,' he told her, then raised his voice as he saw the girl behind the bar staring at them. 'Hello, Rose.'

The girl smiled, but she was assessing Rowan. She was about Rowan's own age, but taller and more heavily built, with curly, copper-brown hair in a *coup sauvage*. Her expression as she looked at Rowan suggested that she was impressed by what she saw, but would have preferred not to see it in Mal Lyndon's company.

'Morning, Mal,' she said, her accent on the harsher side of West Country. 'The usual, is it?'

'Yes, please. And Rose, I'd like you to meet Rowan Vosper – she's Maud Fairfax's granddaughter. Rowan, this is Rose Bastable.'

'Pleased to meet you.' Rose held out a hand, which Rowan shook briefly. 'So you're the one who's inherited old Mrs Fairfax's place? The one from London?'

It seemed everyone in the village knew all about her, Rowan thought. 'That's right,' she said.

'Must be a proper liability, that. Are you going to sell it?'

'I don't know – I haven't decided.'

'Well, there's plenty of time, I suppose. So you'll be around the village for a while, then?' Rose glanced sideways at Mal as she spoke, and he felt uncomfortable. He knew full well why she was so interested in Rowan's plans, and thought angrily that she was being very unsubtle. But Rowan didn't seem to notice, and Mal reflected a little ruefully that she probably wouldn't have cared either way.

'What would you like to drink?' he asked, wanting to rescue her from Rose's curiosity.

'Oh, I don't know. Do they do wine by the glass?'

Mal looked enquiringly at Rose, who said, 'We can do, though there's not much call for it except in the tourist season.' If that was a deliberate dig, it had no effect on Rowan. 'Red or white?'

'White, please.'

'And something for you, Rose?' Mal asked as the barmaid started to pour.

Rose's sloe-like dark eyes met his coquettishly. 'Thanks. I'll have a G and T if it's all the same. There you are, there's your cider.' She turned back to Rowan, and added, 'Our Mal is the only man in Barton Tavey who doesn't drink beer. Personally, I think he does it just to be different. Some men are like that, aren't they?' She gave Mal a mischievous smile. 'But I mustn't tease. Wouldn't do to spoil his image.'

Rowan sipped her wine. She found Rose's little darts embarrassing, and was in half a mind to tell her straight out that she had no need to fear any rivalry. If she wanted Mal Lyndon to herself, she could have him. Rowan's relationship was purely business.

But something – perhaps the look on Mal's face – stopped Rose from going any further. Instead, leaning her elbows on the bar, she said to Rowan, 'It must be very different down here from what you're used to.'

Rowan stared at her glass, her fingers fidgeting on the

stem. 'That's what everyone says, but I'm not so sure. People are the same wherever you go.'

'Yes, but it's not just people, is it? I mean, there must be so much more to *do* in the city.'

'Is there? I don't know.'

'Well, there must be!' Rose looked astonished. 'Maybe you don't realise how dead a place like Barton Tavey really is yet. It may seem okay now, but you wait till you've been here a while. You'll be dying to get back.' She sighed. 'I'd give anything to get out of this dump. It's so boring – I feel like I'm rotting away.'

'Then why don't you?' Rowan asked. 'Go to the city, I mean.'

Rose shrugged. 'You've got to have something to do once you get there, haven't you? I haven't got any qualifications, so what chance would I have of getting a decent job? My dad thinks I've done well for myself being a bloody barmaid!' Leaning further forward she went on conspiratorially, 'That's the trouble with most of the people round here. They're born with blinkers on, and they can't see anything beyond their own back gardens. Of course, there are exceptions.' She glanced at Mal with another of her smiles. 'Though why he wanted to settle back here after seeing the bright lights for himself beats me.'

'If *you'd* seen it for yourself, Rose, you probably wouldn't want to stay either,' Mal told her, with a tinge of irritation in his voice. 'The grass on the other side, et cetera.'

'Don't be daft! I'd give my right arm to get out of here, and you know it. I don't want to waste the rest of my life in this hole.'

Mal was tempted, as he had been tempted on many previous occasions, to say bluntly that she should stop complaining and do something about it. But he kept his thoughts to himself, and looked at Rowan.

'We've got some business to discuss – that's why you came along in the first place. If you'll excuse us, Rose . . . '

Rose took her dismissal in good part, but she stared after them as they headed for a table. She had known Mal long enough to be aware that there would be more than business between him and this girl, if he had any say in the matter. She seemed pleasant enough, though too quiet to be Rose's type – and a bit stand-offish. Chances were she wouldn't last. Either he'd get fed up with her cool ways, or she'd be off back to London soon enough, and the field would be clear again. Until then, Rose thought, she'd have to put up with it and bide her time.

'I hope I wasn't too rude to Rose,' Mal said as they sat down, 'but if you give her the chance to start one of her complaining sessions, she'll keep it up for hours at a time.'

'I don't understand why she doesn't just leave, if she's so dissatisfied,' Rowan replied. 'She's attractive and intelligent.'

'And lazy as hell. Rose is her own worst enemy. She'll moan interminably about how unfair life has been to her, but she'll never get off her ar – off her backside and do something about it for herself. She hasn't learned yet that the world doesn't owe her a living.' He looked at her, watching for a reaction. He had been trying, in a roundabout way, to make the point that he had little respect for Rose Bastable, and therefore little interest in her. But Rowan didn't react, and he was disappointed. He wanted to get through to her, persuade her to lower her defences enough to enable them to at least get to know each other a little better, but he felt helpless in the face of this unrelenting disinterest. All he could do, for the time being, was to keep the conversation on topics that didn't provoke any more hostility, and that meant the writing-desk.

And so for some minutes they discussed the work that was to be done. At first Rowan felt that Mal's estimate was too low, and tried to argue about it, but he refused to agree to a higher price, saying only that he promised to reassess it if the desk proved to need more attention than he anticipated. When at last they were both satisfied, a rather awkward silence fell, not helped by the fact that there were no other customers in the pub to take their attention away from each other. Rowan had finished her wine long ago, but she still played with the glass, twisting it round and round, looking anywhere but directly at Mal.

As so often happens, when they broke the silence they broke it together, and both stopped, confused.

'Go on,' Mal said with a grin.

'No, you – '

'I'm nothing if not a gentleman,' he insisted. 'What were you going to say?'

'Well, I was just wondering how this pub got its name. It's very unusual.'

He looked surprised. 'I've never thought about it before, but I suppose it is. It's a pity Jack's not here – he's the landlord, and he knows a lot about local history. There's probably some old story connected with it. Mind you, there are a lot of oak trees around here, and a lot of oak wood used in building. Maybe that's got something to do with it.'

'Yes, I noticed that in the house. There's a lot of oak furniture. Though of course maybe that was just a little foible of Gran's. When I was looking through some bits and pieces last night – ' She stopped suddenly, remembering the scent bottle and the smell of roses.

Mal frowned, seeing her expression change. 'What's wrong?'

'Nothing. I was just thinking about something. It doesn't matter.' In a way she wanted to tell him, ask his opinion, but she didn't. He'd either think she was stark raving mad, or he would want to get involved.

'You'll break that glass if you don't stop fiddling with it,' he told her with gentle amusement.

'What? Oh.' She set it down and put her hands in her lap like a rebuked child.

'Would you like another drink?'

She shook her head. 'No, thanks. I ought to be getting back in a minute.'

Mal decided at that point that there was nothing to lose by being straightforward. If she wouldn't react to subtlety, maybe she needed provoking. He said simply, 'Why?'

'What?'

'Why do you have to get back? You haven't got anything in particular to do, have you?' As he spoke, his hand unconsciously reached out across the table towards her, and she visibly shrank back.

'No,' she said, 'but you have. You said yourself that you're very busy.'

There was no answer to that. She had neatly cornered him by throwing his own words back in his face. But Mal was not entirely deterred.

'Well, that's true,' he admitted, 'But I don't spend every moment of my life working, you know. I do have *some* leisure. Listen, tomorrow's a quiet day – I don't suppose you've had a chance to see much of the countryside round here yet. How would you like a guided tour? We could drive out on the coast road and down to the beach – '

'No.' The refusal was sharp, almost savagely so. 'Thanks, but I'd rather not.' To soften the blow, she added uncomfortably, 'I'm going to be busy.'

'Then pick a day when you're not busy.'

'Please, Mal.' She looked at him, and her eyes were miserable. 'I'd just rather not.'

Mal sighed. She simply would not be persuaded, and now the hostility was coming back. If he tried to press the point now, she would likely as not snap his head off and walk out. This was like dealing with a wild animal – she rebuffed every friendly overture he made. Of course, it could be that she didn't find him in the least attractive, but Mal, without being arrogant, was convinced that there was more to it.

'I'd better go now,' she said quietly.

'All right, if that's what you want. I'll walk back with you, then I can pick up the van.' He held out her light jacket, but she refused his help in putting it on. With a quick word of goodbye to Rose, who had been watching the proceedings with interest though unable to hear any of it, he ushered Rowan out into the street.

The sun had come out, after the misty and dull start to the day, and the village looked bright and clean under the mellow light. Mal and Rowan started back towards her house, and neither said a word until they reached the gate. Then Mal opened the door of his van and turned to face Rowan.

'I'll give you a ring in a couple of days,' he said, 'then I'll be able to give you some more details about the desk.'

'Thanks.' She didn't meet his eyes. 'And thanks for the drink.'

He smiled a little wryly. 'My pleasure.' Swinging himself into the driving seat he started the recalcitrant engine, and before closing the door added, 'Take care.'

'You too.' But from her it was a meaningless courtesy.

Rowan hurried indoors as the van drew away. The house seemed unnaturally quiet, and she switched the radio on to keep the silence at bay. She wished that she hadn't agreed to go to the Oak and Ash with Mal. It had been a disaster, and now she had probably alienated him. God alone knew what he must think of her – she had verged on the downright rude in the last few minutes, and it had left a sour taste. And recalling the scent bottle hadn't helped, either. She had very much wanted to mention that incident to him, to see if he could shed any light on it, but now that would be impossible. Even if he was willing to overlook her behaviour and forgive her for it, he had made it all too clear that he was attracted to her, and if she gave him the chance to approach her again, no doubt he would take it. No; from now on she would have to stick firmly to business and nothing else, at least until he realised that there was no point in pursuing her.

That made her feel both regretful and angry. In some ways she would have liked to count Mal as a friend, but if he wanted to be more than a friend, that would put her in an impossible position. Why couldn't he have taken the hint in the first place and kept their relationship on a formal level instead of trying to push her into something she didn't want?

She walked into the living-room, then through to the kitchen and filled the kettle to make coffee. She needed to get out of here for a while, right out of the village, get some fresh air to clear her mind a little. A quick bite of lunch – perhaps some cheese on toast – and she might take up Mal's suggestion of exploring the surrounding countryside. But alone. She would have to go alone. And at least it would while away the afternoon.

It was pleasant to be driving again, though even after a mere couple of days' break Rowan found the sensation slightly strange, particularly on the narrow, twisting and hilly roads of the Exmoor countryside. All traces of cloud had vanished from the sky by now, and the sun shone brilliantly in a vast, deep blue bowl. Rowan could feel its warmth through the car window, and the sensation of heat on her skin invigorated her and did a lot to improve her mood. She left Barton Tavey on a road that wound steeply upwards through woodlands, the green and gold leaves almost meeting in a shady canopy over the lane. And then with breathtaking suddenness the car emerged from the woods on to the high coast road, and Exmoor was spread out in an incredible vista around and below her.

Rowan slowed to a halt and just stared. Behind her, the road dipped back down into the trees, deep and secretive. Ahead, the ground fell away in a sweep of hills like gigantic, petrified waves, the colour of honey under the mellow sun, and dotted with darker belts of trees and tiny villages, doll-sized from such a distance. On another road, far below her, the sunlight caught and reflected dazzlingly from the bonnet of a single slow-moving car. And on the horizon was another faraway glint – the smooth, still glitter of the sea.

Rowan wound down the window and took a deep breath. The scents of brambles and hot, dry grass filled her nostrils, mingling with the more prosaic but somehow equally pleasant smell of the Mini's hot engine. Then she slipped into gear, and pulled slowly away, following a signpost that directed her towards Foreland Point and Lynmouth.

For the next two hours she drove with no particular goal in mind other than simply to see what was to be seen. By following the small roads, turning down side lanes that looked intriguing, she soon became aware of the wide contrasts in this land, from the villages such as Oare in its shady and steep valley, to the rocky bays that dotted the coastline. At Foreland Point she stopped the car again and got out to look at the view from the tremendous cliffs. It was reputed to be the highest headland in England, and judging from the vista it presented, Rowan could well believe that. She wished that she had thought to bring her camera. But there would be time enough for that, if the weather didn't break.

At last she consulted her map and turned the car towards home. Strange how she was already thinking of Barton Tavey – or at least the house – as home. The high open spaces gave way to trees again, and the shadows were beginning to lengthen as the sun dipped towards the sea. There were streaks of pale salmon-pink in the sky overhead, heralding a spectacular sunset. Rowan was anxious to reach the village before dusk fell, as trying to find her way on unfamiliar lanes in the dark would be difficult.

She was only three miles or so from Barton Tavey when she caught sight of the westerly sky through a narrow belt of trees. The sun was truly setting now, and she stopped to watch. Nothing like this was ever visible in London, with its high buildings, but here, with nothing to obscure it, the entire sky was a blaze of fiery colour. Small streaks of cloud that had blown up from the south-west showed black against a vast wash of red, and bands of gold seemed to flood from the crimson ball of the sun, making the whole scene wild and surreal.

Rowan got out of her car, again cursing herself for having left her camera in the house. But camera or no camera, she had to see this in its full glory.

There was a narrow farm track that seemed to lead through a copse and out on the other side into fields. This was high ground – she should have an unobstructed view from there. Quickly she walked up the path and through the rustling coolness of the trees.

For some minutes then she stood reverently gazing across the rolling sweep of hills to where the magnificent sunset was gradually changing, deepening, finally fading towards a soft, washed-out pink as the sun sank lower and dusk began to encroach from the east. She could understand why so many civilisations of the ancient world had worshipped the sun. Just to gaze at that sight had given her a feeling of peace, of – she almost laughed at herself, but it was true – of completeness.

She sighed, coming back to earth. The celestial display was all but over now, and before long it would be too dark to read the signposts. Better get back to the car. She turned around – and stopped.

She had been too preoccupied with the sky to notice the field before. It was bordered on three sides by woodlands and it had been left fallow. In its very centre, standing motionless and alone, was an oak tree – a white, bare, lightning-blasted oak tree.

Rowan felt sick as a horrible feeling of déjà-vu flooded through her. This was the field of her nightmare – and the tree was the same dead and threatening tree which had terrified her in that dream!

She shut her eyes tightly for a few seconds. But when she looked again, the tree was still there. Now all the details of that nightmare came back to her: the darkness, the solitary figure standing under the dead tree's branches, the sound of the baying dogs. Very slowly she started to back away, her feet feeling for the ground behind her, wanting only to get back to the car and away from this place, but too afraid to turn her back to the tree in case –

She stopped again. Then she turned her head towards the woods that separated the field from the road.

Someone was watching her. She could sense their presence, and nothing could have convinced her at that moment that it was imagination. Her attention focused on a dense and bushy clump of birches less than fifty yards away, and as she stared harder she thought – no, she *saw* something move. No more than a glimpse, but unmistakable. A human figure, half-hidden among the leaves and too distant for any detail to be clear, but – unmistakable. And a faint glimmer of coppery-red hair.

She bit her lip until the pain overtook her fright, but her hands were shaking. The field was so silent, and the silence was suddenly almost intolerable.

'*Who's there?*' she called out. Her voice sounded unnervingly flat in the empty space; the words seemed to drop away and soak into the ground even as she uttered them. For an instant the glimpsed figure was motionless, then, in less than a second, it had gone and Rowan was totally alone in the field.

She took two great breaths like a floundering swimmer,

glancing wildly towards the dead tree, then to the copse which lay between her and the sanctuary of the car. She couldn't do it, she was too frightened to go back into those trees. Whoever it was she had seen might be there by now, blocking her way. *Who was he?* And what did he want? Why had he been watching her?

Savagely she tried to take a grip on her mind, telling herself that her imagination was getting overwrought. For God's sake, he was probably just a farm labourer, or one half of a courting couple. There was no reason why she shouldn't simply walk back to the car in perfect safety. And anyway, what was her option – to stand out here in the field all night because she was too scared to brave a few trees?

She *was* scared, and no amount of reasoning could dispel it. Yet she had to get back to the car. And the only way was on the path through the copse.

Rowan took another deep breath and, before the little that remained of her courage failed her, ran. She plunged into the gloom of the trees, stumbling on the rutted track but managing to avoid a fall, and as she went she kept her face towards the ribbon of the road between the branches, not looking to either side. And then she was on the road, and the Mini with its driver's door ajar was waiting for her.

She threw herself into the seat, slammed the door and locked it, and fumbled for the ignition key. The engine started, and in her frantic haste she jerked it unceremoniously into gear with a crunch that shook the whole car. The Mini lurched forward with a kangaroo-jolt, and stalled.

Rowan fought with the gear-lever, a fresh wave of near-panic welling up in her. Then, with a great effort, she took a grip on herself. *Calm down, or you'll do something really stupid, like crash the car. This is childish, completely childish!* She forced herself to go through the motions of starting the car properly, telling herself what to do as though she were a beginner taking her first lesson. The engine revved into life again, and this time there was no teeth-rattling stall as she put it more gently into gear and pulled away from the side of the road. But once she was moving she accelerated hard, wanting only to escape from the field and the dead tree, and reach her house before the darkness came down to engulf her.

5

The dream came back again that night. Rowan had half-expected it, and so she was better prepared for it, although the experience was as unpleasant as ever. This time, Neil figured far less strongly, and the dream focused more round the mysterious man under the branches of the blasted oak tree. She saw him no more clearly than before, but Rowan was aware of a change in him, and for a moment could not pinpoint what it was. Then, with a shock, she realised it – rising from his head, like a strange crown and yet apparently part of him, was a pair of huge stag's antlers.

The shock lasted only a moment, and then, in the way of dreams, she found herself accepting the extraordinary fact as if it were the most normal thing in the world. All that mattered to her was that the dream – which somehow she *knew* was a dream – was progressing down the now all-too-familiar path: the lightning, the dogs, the terrible, sweeping darkness.

She woke as suddenly as before, but this time there was no panic, no frantic groping for the bedside lamp. Instead, knowing what to expect, Rowan lay quiet under the blankets, her ears attuned to the soft noises of the night outside, listening for the sound she knew she would hear. The baying of the distant hounds.

But there was nothing. Only the muted voice of the wind blowing across the hills that enclosed and protected the village. No dogs.

Rowan frowned in the darkness. She had been ready to congratulate herself on her level-headedness, her ability to ignore that unearthly sound, but now all her defences were unnecessary.

Why weren't the dogs giving tongue tonight? It was a perverse question – she should have thanked her lucky stars and left it at that – but the thought nagged at her, suggesting that something must be wrong. She had resigned herself to the idea of the nightly howling, and its absence now was more disturbing than its presence would have been.

She turned over, trying to find a more comfortable position. Forget the wretched dogs, she told herself. Go back to sleep.

But she couldn't sleep. For half an hour she tossed and turned, shifting her position but finding no relief from her restlessness, until at last she knew she would have to get up for a while. With a sigh she switched the lamp on, wishing she had moved the electric fire into her bedroom as she had intended. The room was like a refrigerator.

Maybe if she went to the bathroom she would be able to get back to sleep afterwards. Reaching for her dressing gown, which was designed more for centrally heated flats than chilly old country houses, she pulled it on and padded to the door. She still did not feel entirely happy about the long, dark landing, despite the fact that her grandmother's room was now locked, and she ran quickly down to the far end to switch on the stairs light.

The bathroom was at the front of the house, overlooking the village street. It had a distinctly Edwardian air: the bath stood on four squat pedestal feet with the water tank hanging above it like some Sword of Damocles. Every time she sat in the bath, Rowan had the unpleasant feeling that the tank could at any moment break loose and fall on her head. The rest of the fitments, though, were fairly new, although she might have wished for a more pleasant wall covering than the pale green ceramic tiles.

She was washing her hands when she heard a sound beyond the window. For a moment she thought she must have imagined it but then, as the wind blew more strongly, it was carried clearly to her – the sound of a single horse trotting along the road.

Who on earth could be crazy enough to go out riding in the middle of the night?

Wondering if perhaps the animal had escaped and was

running loose, she leaned across the washbasin to the small window and pulled back the flowered curtains. The light from the room made it impossible to see the dark street, so she eased the window open for a better look.

The night air rushed in, bringing the sound of hoofbeats suddenly much closer. The horse was coming from the left, but as yet she could make out no silhouette in the darkness. It was cloudy and there was no moon.

Rowan stayed at the window, listening and watching. It was only when she had been standing there for some time that she realised the hoofbeats were now very close indeed. Too close, in fact. They were passing directly by the house. And yet the road was empty.

The brisk clopping gradually diminished while Rowan stood rigid at the window, staring disbelievingly into the night. Then, at last, the sounds faded and were gone.

Rowan's muscles unlocked and she stepped slowly back from the window, her eyes still focused on its black square. This just wasn't possible. She had been dreaming again – she *must* have been. Wildly she looked around the room, searching for something, some discrepancy that would tell her she was still asleep and this was all in her imagination. But there were no blurred edges, no out-of-place doors, no unexpected shifts of perspective. Everything was normal. She was wide awake.

But how could she be awake, when she had just witnessed the passing of an invisible horse? Those hoofbeats had been clearly audible, *real*.

Suddenly she wanted to get out of the bathroom. She pulled open the door and, leaving the landing light on, ran back down the passage to the sanctuary of her room, where she scrambled quickly into bed. The house felt appallingly empty, and she wished that there were another living soul, *anyone*, under the roof with her. One thing was certain – what she had just heard had not been her imagination. And there was no possibility that she might have missed the horse in the darkness. If it had been visible, she would have seen it.

That left two possibilities. Either she had had a serious hallucination which put her mental state on very rocky ground indeed, or the horse had been a ghost.

Did she believe in ghosts, she asked herself? She would rather not have faced that question alone, in the middle of the night. As a child she had been terrified of a whole range of imagined bogey-men, but that was not the same thing. Did she believe that spirits of the dead could actually exist, and be seen – or heard – by the living?

She didn't know the answer. It was more comfortable not to credit any such superstitions, but she had to admit to at least an open mind on the subject. And in some ways it would be better if it had been a ghost. Better than the thought that she was more than half-way to a mental hospital.

Suddenly all the events of the past few days crowded in on her at once, the fear they had brought mingling with tiredness and a desperate longing for something that was familiar to comfort her. Neil. If he were here, he would understand. He would help her. If only . . .

She hardly realised what she was doing as she reached out and took Neil's photograph from the dressing table where it stood. Tears were streaming down her cheeks in silent, resigned, hopeless grief. The edges of the picture frame dug into her as she clutched it tightly to her body, and by the time she finally fell asleep her pillow was wet with tears.

It was lucky that the following day turned out to be a busy one. Rowan hadn't planned it that way, but by one of those odd chains of coincidence everything seemed to happen at once. She overslept and had only just sleepily pulled on her clothes when a ring at the bell announced Agnes Teale.

Agnes had called round on the pretext of borrowing sugar, but she was obviously in the mood to stay and chat. She had seen Mal Lyndon's van outside the house the previous day, and was agog to know what he was taking away from the house. With a smile, Rowan told her that he was going to renovate the Queen Anne bureau, and Agnes looked delighted.

'Well, now! There's a turn-up! I told you, didn't I, that he'd be the one to see?'

'Yes, and I'm very grateful to you.'

Agnes dismissed her thanks with a slightly coquettish wave of one hand. 'When you've lived in one place as long as I have, you get to know what's what.' Then she added casually, 'I expect you and him got on well, did you?'

Agnes was fishing again. Rowan shrugged. 'Yes, I suppose so. He's very professional, anyway.'

'Ye-es. Nice young man, like I said. Does he think the old desk's worth a lot of money?'

'It's hard to tell, as yet. We'll have to see when it's finished.'

'Set you up nicely for a bit that will, I expect.' Agnes glanced round the living-room, and Rowan could see her mentally calculating how she would have refurnished it, given the money and the chance. She suspected that their ideas would be very different indeed.

Agnes was something of a limpet, as Rowan soon discovered. Once she had made herself comfortable with a cup of tea balanced on her knee, it was difficult to move her if she was in the mood for a gossip. It seemed that in her mind Rowan had already taken Maud Fairfax's place as a neighbour and friend with whom to while away the hours. And Rowan's youth was an added advantage to Agnes; it enabled her to give rein to the motherly if somewhat patronising side of her nature, so that her conversation was liberally sprinkled with such phrases as, 'Well, you're so young yet, aren't you?' and 'but of course, when you get to my age . . . ' Rowan was not willing to take too much of that today, and she soon found herself growing irritated and having, for politeness's sake, to keep a check on her own tongue. However well-meaning Agnes might be, Rowan's patience was wearing thin.

At last, having hinted broadly but unsuccessfully that she had a lot to do, Rowan stood up and, interrupting Agnes in mid-flow, said that she really must excuse herself, as she had some shopping that couldn't wait any longer. That proved to be a mistake, for Agnes instantly said that in that case Rowan could do her a great favour, and she was sure it wouldn't be too much trouble, just one or two little items from the grocer's, and it would give her a chance to get on with her ironing. Rowan acquiesced with as much grace as she could, well aware that she had walked into her own trap. Agnes wrote her a list, which comprised considerably more than 'just a few' items, and finally left her to it.

Disgruntled, Rowan went upstairs to fetch her jacket. She was beginning to feel like a housewife with this daily round of shopping and gossiping. If she spent too long here, she would be middle-aged before her time. Perhaps Rose Bastable at the pub had a valid point when she called Barton Tavey a dead end.

She left the house with a basket on her arm, and turned towards the village high street. The clouds that had been gathering throughout the night had thickened, and the sky was a dull grey laced with small, low wisps of darker, damper cloud that blew like smoke across the heavier backdrop. There was a bite in the air, too, and a smell of imminent rain; it might be a good idea to light the fire when she got back. God, she was even thinking like a housewife.

'Rowan?'

The voice was unfamiliar, and she looked up, startled. For a moment the middle-aged man's face didn't register at all, and then, seeing the clerical collar above the brown tweed jacket, she remembered the funeral and Tom Rushford.

'Oh, hello, vicar.'

'I was just on my way to visit you,' Rushford said with an apologetic smile. 'And feeling very guilty that I haven't been round earlier, to see how you're settling in. Are you going shopping?'

Rowan glanced at her basket. 'Well, yes.'

'Do you mind if I walk with you?'

She wasn't in the mood for more idle chit-chat, but she couldn't very well refuse. 'Of course not.'

Rushford fell easily into step beside her, slowing his pace to match hers. 'How's the house?' he asked after a few moments. 'Are you beginning to feel at home?'

'Yes, I – I think so. In an odd way.'

'Odd?' He sounded curious, and she wished she hadn't said what she had. How could she explain to this virtual stranger the effect the house was having on her? Despite the fact that he was a vicar, and vicars were theoretically supposed to believe in strange happenings, she was sure that he would not understand.

'Well, I suppose it's just a matter of getting used to a new environment,' she said lightly. 'And with Gran having died there recently – '

'Of course.' He was looking at her, too astutely for her liking. 'You haven't had any bad feelings about the place?' he asked after a few moments.

Rowan almost stopped walking but forced herself to go on. She mustn't let him see that his question had disturbed her. Not meeting his eyes, she said, 'No, nothing like that.'

'I'm relieved to hear it! A lot of people would be very chary about moving into a house in which there'd just been a death, I know. I'm sorry, am I being morbid?'

She smiled. 'Not at all. I don't think I'm really superstitious.' Was that a lie? She didn't know. 'Anyway, there aren't any funny stories connected with the house, are there?'

'Not that I know of. And I think if there were, I'd be one of the first to hear about them.'

Rowan knew she must not give too much away, but she couldn't help asking, 'Have you ever performed an exorcism?'

'An exorcism? No, I haven't.' He grinned. 'I hope this isn't the prelude to a request for one, because I don't think I'm qualified!'

She shook her head. 'It isn't. I just wondered. In a village like this, I mean . . . '

'Oh, it's certainly the perfect setting for ghoulie and ghostie legends, and there are plenty of stories around the area. But no, I've never been called in to exorcise anything. Perhaps I shouldn't say this as the vicar of a little village church, but to tell you the truth I think most of these so-called "manifestations" that one hears about are attributable to other causes. Either there's some perfectly logical explanation, or the person concerned has an over-active imagination.'

He couldn't possibly be aware that he had touched on a sore spot, but Rowan immediately put out of her mind any idea that Tom Rushford might after all provide a sympathetic ear. The smell of roses and the scent bottle: coincidence, he would call that. And the hounds, well, he would agree with Agnes. As for the lightning-blasted tree and the figure watching from the woods, and the invisible horse, she could almost hear him saying in his quiet, pleasant way that the first was obviously a mistake on her part, that there had been no threat and maybe even no watcher, and that the second was all in the mind and she had better see her doctor as it sounded like overstrain. Exactly what she had tried to tell herself.

They had reached the grocer's, and Rowan turned to take her leave. Before she could speak, someone bumped against her and a gravelly voice said, 'Avnoon.'

An old man shuffled by, apparently unaware that he had jostled Rowan, and as he passed he grinned lopsidedly at the vicar, showing decayed teeth. He wore an old coat and older baggy trousers, with working-men's heavy boots and a shapeless felt hat crammed on his sparse hair. He was unshaven and unsavoury, and Rowan looked at Tom Rushford in surprise.

'Hello, Tully.' The vicar smiled after the departing figure then, seeing Rowan's expression, said, 'That's Tully – haven't you come across him before?'

She shook her head. 'No.'

'Ah. Well, he's harmless, if a bit off-putting at times. Poor old chap. I suppose in the old days he'd have been known as the village idiot. He's certainly not quite all there – people call him "Cracky Tully" behind his back, which is bit unkind.'

'Where does he live?' Rowan was suddenly struck with the thought that the old man might be a near neighbour.

'Nowhere in particular. He's a tramp really. He's been here as long as anyone can remember, and he gets by on what he can scrounge, as far as I know. He even turns up in church on the occasional Sunday – sits at the back and mumbles all through my sermon.' Rushford laughed indulgently. 'I suspect he sometimes sleeps in the church as well. Now and again the verger's complained of a smell in the vestry.'

Rowan could well imagine it, and despite the vicar's goodwill towards the old tramp she thought privately that the village would be better off without him. With a final glance at the shuffling figure, she said, 'Well, I suppose I'd better get my groceries.'

'Oh dear, have I detained you? I am sorry. Oh, by the way, will you be coming to our Harvest Festival?'

'I didn't know you were having one.'

'Yes indeed, and it's quite an occasion. There's a church service, of course, but I think most people only go to that as a matter of form. But there's a very good fête afterwards, and the local morris team will be dancing. It's an old tradition in Barton Tavey, to celebrate the end of the grain harvest.'

A village fête wasn't Rowan's idea of the high life, but nonetheless she smiled. 'I'll certainly come if nothing intervenes that I can't get out of,' she said non-committally, hoping she didn't sound too unenthusiastic.

'Good! Sunday week. There'll be posters put up around the parish, of course, but you might not think to look at the local notice boards. And sometime before then you must take up that invitation to dinner at the vicarage.'

'I will,' she promised.

'Right. Well, I've taken up more than enough of your time. See you soon.'

'Yes.' She stepped into the grocer's as Rushford walked away.

By the time Rowan had made her purchases, a fine, soft drizzle was falling and the village street gleamed leadenly with a wet sheen. It was an insidious kind of rain; it didn't seem much while she was walking in it, but by the time she reached the house her hair and outer clothes were sodden.

As she opened the front gate, she could hear the telephone ringing. Instantly an irrational thought leaped into her mind – this was the first time anyone had tried to call her since her arrival, and she wondered if it could possibly be Neil. Running up the path, she fumbled with the door-key, dropped it, snatched it up again and in her haste could not get it into the lock. By the time she had taken a grip on herself and got inside, the bell had stopped.

Rowan stood in the hall, listening to the silence, her heart thumping painfully. She wanted to scream with frustration that she hadn't reached the phone before whoever it was hung up. Whoever it was . . . Neil?

Throwing her jacket over the hallstand, she went into the living-room and stared at the phone, willing it to ring again; but it stayed mute. It couldn't have been Neil, she told herself, because Neil did not know where she was. But could he have found out? It seemed unlikely, but Rowan clung obstinately to the thought that it was possible. And who else would want to phone her? Who else?

Ring, damn you! she thought. Maybe she should unload her shopping to take her mind off it. It had always seemed to be a true maxim that things never happened when you were expecting them to or hoping that they would. If she concentrated on something else, maybe it would ring again. But then there were Agnes's groceries; if she took them next door, Agnes would keep her talking, and she might miss the call. Her hand hovered over the receiver as it occurred to her to call Neil herself. But what could she say? If he wasn't her mystery caller, how could she explain herself? 'I'm in Somerset, my phone was ringing and I thought it might be you.' No, she couldn't do that. She would just have to hope and pray that the unknown person tried again.

She took her basket through to the kitchen, leaving the connecting door wide open, and started to unload her shopping. She worked slowly, subconsciously trying to waste time, to put off the moment when she would have to go round to Agnes's house. Sugar, eggs, plain flour; she set them all neatly on the table, then began to put her own purchases away in the larder. *Come on, come on – ring!* Rowan shut the larder door and looked at the things she had bought for Agnes. Perhaps if she put them back in the basket slowly, the phone would start to shrill before she had no more excuses for hovering in the house.

Even as the thought came into her mind, the telephone bell pinged once and then started to ring.

Rowan almost dropped the eggs she was holding, and ran

into the living-room. Snatching up the receiver, she said breathlessly, 'Hello?'

There was a brief pause. Then a voice said, 'Rowan?'

It was Mal Lyndon. Rowan felt a leaden weight of disappointment settle within her. She should have guessed it would be him.

Trying to keep the edge of resentment out of her voice, she said, 'Hello, Mal.'

She must have failed, because he asked, 'Are you all right? You sound a bit tense.'

'No, I'm fine. What can I do for you?'

'Well, it's about the bureau. I tried to call you a short while ago, but you were out. I started work on it this morning.' He laughed self-consciously. 'Couldn't resist the temptation! The thing is, I found something inside it which I think you ought to see.'

Rowan felt a mixture of interest and apprehension. She had had enough of odd finds in the house to last her for a while yet. 'What is it?' she asked.

'A bundle of papers, notes really. They were tucked under the lining of one of the drawers. I don't know who wrote them, though it looks as if some are pretty recent.'

That *was* intriguing. 'What sort of notes?'

'I didn't read them. They're not intended for me, obviously, and they don't belong to me either, so I felt I should hand them straight over to you. Are you busy at the moment? I thought I might bring them round.'

She didn't want to see him, but she did want to look at the notes. And it would give her an excuse for not staying with Agnes for more than a couple of minutes. She considered for a few moments, then said a little cautiously, 'Fine. Come round, if you've got the time.'

'I've got the time. In half an hour?'

'Okay.'

'See you later.' And he hung up.

When Mal arrived, Rowan was still unreasonably angry with him for being her mystery phone caller, and greeted him at the door with little more than a cursory nod.

He was carrying an old cardboard folder under one arm,

and followed her into the living-room a little chagrined at the reception he had received. She didn't offer him tea, coffee or even a smile, and, deciding that discretion was probably the better part of valour for the time being, he sat down and held the folder out to her.

'Here they are. Be careful, I just put them in there to keep them together, and they're in a bit of a mishmash.'

A couple of yellowed sheets of paper slid out of the folder as Rowan took it, and drifted like feathers to the floor. Rowan sank down cross-legged on the carpet and opened the folder before her.

It was, indeed, something of a mishmash. For perhaps a minute she gazed at the papers, experiencing strongly mixed feelings. On the one hand, she was eager to know what the papers were, what they referred to. On the other, she had an intuition that they were of a private nature, and never intended for the eyes of a casual investigator.

Her hand hovered over a sepia photograph, badly dog-eared, which lay half-hidden under a small package of letters tied with yellow ribbon, and finally she pulled it out. It showed a bearded man in a Norfolk jacket posed, in the typical way of an Edwardian photographer's studio, with one foot on a small wooden chair before a black backcloth. There was something familiar about the eyes, the shape of the mouth, and Rowan turned the photograph over. On the back was an inscription in an elegant though now faded hand.

> *'To dear Maud with much affection on her Birthday, June 3rd 1909. With fondest regard, Geoffrey Fairfax.'*

Rowan put the picture down, aware of a hard little lump that had formed in her throat for no good reason. Blinking quickly, she looked at Mal.

'My grandfather.' She held the print out as though urging him to take it away from her. 'This must have been taken before they were even engaged.'

Mal studied the photo. 'Did you know him?' he asked.

She shook her head, her memory of the family history coming back to her.

'They were married in about 1912, I think, and my mother was born in 1917.' She paused. 'My grandfather was in the army by that time. He was killed right at the end of the Great War. I can't remember where.' She felt suddenly guilty, as if her forgetfulness were somehow disloyal.

Mal looked keenly at the youthful Geoffrey Fairfax. 'I can see a likeness. In the mouth. Particularly when you're not smiling.'

Rowan didn't feel like smiling, and so she did not rise to the gentle bait. Mal let it pass, giving the photograph back. 'So your grandmother was a widow for all those years? That must have been hard.'

'It's funny, I can never think of her as a sad woman,' Rowan said. 'When I was very young, and we used to come here and visit her, she always seemed lively and cheerful. Yet she must have been so lonely.' Her voice tailed off as if she had suddenly realised that she was touching on something more personal than she had intended.

To cover her sudden embarrassment, she turned her attention to the pile of papers that lay scattered on the floor. There were two ribbon-tied bundles, and one glance at those, in which she recognised her grandmother's thin, upright script, told her that they were love-letters, and therefore not intended for anyone other than the long-dead Geoffrey. She put them aside, and picked up at random a few loose sheets of varying colours and sizes. These, too, were covered in Maud Fairfax's hand, and for a minute or two she was silent as she scanned the first of them. Then she frowned.

'Mal, where did you say you found these?'

Mal looked up from toying with a loose thread on his pullover. He had been feeling superfluous, not liking to join in Rowan's examination of the papers without being invited, yet too curious to get up and leave. 'In one of the bureau drawers,' he said. 'There was some old lining paper in the bottom, and these were spread out underneath. Have you found something interesting?' he added a little diffidently.

'Interesting, yes. Perhaps odd is a better word. I think it's a series of notes, but I can't work out what they refer to.'

'Did your grandmother write them?'

'Yes, it looks like it. The trouble is, I can't make out some of it; it's been scribbled in a hurry. Have a look – see if you can make any sense of it.'

He took the paper. It was badly faded, and stained darkly at the edges, and certainly the writing was very hard to read. Holding it up to get a better angle of light, he managed to make out a few lines.

' " . . . *in the family for generation after generation* . . ." ' He was speaking aloud, hardly realising that he did so. ' " . . . *although the name changes, the basic essence*" – can't read the rest of this bit! – hold on, it's clearer here – "*finding the Crown of Horn as my own grandmother did*. . ." another blank here, I'm afraid, and then it says something about Margery.'

'That was my mother's name,' Rowan interjected.

'Yes, it says – "*Why Margery could never understand the importance of it; she still believes that as my daughter she has the right . . .*" '

'The right to what?'

Mal shook his head with a sigh. 'I can't read it from there on.'

'Give it to me.'

Rowan scanned the paper for some time, then sat back, her face disappointed. 'It's stained too badly. Damp must have got to it, and it's ruined the writing. Here, let's look at some of the others. They might tell us something.' She had forgotten her reserve in the light of this discovery, and together they searched through the scattered sheets, looking for some clue, some continuation.

But their hopes were unfounded. The remainder of the papers consisted of only the vaguest notes on a variety of subjects, even down to what appeared to be a list of library books. The only other promising find was still more cryptic than the first: a torn-off scrap from a notepad which said, '*Traditional attribute of the Crown of Horn – from Dwyer down – find out whether the hiding place has always been the same*.'

'Ye gods,' Mal said when she showed it to him. 'That tells us precisely nothing. It only makes the whole thing more confused!'

'That's the second reference to the Crown of Horn,' Rowan murmured half to herself. 'Have you ever heard of that before?'

'Never. It's double-Dutch to me. But it obviously meant something to your grandmother, and she implies that it has a strong connection with your family.'

'And my mother.' Rowan looked up. 'That's one thing that rings a sort of bell. You see, my mother and my grandmother quarrelled when I was about eight. I still don't know to this day what the row was about, because my mother would never say a word to me about it, and now she's dead I haven't a hope of finding out. But we never went to visit Gran again after that, and I suppose by the time I grew up and became independent I'd lost the habit of coming here altogether. I feel so bad about that now, and not just for that reason.'

Mal glanced at the crucial paper again. 'She makes a point about your mother believing she had a right to something. Could that have been at the root of it?'

'I'm sure it is, but that doesn't bring me any closer to finding out the cause. This Crown of Horn, it must have some connection with that, but what *is* it?'

'Perhaps it's an heirloom, or – ' Mal fished for the right words. 'I don't know, maybe a principle, an idea – something abstract.'

Rowan did not reply at first. *Crown of Horn* – that phrase had triggered off an apparently unconnected image, but one which nonetheless made a strong impact. The tree in her dream, and in the field, and the man with the antlers rising from his head.

No, she decided, it made no sense. She was simply allowing her present preoccupations to colour everything else, and inventing illogical and far-fetched links that did not exist. Groping in the dark as she was, it wouldn't do her any good to latch on to any theory simply for the sake of solving the mystery, if the answer she came up with was way off beam.

'What are you thinking?' Mal's voice broke into her thoughts. 'Have you got an idea?'

She shook her head quickly. 'No. Just a thought, but it doesn't fit. I'll have to admit defeat.'

'Well, before you ask, I *did* check the bureau thoroughly. There was nothing else.'

She considered telling him about the dream – not to gain some assurance that she was not cracking up, but to see if he could find any connection. But she decided against it. Some other time, perhaps, but now it would surely only cloud an already confused issue further.

Mal rose, stretching stiffened legs. 'I'd better go,' he said, 'if I'm going to get any more work done today. Look, if there's anything I – '

Her look silenced him; it was suspicious, closed, verging on hostile. 'Thanks, but I don't see how you can shed any light on this, Mal. If there *is* anything to it, I don't doubt I'll find out eventually.' Her tone was unconvincing and he knew she didn't feel as indifferent as she pretended. It was frustrating to leave her to pore and puzzle over the notes alone, knowing that even if he had concrete help to offer it would not be well received. But he had already learned how stubborn Rowan could be.

'Well, if you need me, you know where I am.' He had the distinct feeling he had said that before.

'Yes. Thanks.' She wasn't really listening.

'I'll see myself out,' he said with a touch of irony.

Rowan looked up, but the guilt in her eyes was very faint. 'I'm sorry, I was miles away. Mal, thank you for bringing these round. It was very good of you to take the time and trouble.'

He wanted to pick her up and shake that careful formality out of her, but instead he smiled. 'My pleasure. Give me a ring if you find anything out, will you?'

'Of course.'

She was bent over the papers, hair falling across her face and hiding it, as he closed the door behind him.

Despite Rowan's efforts, the mystery of the papers remained stubbornly impenetrable. After Mal had gone, she spent the afternoon poring over the sheets and trying to make some sense of them. And by the time she finally gave up, the light outside was fading and the room had taken on an air of shadowed gloom that drained all life and colour from the very walls.

Shivering, she glanced at the fire, which she had lit before Mal's arrival, and saw that it was almost out. The room no longer felt friendly, and quickly she switched on some lamps and added a few logs to the hearth. Then she gathered up the papers and put them carefully away in the folder. Her mind was too tired and too confused to continue worrying at them now; she needed time to let her muddled first impressions clear away before she had another try at unravelling their secrets.

It was when she was in the kitchen, making herself a long overdue cup of coffee, that she realised suddenly just how her original plans had drastically changed, and changed in such a way that she had been unaware of the subtle shifts until it was too late. She had arrived in Barton Tavey intending to stay only a few days, just long enough to sort out her grandmother's affairs, before returning to London. But as time went by, events seemed to be conspiring to keep her in the village. Intriguing questions had begun to pose themselves, questions that would not let her alone, questions that were putting other and theoretically more important matters out of her mind. It had begun simply with disturbing dreams, but now it was escalating rapidly. The dogs baying in the night, the scent bottle that smelled of roses, the papers in the bureau drawer, even the tree she had encountered in the field – they were all pieces of a jigsaw puzzle, and she knew herself well enough to be aware that she could not be satisfied until the puzzle was complete.

She went to the kitchen door and opened it, breathing in the soft autumnal air that was already damp with dew, and stared out across the garden and beyond. There was still enough light in the sky to see the impressive rise of the Exmoor hills in the distance, and she remembered thinking how the hills seemed to enclose the village, both protectors and jailers. Was she, too, beginning to fall under their spell? Was she gradually becoming caught in the gentle but inexorable snare that held this small, close and self-contained community together in the hills' embrace? She was starting to think of Barton Tavey as home now, the house as a sanctuary. And she was making friends – or at least friends of a kind, like Agnes Teale, Mal Lyndon, Tom Rushford. Even the dissatisfied Rose Bastable was a pleasantly familiar face now. Rowan shopped at the local shop, visited the local pub, had half-promised to join in the fun at the Harvest Festival. Dangerous signs that she was becoming parochial, losing the sense of anonymity and independence which London had fostered on her, and taking on the new identity of a village-dweller.

But was that so very dangerous, she asked herself? What, exactly, did she fear? The only threat that Barton Tavey posed was in the way it forced her out of herself and made her relate, however reluctantly, to the people around her. Surely no bad thing, if she was dispassionate about it?

Rowan sipped her coffee, still gazing out of the open door at the gathering dusk. If she really did feel that Barton Tavey was trapping her, turning her into something she did not want to be, then the best thing to do would be to finish this cup, go upstairs and pack all her clothes, then lock up the house and drive back to London right now, before the rot could set in any further. For if she left it too long, the web would close too tightly and she would find a hundred and one excuses to keep her here. If she wanted to survive unchanged, she should go now. And to hell with the jigsaw puzzle.

She closed the door and bolted it, then stood in the kitchen for a minute or so, unmoving, a thoughtful frown on her face. It was not an easy decision. Picking up her coffee again she took it through to the living-room. Here the fire was burning up, and the cheerful blaze sent patterns of light and shadow skipping across the walls. The room was warm now, recapturing its sense of drowsy comfort that had already become so familiar to her.

Rowan paced uncertainly across the floor. She was tired of thinking, tired of trying to make decisions about herself and her future. Tired, too, of the dark miasma of depression that was constantly at the back of her mind, and of its cause. All she wanted was a little peace and quiet, time to allow her thoughts and ideas to sort themselves out into comfortable order, without too much conscious effort. Time to let herself relax.

She sat down in what had become her favourite armchair and, seeing that it was nearly half-past seven, leaned forward to switch on the television to see if she could catch the mid-evening news.

6

If Tom Rushford had been praying for good weather to attend the harvest celebrations, it looked as though his prayers would be answered. During the week preceding the festival, Exmoor basked in an Indian summer; barometers went sharply up, and the noon temperature hovered above seventy. Agnes Teale, during one of her increasingly frequent morning chats with Rowan over tea, predicted with gloomy relish that it couldn't possibly last; if she knew anything about weather there'd be a storm before Sunday, and the fête would probably be washed out.

'Not that it'll make that much difference,' she added. 'The Harvest's not like it was a few years ago. Oh, the church service hasn't changed much of course, but the fête now – that used to be quite an event! People'd come for miles for the Barton Tavey Harvest Fête. Now, of course, it's just a few stalls and a bit of morris dancing and all that litter to clear up afterwards. Personally, I don't know why the vicar bothers these days.'

Rowan thought that if her attitude was typical of the village, it was little wonder that the fête had gone downhill. But Tom Rushford's enthusiasm seemed boundless; the posters were up and she knew that he had been scouting around, determined to rope in anyone who could help in any way. She herself had been mercifully excluded, either because Rushford was sensitive enough to take her original hint or because she was too new an arrival to be of any use. But she had finally run out of excuses to avoid dinner at the vicarage, and had promised to join the Rushfords for a meal after the festivities on Sunday.

She had met Mrs Rushford once, though only briefly, and her first impression was of a broad-faced, cheerful but not too overbearing woman who made the perfect social foil for her enthusiastic husband. She was, Rowan imagined, far more of a traditional countrywoman than Agnes – the type who baked her own bread and won prizes for bottled fruit. The dinner, she suspected, might well be something of an ordeal.

She sat back in her chair, gazing out of the window and only half-listening as Agnes chattered on. Vaguely it occurred to her that before long she would have to start putting her foot down about these morning visits, or they would become a habit that she would feel duty-bound never to break. All part of the trap? She wondered why she hadn't taken the decision to bolt back to London when it occurred to her a few days ago, why she had allowed lethargy to get in the way of her survival instinct. Since then, she hadn't considered the idea seriously again. Other things had got in the way, like the papers – and she was still no nearer to solving that particular conundrum.

'Rowan?' Agnes's bird-bright gaze darted to her face, taking in every detail of her expression and sifting it for clues. 'You're miles away, dear. Thinking about something special?'

Rowan started guiltily. 'What? Oh – I'm sorry, Agnes, I *was* drifting.' And looking hastily for something that would soften the insult she added, 'I was thinking about something, something Gran left, that's a bit of a puzzle.'

'Oh?' Agnes waited for her to say more.

'Agnes, have you ever heard of anything called the Crown of Horn?'

'Crown of *Horn*?' Her neighbour repeated the words. 'No, dear. Should I have?'

'I don't know. It was just a phrase Gran mentioned in a paper that she wrote.' Rowan didn't want to elaborate too far, and certainly she did not want Agnes's prying eyes to see the notes themselves. 'She mentioned it only briefly, but I wondered what it was.'

'Well, Crown of Horn . . .' Light dawned in Agnes's eyes. 'You mean Crown of *Thorn*, don't you? The one they put on Jesus at Easter.'

'No.' Rowan shook her head. 'It was Horn, definitely.'

'Perhaps you misread it, dear. Maud's writing was never very clear.'

'I didn't misread it,' Rowan insisted, somewhat vehemently.

Agnes looked piqued. 'Well now, then maybe it was Maud who made the mistake. I don't want to be disloyal, but then I know you won't mind me saying it, seeing as we're friends, but she *was* a bit inclined to wander, you know. Particularly this last year. I expect she meant thorn and wrote horn, don't you?'

'Possibly.' That hadn't occurred to Rowan before, but somehow she knew in her bones that it wasn't the answer.

'There we are, then.' Typically, Agnes had decided that once an explanation of sorts was found, that was an end to it. 'She wrote you a letter, did she? Before she passed on?'

She was probing, and Rowan was not about to give way. 'No, not a letter, Just a scrap of paper I found with a few notes on it. It isn't at all important, but I wondered what she meant.' Rowan smiled sweetly. 'As you said, it must have been a mistake.' Her tone implied firmly that she was not going to elaborate any further, and Agnes was wise enough to let it go at that.

Agnes's predictions about the Harvest Festival weather were proved wrong when the following Sunday dawned with a clear sky, a south wind and a steeply climbing temperature. To her own surprise, Rowan found that she felt quite enthusiastic about the afternoon's festivities. During the week she had been busy with a lot of small, mundane, but nonetheless time-consuming things and, had she stopped to think, she might have wondered at the easy and absorbing way in which the last few days had passed.

Mal had been in frequent contact, ringing up on the pretext of giving her a progress report on the Queen Anne bureau but somehow never failing to drop a hint about meeting for a drink. Each time she had refused him, but he still persisted, and at times, particularly when she lay alone in her bed late at night, that worried her. Mal was neither thick-skinned nor arrogant; if he continued to pursue her it could only mean one thing – that his interest was genuine, and not just a means of gratifying his ego. She was disquieted by his determination in the face of her repeated rebuffs, and because of that she was becoming afraid of him. He would make such a good friend, if only he would be content with leaving it at that. But anything else was unthinkable. And so she avoided Mal, keeping contact only on the formal and therefore safe level of a few phone conversations.

She had called in at the Oak and Ash on a couple of occasions, always carefully picking times when the bar was unlikely to be busy. A slightly wary friendship had developed between herself and Rose Bastable. Rose was jealous of her, Rowan knew, but it was an easy-going kind of jealousy, and if there was malice in it Rowan did not see the signs.

And so Rose and Agnes Teale formed the nub of Rowan's social life. She knew most village people to nod to when they passed in the street, and occasionally they stopped to chat idly. On the surface at least, she was settling into the comfortable and narrow routine of village life.

And the nightmares had stopped. After the nerve-racking occasion when she had heard the invisible horse, Rowan's dreams had reverted to something like their normal state. Sometimes they were disjointed, sometimes filled with everyday anxieties; but the dreams of Neil and of the grim pack of hunting dogs no longer troubled her. And there had been nothing else to disturb her in the night. If the 'Major's hounds' had kept up their nocturnal baying, she now slept through the din as peacefully as a child.

And so today, although perhaps she was not consciously aware of it, she was feeling more at ease than she had for a considerable time. The routine of her days had become alluringly simple. She could get up when she liked, go to bed when she liked, spend the day doing whatever she liked. Of course, it could not last; the money she had saved in the starry-eyed days of her engagement to Neil would not last forever. It would see her through the winter, but before next spring was under way she would have to start thinking about picking up the threads of her abruptly-abandoned career. That, or something less ambitious. But in the meantime she was content to drift on as she was.

The Harvest Festival service was due to take place in the church at two-thirty, and at three-fifteen, when the congregation came out, the real fun would begin. The modest area of the village green had been set aside for the fête and, watching the preparations, Rowan could see what Agnes had meant when she said the event was going downhill. A few stalls – probably for home-grown produce, raffles and white elephants – flanked the small green area, decorated with limp bunting, and the centre had been left clear for the morris dancers. The efforts of Tom Rushford notwithstanding, Rowan had her doubts about its chances of success.

Agnes had suggested that they went together to the church, and Rowan felt obliged to agree. Shortly after two, her neighbour appeared at the door dressed in her usual Sunday coat, crowned with an extraordinary straw hat on which a cluster of fake cherries and flowers nodded and shook. Clutching her prayer book in one gloved hand, she looked Rowan up and down, but if she did not approve of what she saw, she thought better of saying so. Rowan herself felt vaguely incongruous in a print dress – these days she had almost forgotten what it was to wear anything other than trousers – and they set off together to walk the quarter of a mile to the church.

It seemed that, as with funerals and weddings, just about everyone in the village turned out for the harvest service, and a good few outsiders helped to swell the congregation. Rowan saw a lot of unfamiliar faces, men mostly, with wind-browned skins and slightly embarrassed expressions. Agnes, in a whispered running commentary, told her that most of them were farmers from the outlying regions, not that they ever went to church normally, that was why Rowan wouldn't have seen them before, but somehow they always turned up for the Harvest, and if you asked her opinion they were a lot of hypocrites, coming in to give thanks for something that mattered to them, that they got profit out of, and ignoring it the rest of the year. It just showed, didn't it, that they must *believe*, otherwise they wouldn't turn up at all, so if they believed, why was it too much trouble to come other Sundays, that was what she'd like to know.

Rowan nodded without really listening, watching a small gaggle of children, each carrying some small token like a polished apple or even, incongruously, a bunch of bananas, who were filing in untidy order through the church door. She and Agnes fell in behind them, moving out of the bright sunlight into the dusty gloom of the interior.

The little church, which Rowan only faintly remembered from her grandmother's funeral, had been transformed. Sheaves of corn were propped on either side of the altar, and garlands of late summer flowers decked the severe stone pillars and their gargoyle heads. Someone had fastened a small posy of cornflowers to the end of each pew, and all this, together with the piles of votive fruit that were already building up by the chancel steps, lifted the atmosphere from its usual restrained solemnity to a brightness and gaiety more reminiscent of pagan times. Rowan and Agnes walked slowly along the cracked flagstones of the aisle, and Agnes fussed her way into a pew near the front, where she could get a good view of Tom Rushford.

As they sat down, someone in the row behind tapped Rowan on the shoulder, and she turned to see Mal Lyndon smiling at her.

'All good people met together!' he said in a stage-whisper, nodding his head in the direction of Agnes, who was now on her knees, lips moving soundlessly in a prayer while her eyes watched the newer arrivals through a gap in the lattice of her folded fingers.

Mal had made some concession to formality, in that he was wearing a jacket and cravat instead of simply an open-necked shirt, but he still managed to look cool, relaxed and totally at ease. As Rowan returned his smile and made to turn back, he added, 'I gather you've been invited to the vicarage revels this evening.'

She realised what he was implying. 'Will you be there too?'

'Yes. I think Mrs Rushford suspects that I need a square meal for once in my life.'

'Oh. Good.' At that moment, to Rowan's relief, the organist started up the first wheezy notes of a hymn, drowning out anything more Mal might have wanted to say. She rose with the rest of the congregation, hastily thumbing her battered hymn-book for the right page and privately wishing that the Rushfords had not invited her and Mal to dinner on the same occasion. All week she had tried to avoid Mal, and now circumstances had thrown them together again. Rose Bastable would be furious. She smiled faintly, then turned her attention to the singing as the small church choir, with Tom Rushford bearing the tall cross, began their procession from the door towards the altar.

Rowan had never been interested in religion, but she had to admit afterwards that she enjoyed the Harvest Festival service. There was something quite moving about the sound of a West Country congregation singing – the deep, rich and powerful voices of the farmers blending with the higher, shriller sopranos of children – and when the organ struck up 'We Plough the Fields and Scatter' and the younger ones began to scramble out of their seats and walk in self-important procession to place their harvest tokens on the chancel steps, Rowan saw Agnes surreptitiously wipe away a tear. Tom Rushford, tactfully aware that everyone would be eager to get on with the fête, kept his sermon short, and after a couple more hymns, a prayer and the blessing, the organist began a lively Handel piece that he played with gusto, if not great skill, as if to put everyone in a fair-going mood.

Mal fell into step beside Rowan as she emerged from the church, Agnes having taken herself off to chat with an acquaintance.

'Well, that wasn't too much of an ordeal, was it?' he asked.

Rowan laughed. 'I enjoyed it.'

'Then you should enjoy the fête, too. Despite Agnes's gripes, it's still the high point of village life.'

As they waited to pay polite respects to Tom Rushford, who at that moment was talking to a group of farmers, Rowan's gaze travelled casually over the stone walls of the church, and then she paused, a slight frown crossing her face. Mal said, 'Something wrong?' and she shook her head.

'No, not wrong. I've only just noticed those gargoyles.'

'What, the demonic-looking faces? Yes, our church seems to have more the usual share of them, doesn't it.'

He was right; but that wasn't what had caught Rowan's attention. The grotesque stone faces which seemed to leer down at her from under the eaves almost all had an unusual feature in common – on their heads, sprouting above their over-large ears, were horns. Horns of different shapes and sizes, some forward-curving like those of a goat, others like stubby, branching antlers.

Rowan recalled something she had seen before, and then forgotten. She looked back towards the church door, and they were there, as she had thought – a pair of perfect large stag's antlers mounted over the door, at the apex of the arch.

'Mal,' she said, 'Something's just occurred to me. Look at the figures – they've all got horns of one sort or another, and the antlers over the church door . . . well, it made me think about that phrase in Gran's notes.'

Mal's eyes were alight with interest. 'Crown of Horn – of course! That's a perfect description, isn't it? But what could possibly be so significant about a set of antlers?'

'That's the trouble, it still doesn't make any sense.' Rowan sighed. 'In fact it only makes everything more confusing than ever, when I think about it. Crown of Horn *could* refer to deer horns, but then on the other hand, what connection could they have with some family heirloom?'

'Maybe it isn't an heirloom. As I said before, it may not even be anything concrete. But I think this is at least a clue.'

She grimaced. 'Some help!'

'You ought to start making enquiries about local legends – the Crown of Horn could be an allegory for something.'

The idea both interested and alarmed Rowan, and her mixed feeling showed in her face. 'Perhaps I'll think about that,' she said cautiously.

At that point Tom Rushford moved on from his group of farmers and was asking them if they had enjoyed the service, and saying how much he and Jennifer were looking forward to seeing them both that evening. They thanked him and returned the sentiments, then Mal led Rowan away towards the lych-gate.

'Duty has been done, and seen to be done,' he commented. 'Now we can get down to the serious business.'

By the time they arrived at the village green, the fête was under way. The event had attracted a surprising number of people; far more, it seemed, than could be provided by Barton Tavey and the surrounding villages.

'I reckon a lot of them are tourists,' Mal said when Rowan remarked on it. 'If you go into Minehead or Lynton you'll find that most of the hotels are still pretty full. And I expect the weather's brought a few weekenders out of the woodwork too.'

It was, she thought, certainly a more colourful and lively scene than Agnes had led her to anticipate. As well as the usual fête stalls – tombola, white elephant, home produce – there were other entertainments, including an Aunt Sally, hoop-la, and even the chance to bowl for a small, pink, and very vociferous pig that snuffled about in a small pen off to one side, much to the interest of several dogs. From the pond at the edge of the green the local ducks watched, commenting on the activity with an occasional disgruntled outburst of quacking.

For an hour, Rowan threw herself into the spirit of the fête. She let Mal persuade her to try her hand at bowling for the pig, and she was relieved when she lost; then she won a large tin of Indian tea on the hoop-la. Afterwards they went to the refreshment tent for ham sandwiches and lukewarm orange squash, and she realised that not only was she enjoying the fête, she was also enjoying being in Mal's company. In the midst of this crowd she experienced none of the unease that she felt alone with him; there was nothing to intrude on their light, easy friendship. If it could be like this all the time, she told herself, they would see a lot more of each other than they did at present.

By the time they came out of the tent, people had been herded to the fringes of the green and the central space cleared. The morris dancing was about to begin, and three musicians, a fiddler, tin-whistle and hand-drum player, all dressed in the distinctive white shirt and trousers with crossed bands of red and green on their chests, were already in place. The fiddler – whom Rowan recognised as the local baker – adjusted his jaunty straw boater and nodded to his companions, and a ragged burst of applause broke out as the morris men themselves came dancing in to the first lively strains of 'The Cuckoo's Nest'.

London wasn't exactly rife with morris dancers, and so Rowan was fascinated by the entertainment, which brought back long-lost memories of childhood holidays spent with her grandmother. The rhythm of the music and the jingling of the dancers' bells had a hypnotic appeal, and soon she was clapping along with the rest of the spectators. They danced a stick-dance, a kind of ritualised mock battle with long staves, then another in which each man held a 'sword' made of a strip of flexible steel, and the 'swords', after some incredibly complex manoeuvres, combined to form a great star which the leading dancer carried off in triumph.

'Enjoying it?' Mal asked.

'Yes! But why don't they have any women in the team?' she asked.

Mal threw up his hands in assumed horror. 'Women? Good God! No, seriously, though – it's strictly against tradition to have female morris dancers. Something to do with the origins – they're fertility dances, you see, and it's all connected with the –' he stopped speaking suddenly as something caught his attention, and Rowan, following the direction of his gaze, saw what it was.

The morris men were beginning a new dance, and this

time another character had arrived to join them. One of their number had put on a dark blue blanket which hid the top half of his body completely, and crowning this was a huge wooden head with a hinged mouth that clacked noisily open and shut. And sprouting from this pantomime head were two tall antlers.

'There you are,' Mal said, as if the connection had only just occurred to him. 'There it is again – your Crown of Horn!'

Rowan stared at the figure, which was now capering at the edge of the line of dancers. Now and then it dipped its head and rushed towards a knot of onlookers, the mouth flapping. Children scattered with screams of mock terror.

'What is it?' she asked. 'What does it symbolise?'

'I suppose that's an arguable question these days, but I think it's the sort of central symbol of the masculine principle, if that doesn't sound too high-blown. Originally he was probably the stag-king, but nowadays they call him the Hobby-Horse.'

She glanced keenly at Mal, surprised by this unexpected store of folkloric knowledge, but before she could say anything the Hobby-Horse decided that they were a likely target for its attentions, and rushed at them in a zig-zag charge. Rowan squealed and jumped back, then laughed.

'He'll be coming round collecting money at the end,' Mal told her. 'Better have a few pennies ready, or he'll give you a hard time!'

She nodded and agreed, but her mind was suddenly elsewhere. Antlers. The Crown of Horn. It was beginning to look as though her first instinct had been right after all. But the connection? She was still no nearer to finding it.

They continued to watch while the morris men danced 'Old Tom of Oxford' and 'Shepherds Hey' (which even Rowan knew, it was such a popular tune), and then the display was over. Along with the rest of the crowd Rowan put some coins into the leather bag which the Hobby-Horse brought round, and then, as people began to mill back on to the green, she turned to Mal.

'I'd better go home and get myself ready. I'm due at the vicarage at seven-thirty, and I don't want to be late. I expect Mrs Rushford's gone to a lot of trouble.'

'Ah, yes. She usually does. I suppose I ought to get back and at least have a wash or something.' He paused, but if he had hoped that Rowan might invite him back to her house, he was disappointed. 'Do you want a lift?' he suggested.

She shook her head. 'No, thanks. I'd rather walk; it's such a lovely afternoon. Well, I'll see you later, I expect.'

'Count on it.'

'And thanks for – well, I've really enjoyed myself today.' She meant it. For the moment, at least, the barriers between them were down.

'My pleasure. See you at the ordeal!' And he was gone, striding across the green to where he had parked his van.

Rowan exhaled a long, slow breath and looked around her. The September light was losing its brilliance, turning gold and mellow, and the fête was beginning to wind towards its close. Visitors were luring their children away with promises of ice-cream later, the morris team's musicians were packing up their instruments, and even the noisy pig had been won by a farm labourer who was stoically suffering the jokes of his friends. Some of the bunting fluttered as a small, quirkish breeze – the first today – made itself felt, and the shadows were growing longer. Somewhere, audible even above the sounds of the fête, a blackbird was singing its heart out.

Rowan scuffed at the churned grass beneath her feet, then turned slowly away and moved across the green to the high street, where the late sunlight still glinted off the bonnets of visitors' cars. She looked back once more at the coloured tableau of stalls and people, and then with a contented smile started along the street in the direction of her home.

7

Dinner with the Rushfords turned out to be far less formidable than Rowan had feared. She arrived at the vicarage to find Jennifer Rushford alone. Evensong had not quite finished, and the vicar's wife took the opportunity to show her something of the house and its garden.

The house had been built in the eighteenth century, but had echoes of an earlier, Jacobean style. It was, Jennifer explained, far too large for them, as their two sons had left home, and half of it was never used. Rowan admired the high-ceilinged library with its glass-fronted bookcases (walnut, she noted, and good walnut at that), was shown the lounge with its French window and marble fireplace, and then, as dusk started to fall in earnest, Jennifer took her on a lightning tour of the garden, during which she cut a very generous spray of floribunda roses and pressed them into Rowan's hands, saying that she must take them home with her.

Rowan was fast growing to like Jennifer Rushford. Underneath her rather forceful and off-puttingly efficient exterior, she was warm-hearted and generous, with a reassuringly scatty side. And, as Rowan found out, she was not the sort of hostess who put her guests to shame by serving a perfect cordon-bleu meal. At a quarter past eight, Rowan and Mal sat down with the Rushfords to roast lamb and two veg, with a lumpy gravy for which Jennifer profusely apologised – something had distracted her attention while she was making it, she said, and she had forgotten to stir it whilst it was coming to the boil. That did a lot to put Rowan at ease and, as Mal seemed perfectly at home here, which suggested he was a fairly regular vicarage guest, she quickly managed to relax and join in the talk.

The Rushfords, it seemed, had been in Barton Tavey only six years. According to Tom, the previous incumbent – a bachelor – had not been very popular; on the more than one occasion he had arrived at the church to take a service drunk, and the number of whisky and gin bottles which had found their way into the vicarage dustbins had been at the centre of a lot of outraged gossip. And so the people of Barton Tavey had been heartily relieved when their new parson proved to be a sober – 'relatively sober, anyway' Jennifer put in – family man who took an active interest in his parish, and the Rushfords had been wholeheartedly accepted, despite the fact that they were not Exmoor natives.

The conversation after that turned to the afternoon's fête and, as Tom refilled her glass with a red wine that caught the firelight and glowed like liquid ruby, Rowan thought back to the ideas which the antlers had triggered off in her mind. She decided to see if the 'Crown of Horn' meant anything to the Rushfords. Tom in particular, she knew, was interested in local lore.

But her hopes were disappointed. When she broached the subject, both Tom and Jennifer shook their heads blankly.

'It's a new one to me, I'm afraid,' Tom said. 'Where did you come across it?'

'In some notes of my grandmother's, but she doesn't give any more clues,' Rowan told him. 'Mal and I both puzzled over it, but we couldn't get anywhere at all.'

Jennifer glanced surreptitiously at Rowan and Mal in turn, as if interested to hear that they had been seeing something of each other, and a small, pleased smile quirked her mouth. Fortunately Rowan did not see it, but Mal returned Jennifer's look with a faint raising of his eyebrows.

'Crown of Horn . . . ' Tom said reflectively. 'It almost sounds like a pun, doesn't it? On Crown of Thorn.'

'That's what Agnes said,' Rowan replied, then added, 'but to be honest I don't think there's any connection. Whatever it is, I – well, I don't think it's got anything to do with the Bible.'

She wondered if she had said the wrong thing, but Tom, surprisingly, agreed with her. 'You're quite probably right. If it does have any link with local legend, then the chances are that the Christian church doesn't come into it at all. Perhaps I shouldn't say this in case I talk myself out of a job, but most folklore was well and truly established long before our lot came along. All the church did was to change it to fit a bit more closely with its own creeds. Well, I have to admit it, Rowan, you've got me foxed!'

Jennifer laughed. 'He won't be satisfied now until he's got to the bottom of it.'

'Too true! I'll start digging and see what I can come up with. If you don't think I'm interfering, that is?' He looked quizzically at Rowan.

'No, of course not.' She quashed a faint flicker of doubt. 'If you can help, I'd be very grateful.' Of all the people in Barton Tavey, Tom Rushford was the most likely to be able to come up with a few answers. And any misgivings she might have felt about her grandmother's private notes being revealed to people for whom they were not intended were surely outweighed by the possible advantages.

And so, when the meal was over, they moved through to the lounge to drink coffee out of bone china cups with a pattern of primroses, and Jennifer firmly vetoed Rowan's offer to help with the washing up. At last, at a little after eleven, Jennifer began to yawn and the two guests rose to leave.

At the door, as Rowan clutched her bunch of flowers, Mal said, 'I walked down here tonight, so I'll see you home before I go back. And don't argue, it's only a courtesy!' His smile took the edge from his words, and she acquiesced with a small nod.

The village was in darkness. Only one street lamp glowed ghostly white like a tiny moon at the end of the road. Windows were dark – hereabouts, people went to bed early – and their slow footsteps as they walked past shuttered shops and curtained house-fronts echoed clearly in the quiet air.

Something in the atmosphere reminded Rowan of the

night when she had heard the horse's hooves, and, involuntarily, she shivered. Mal glanced at her.

'Cold?'

'No. I was just thinking about something.' Defensive, she waited for him to probe further, but he said nothing. After a few more seconds she wondered, would it do any harm, any real harm to tell him about that incident? She had kept it and the other things, like her strange dreams, bottled up inside for a long time now, and yet she knew that to bring them out into the open would do her a lot of good. And Mal – well, Mal wasn't like Agnes, nor even Tom Rushford. She had the feeling that he wouldn't automatically pounce on the first 'logical' explanation that came to mind and leave it at that. He was more open-minded; he would weigh up what she said, give her an opinion that was less likely to be based on prejudice. And, if he ended up as baffled as she was, he would have the honesty to admit it.

She looked covertly at him walking beside her. His face, the profile sharpened as they came within range of the street-lamp, was thoughtful, and the chilly white light had drained the colour from his hair so that he looked suddenly older, a hint of how he might be in twenty years' time. He wouldn't lose his good looks, she thought; they were ingrained in him, in his very bones. She felt a sharp pang then of something unnameable, some emotion that she couldn't analyse beyond the fact that it hurt.

'Mal.' She stopped walking and turned to face him fully. He gazed back at her, surprise and something akin to hope showing before he could mask it.

He didn't speak and, encouraged by this gentle tact, she said, 'Mal, there's something that's been bothering me for a long time now, almost since I first came here. I haven't talked about it to anyone, but, well, I don't think I can keep it to myself any longer.'

'Another puzzle?' Mal asked quietly.

She nodded quickly, gratefully. 'That's exactly it! It doesn't seem fair to foist it on you, but – '

'Look,' he said, 'there's no question of fairness or unfairness, all right? You've got something on your mind; you want to talk it over with someone and see what a second opinion does. I'm interested. Shall we talk now, or wait till we get back to your house?'

'Now, I think.' She smiled apologetically. 'It'll be easier to sort my thoughts out while we're walking.'

And so, as they strolled on, the story came out. She told Mal first about her dreams and about the baying dogs she had heard when she awoke in the dead of night. Then came the account of her drive out to the coast, and of how she had found the very same tree that figured in her nightmare. At this, Mal showed sudden interest.

'I think I know that place,' he said. 'It's not far from Countisbury, if we're talking about the same field. Now that *is* something to think about – the fact that you dreamed, in completely accurate detail, about a place you'd never seen before, but which actually exists only a few miles away. Is there any more?'

'Yes.' And she described the night when she had heard the horse, and yet had seen nothing.

Mal was quiet for a while after she had finished. The dark shape of her house was visible ahead now, and as they neared the gate he said, 'Look, Rowan, would you mind if I came in for a few minutes? I'm not trying to invite myself under false pretences, but something's occurred to me, and I want the chance to chew it over for a bit longer before I put it into words.'

He was walking a pace apart from her, deliberately keeping his distance, and that assuaged the reluctance she might otherwise have felt.

'Of course,' she said. 'I was going to offer you a cup of coffee before you go home anyway.' A white lie, maybe, but it was only common courtesy as he had been gentlemanly enough to escort her home in the first place.

They reached the gate, and Mal turned, looking towards the hills.

'Take a deep breath,' he said softly. 'Smell the sea?'

Rowan inhaled, closing her eyes momentarily, and her nostrils caught the faint, salty tang that mingled with the more familiar scent of warm, night-damp grass. Looking where he looked, she could see that the sky to the north-west, where the sea lay, was perceptibly paler, a chilly silver-grey glow reflecting from the water beyond the horizon. She looked away, and the house met her gaze, mysterious in the darkness.

Suddenly she was irrationally glad that she was not alone.

They entered the hall, and Mal saw that Rowan relaxed as soon as the lights came on. He followed her into the living-room, and on the threshold paused.

'Those roses of Jennifer's have a strong scent,' he said when she glanced inquiringly at him. 'Or have you already got some in here?'

Rowan's face became a mask, stunned into immobility. She was almost afraid to breathe in; but there it was, that unmistakable fragrance. She brought the bunch of flowers she held quickly up to her face, silently praying that the scent came from them. But their perfume was different; the scent that hung in the room was all too familiar, and she looked at Mal, her eyes suddenly haunted.

'Did I say something wrong?' Mal asked.

'No. You only stated the obvious, I'm afraid. Mal, I – I've smelled this scent before on several occasions. Always in this room.' Her eyes scanned their surroundings quickly, as though she were afraid of seeing something that shouldn't have been there. 'I don't know where it comes from, or what it means. But there's no possible *physical* source that I can find for it.'

Mal's nose wrinkled as he sniffed the air again. 'It's fading now. That really *is* odd. That, tied in with the other things you've told me.'

'Do you believe me?' Rowan was uncertain, suddenly wondering if she had been wise to confide in Mal.

'Of course I do. You don't have any possible reason for making it up, do you? Why on earth should you invent something like that?'

Her face closed up as he spoke, and when he looked at her she was staring at her own feet. 'Oh, I don't know,' she said, half-challengingly. 'There could be an explanation.'

'What do you mean?'

'Maybe I didn't invent them but maybe I imagined them.' She raised her head and gave him a look that defied him either to argue or to agree; he wasn't sure which. 'Maybe I'm not quite right in the head, Mal. I had a sort of breakdown a few months ago. I haven't told you about that before.'

Mal felt acutely uncomfortable. He wanted to dismiss her suggestion as nonsensical, to say that she looked and acted as sane as anyone else, but somehow he knew that she would take it as an empty and insincere assurance.

Non-commitally, he said, 'No, you haven't told me. But if it was just a straightforward and temporary illness – '

'*Just* a – ' Rowan began in furious protest, but he forestalled her.

'For God's sake don't get me wrong. I'm not trying to make light of it! What I meant was, I don't think that anything short of a real psychosis could produce hallucinations of that order. And if your illness was a psychosis, you wouldn't be here now. You'd be in a mental hospital, or at least under close supervision.'

Rowan thought that over for a few moments, then said grudgingly, 'Okay, fair enough. But how the hell do you know that what you're saying's true? You're not medically qualified. How do you *know* that I couldn't have imagined these things?'

There was a potentially explosive build-up to the atmosphere, and Mal felt his own temper quickening in the face of her cussedness. Trying to keep a note of impatience out of his voice he replied, 'No, I'm not medically qualified. But you wanted my opinion and I gave it. You don't have to take any notice of it if you don't want to.'

Briefly, anger flared in Rowan's eyes, then her shoulders sagged. 'I'm sorry, Mal. I'm getting too tetchy for my own good, particularly on this subject. It's just that it's been preying on my mind so much lately.'

'That's hardly surprising.' He smiled, thankful that some of the tension, at least, had been siphoned off. 'Look, I don't want to be a bad guest, but you did say something about a cup of coffee, and that wine's given me a dry mouth. Give me a minute to think while you're making it, then I'll give you an amateur opinion of what's going on.'

Five minutes later, when they sat at opposite sides of a

small table with a tray between them, Rowan said, 'Well?'

It was both a challenge and a plea. Mal leaned back in his chair. 'First off, do you know of any peculiar stories connected with this house?'

She shook her head. 'Nothing. And I don't think there can be any; if there were, Agnes would surely have heard of them, and you know what she's like. She'd have relished the chance to scare me witless by telling me all the details.'

'True. All right, so there's no direct connection in that sense. But this area – the whole of Exmoor, in fact – is rife with legends.' He paused, then added, 'Tell me something – have you ever heard of the Wild Hunt?'

The phrase disturbed her with a sense of vague familiarity. 'I don't know,' she said slowly. 'I've heard the name.' Shadows moved on the wall, and she wished suddenly that the light in the room were brighter.

'It's just that a lot of things that have happened to you seem, well, reminiscent of that legend.'

'Tell me about it.'

'It's a very common legend, about a pack of ghostly dogs which roams the countryside at night. They're supposedly led by a single huntsman, and there are various stories about the huntsman's identity. Down in Dartmoor, people used to believe he was the ghost of Sir Francis Drake!' He paused, but Rowan didn't laugh. 'Most stories say that the huntsman is the devil, but the legend of the hunt goes back a long way before Christianity, so who he originally was is anybody's guess. I suppose a Viking would say he was Odin, and an ancient Briton would say . . . ' he shrugged. 'I don't know.'

Rowan's mind slipped back to the fête that afternoon and to the morris men with their stag-headed Hobby-Horse. Stags, antlers, huntsmen: the links were becoming all too neat, too obvious.

'This man I saw in my dreams,' she said uneasily, 'he had antlers on his head. Do you think – '

'That he might have been a representation of the huntsman? Yes, it's more than possible.'

Rowan held her coffee-cup in both hands, warming them on the bowl. 'And that brings us back to the Crown of Horn again, doesn't it?'

'That's occurred to me, too,' he said. 'It's all starting to fit.'

Rowan did not doubt that all these strange events were connected, but *how* did they link up? That was the most important question, and the answer eluded her still.

'Mal,' she said, 'do people still believe in the Wild Hunt stories? Surely, in this day and age, it's just an old tale?'

'Oh, I don't know. There are a lot of superstitious individuals around, especially in an area like this. Some people still believe in it. I've met one or two myself.'

'And you?'

'Me?'

'What's your opinion?'

'Christ!' Mal drank some of his coffee, as if giving himself time to prepare an answer. Then he said, 'I don't really think I'm in any position to judge. I've never had anything happen to me that would make me believe in it, and I'm not inclined to take things literally without some evidence. But then, just because I've never met the Wild Hunt face to face on a windy night, that doesn't mean it doesn't exist. I wouldn't like to commit myself either way.' He smiled. 'Sorry if that sounds like I'm sitting firmly on the fence, but I'd rather be honest.'

Rowan did not respond to his smile. Instead she rose from her chair and walked restlessly towards the empty fireplace. Her voice, when she spoke, carried an edge to it, as if she might break down and cry at any moment.

'That's just it, Mal, that's what worries me! You keep an open mind, but you're not superstitious. And you've never experienced anything that might have convinced you one way or the other. Well, don't you see, I'm not superstitious either – even less so than you, in fact, because I wasn't born in the country and I haven't lived in the country until now. I've got a London mentality, and London's very down-to-earth and mundane; nothing exists that you can't touch. By that standard, if either of us was going to start seeing or hearing the Wild Hunt, surely it should have been you rather than me? I'd hardly even *heard* of the damned legend before tonight! So why has all this happened to me? *Why?*'

Her fists had clenched into tight, bunched balls, and her hair fell chaotically over her face as she leaned against the mantel. Mal stood up and came across to her, unthinkingly reaching out to touch her shoulder, wanting to comfort and reassure. But when his fingers made contact she instantly flinched away, almost stumbling over the electric fire in her haste to put a safe distance between them. There was more to that reaction than momentary distress, Mal realised wryly. He had overstepped the mark, tried to go beyond the bounds she had imposed, and it would be a while before she forgave him for that. He opened his mouth to apologise, but changed his mind in case it only alienated her further.

'I can't answer that question,' he said, anxious to put matters back on to their original footing. 'Not for certain, anyway. But don't you think it's possible that this family connection might have something to do with it?'

She watched him, hope and doubt mingled in her expression. 'What do you mean?'

'This Crown of Horn business. Your grandmother's notes suggested that it had something to do with your family, on her side at any rate. Maybe you've inherited some characteristic, some – I don't know – sixth sense or whatever, that's made you pick up on something. Maybe you're a lot more susceptible than you realise.' And, warming to his theme, he went on, 'Take the smell of roses, for instance. That could be connected, too. Could they have been your grandmother's favourite perfume?'

Rowan remembered the cut-glass scent bottle. 'I'm not sure,' she said, 'I think they might have been. But in that case, how was it that you could smell them too? You noticed it this evening before I did.'

'All right. But there was no physical source, we're certain of that. There couldn't have been. But I smelled them as clearly as you did, so you couldn't possibly have imagined them. Perhaps I am psychic after all!'

'You don't believe you are, though,' Rowan argued.

'Oh, don't I? I've always had a sneaking wish at the back of my mind that some of the things that seem to happen only to other people would happen to me once in a while.

I'm not quite as unromantic as you seem to think!'

'So what you're saying is, you think that I'm mentally attuned, because of the blood relationship, to something that happened to Gran, or something that's connected with this Crown of Horn business? Like an echo?'

'I can't think of a better way to explain it. It's almost as if her memories, or her knowledge, are imprinted on this house somehow, and as soon as you, her grand-daughter, arrived here those echoes started to affect you, as though your grandmother had something she wanted to communicate –'

'*Don't!*' Rowan shuddered suddenly and violently. 'Don't say things like that, Mal, please! It makes me start thinking of ghosts, and this place can be bad enought without that!'

'I'm sorry. But that wasn't what I meant. All I said was –'

'That I'm picking up all these things because they've got something to do with the Crown of Horn and that's got something to do with my family. I know that. But I don't want to think about Gran, not right now.' It would be different in the light of day, she knew, but right now her grandmother might almost be a tangible presence in the house, and that idea terrified her.

'So, we've got a theory.' Her voice was over-bright. 'But there's one question we haven't answered yet.'

'And that is?'

'The things I saw. Even assuming that this theory is right, and I've become "sensitive" to things that wouldn't have affected me before – what were they?'

Mal pondered. At length, he said, 'I can give you a comparatively rational explanation, or a totally irrational one. Which do you want?'

'That's up to you.'

'All right, I'll give you both and you can decide for yourself which you prefer. Rational – or at least, rational in the context we're talking about – is that your imagination was fed by these "echoes" and interpreted them in the most obvious way, by making you think that you saw and heard things that weren't there in any physical sense.'

Rowan digested this, then asked, 'And the irrational explanation?'

'That the things you experienced were as real as the fact that you and I are sitting in this room.'

He said it baldly and matter-of-factly, and Rowan felt a frisson run through her, as if a small kitten with sharp claws were climbing up her back. *Real?* That sound of hooves, with no horse visible? *Real?* Suddenly she wanted to back out of what was becoming alarmingly deep water, to clutch at a saner and more comfortable kind of reality. After all, Agnes could have been right about the hounds. The dreams could easily be put down to an upset mind and, God knew, there was enough justification for that. Maybe she had seen the field with the blasted tree when she was a child, and her subconscious had thrown it to the surface in a nightmare after all these years. That sort of thing often happened. And the horse? She could have dreamed it. She might not really have been awake at all.

She wanted to believe what reason was trying to tell her; wanted it so much that she didn't even try to explain to Mal. She preferred to ignore the small voice which told her she was afraid of being argued with, for now she needed this slender thread which held the familiar world close to her.

Mal was waiting for some response and, suddenly self-conscious, she gathered up the tray and carried it towards the kitchen. 'I'd rather believe it was imagination,' she said lightly.

The latched door swung behind her. The kitchen was unpleasantly dark and she put the tray down in the nearest space she could find, then hurried back to the living-room.

She was beset by strongly mixed feelings. Half of her was glad to have been able at least to share the burden of her worries with such a sympathetic listener; the other half wished fervently that she had not said a word. It would have been so much better if Mal had somehow been able to reassure her that there was a reasonable explanation that had nothing to do with either hauntings or the possibility that she was cracking up. Something comfortable. Instead, he had only succeeded in making her feel worse than ever, and now she only wanted him to go, to leave her alone so that she need not dwell on Wild Huntsmen and roses and ghostly dogs any longer.

Without realising it she glanced at the clock, and Mal took this as a hint. He stood up.

'You must be tired. I'm sorry, I've kept you talking too long.'

'Don't worry.' She smiled, then felt a yawn coming on. It was genuine, but she hoped it didn't look like an obvious ploy. 'I'm grateful to you for taking so much trouble, Mal, and anyway, I'm the one who should apologise for boring you all this time.'

'Oh, no. You haven't bored me – far from it! I'm fascinated by all of this. Look, have we said all that there is to say? I don't like the thought of leaving you with anything unresolved. And that question about whether it was real or imaginary – '

Rowan hastily interrupted him before he could say any more. 'I think we've covered all the ground we can for now. Anyway,' she smiled ingenuously, 'I think my brain's had too much stimulation for one day! I'll only start getting confused if I think about it any more tonight.'

Mal was not convinced. He knew that something else lay behind this easy dismissal. She had withdrawn in the space of a few minutes. Something during their conversation had upset her; perhaps that ill-chosen remark about her grandmother which she had misinterpreted. But there was no point in trying to get to the root of it. She was as close as a clam when she wanted to be, and now was one of those infuriating times.

She saw him to the front door, then walked with him down the overgrown path to the garden gate. The seaward glimmer in the sky was beginning to fade as the night deepened, and the street looked daunting in its dark emptiness. Something – a shadow – moved a little way off, and Rowan started. '*What's that?*'

Mal narrowed his eyes, trying to make out the shape that was moving away towards the village. Then he laughed softly.

'Old Cracky Tully, by the look of it. Our local tramp.'

'I know, I came across him a couple of weeks ago. Everyone says he's harmless.' Rowan sounded sceptical.

'He is,' Mal assured her. 'Anyway, every place like Barton Tavey has to have its village idiot, doesn't it? It's all part of English tradition.' He gazed after the departing Tully. 'Poor old devil, we probably disturbed him in the middle of rummaging through someone's dustbin. He'll have to go poaching if he wants his breakfast now.'

Rowan glanced sharply at him. 'Does he really do that?' she asked. 'Go through dustbins, I mean?'

'I don't know. Probably. Why?'

She shivered. 'I don't like the idea of him hanging around at night, that's all. He gives me the creeps. I'd rather give him some money to buy his food, if he's that desperate.'

'God, don't do that, or you'll have him following you wherever you go!' Mal caught sight of her face. 'Sorry. I shouldn't have said that. But honestly, you needn't worry about him. He does quite well out of people in the tourist season. Everyone thinks they're doing their public duty by slipping him a couple of coins, and he sells poached rabbits on the side, when he can find someone to buy them.'

Rowan hunched her shoulders. Tully had vanished by this time, and she was suddenly aware of how cold she was. The wind had still not risen above a breeze, but it was a sea breeze and it carried a bite.

'Will you be all right?' she asked Mal. 'It's quite a long walk, and there won't be any street lights for most of the way.'

'This isn't London,' he told her with a smile. 'No one's going to ambush me, and I won't get lost! But thanks for being concerned – I'm flattered.'

She didn't reply, and he thought how much he would have liked to kiss her, take hold of her tense, hostile body and hold her until all the resistance went out of her muscles, tell her the thoughts that were in his mind, *force* her to react to him.

But that was a fantasy. Rowan was rebuffing him, and would continue to rebuff him while those blocks she had put up in herself, those mental barriers, stayed in place. He could not destroy her barriers for her, so he must either be patient and hope for the best, or give her up as a lost cause and find other fish to fry.

He smiled at Rowan, and she wondered at the sadness in his smile. Then he said softly, 'Goodnight,' and was walking away along the village road.

8

'Gran . . . ?'

That one word brought Rowan out of a confused dream. She opened her eyes in the darkness of her bedroom and instantly became aware of something odd, something different in the atmosphere. At first she thought there was a faint glow of light in the room, but it was only an illusion, her mind adjusting to the fact of being suddenly awake.

Someone had said, 'Gran.' She had heard it distinctly. Now she realised that it was she herself who had spoken. And for some reason it seemed the most natural thing in the world, that soft, questioning call to her grandmother.

Despite the stillness, she felt certain that she was not alone in the quiet house. It wasn't a frightening sensation, far from it – it brought back echoes of something peaceful, something protective, something she wanted to reach out to.

The room swam as though seen dimly through a great depth of water as she slid out of bed and felt about for her dressing gown. Pulling it on, she moved to the door, opened it and looked out along the deserted landing. Something creaked: the house settling, sleeping. It didn't alarm her. And there was the fragrance of roses in the air.

Rowan knew even before she looked that she would see a glimmer of light under the door of her grandmother's bedroom, and for a brief moment rationality tried to assert itself. There *could* be no light there, for Gran wasn't there any more. The Maud Fairfax that this world had known was away in the churchyard. Perhaps, then, she had not really woken at all, but was still lying in her bed, and this was a dream. The truth of it didn't seem to matter. What mattered was that she was walking down the landing towards her grandmother's room, reaching out to open the door with its bar of pale grey light.

The door hardly seemed to need her touch but swung slowly open as her fingers made contact with the wood. There was the room, unfamiliar, the curtains open and shifting as the night wind insinuated through the ill-fitting window frame. There was the bed, and there too was the other thing she had expected to see – the small, frail figure propped up by pillows, the hands arthritic and all but useless, only the eyes as bright and as lively as she remembered them from twenty years ago.

'Gran?' She remembered the welcoming smile, too, but when her grandmother's lips moved she could not hear what was said. The old woman's face blurred as what seemed to be a mist drifted over her features, and all Rowan could see now was the hand that lifted awkwardly from the coverlet and reached out towards her, palm up, as if to convey what the voice could not; a welcome and a plea together.

How it was that she came to be downstairs she did not know, but suddenly she was surrounded by the more familiar setting of the living-room, as dark as the landing, but warm, and still filled with that perfume. The fire had gone out and the old lady upstairs wanted her to find something or fetch something, and she could not remember what it was. She turned hesitantly, torn between searching for it and running back up to the bedroom to ask, *What? What is it? What do you want?* and realised that the furniture was not where it should have been. Surely there was a chair here, an occasional table there? Things were missing, newer things. Only the old ones remained. She had to go upstairs, tell Gran what had happened, ask her –

She turned, as if breasting through deep water, and moved towards the stairs. But her co-ordination was awry, and she collided with an armchair, the impact seeming to jar through her.

She was on the floor, her head resting against the arm of that same chair, and in the space of less than a second the surreal atmosphere had broken into fragments that remoulded themselves, with a violent shock, into a sharp, painful reality.

Her shin and the side of her head hurt, and her heart was hammering with ugly force against her ribs, but this time she was awake. She let out a harsh, grunting breath, trying to work out where she was, what had happened. After a few more seconds the dividing line between the dream and the present grew clearer, and as she looked around she had her second shock.

She *was* in the living-room. She had been sleepwalking. Somehow she had manoeuvred her way down those narrow, twisting stairs and had come in here, guided by nothing more than unconscious instinct. And only the fact that she had blundered into an armchair and fallen had woken her.

A very real and logical fear began to replace the sense of disruption in Rowan's mind. She might have fallen at the top of the stairs, broken her neck and never known anything about it. And there was nothing she could do, nothing at all, to stop the incident from recurring. She had never sleepwalked in her life before, and the possible implications were very disturbing indeed. Certainly it gave weight to the thought that there was something wrong with her. That, and the details of the dream which had caused her to do it.

It *had* been a dream, she told herself, it could *only* have been a dream. Damn Mal Lyndon and his ideas – they must have triggered off something in her subconscious.

The room was chill with the old air of damp that the log fire hadn't yet completely dispelled. Rowan wondered what time it was. Turning towards the window she thought she detected a lightening of the rectangle behind the curtains, and hastily rose to her feet and crossed the room to look more closely. The curtain swung back, and she felt disappointed and discomfited; it was the false dawn, the deep, late hour when light in the sky is no more than an illusion. For a few moments she stayed by the window, idly looking at the indistinct tangle of the garden and trying not to think about the last half hour. And then she was certain she saw something move among the overgrown bushes.

She stood very still. Had it been an illusion, a trick of her mind? She tried to tell herself it was, but now she had the strongest feeling of being observed from somewhere out there, by a watcher whose presence she could not detect, but who could see her clearly.

Quickly she let the curtain fall, crossed the room and switched on as many lights as she could find. If there was someone out there – *if*, she reminded herself fiercely – then they might be scared away by the realisation that the owner of the house was up and about. She took several deep breaths, trying to reassure herself, and remembered that she and Mal had seen old Cracky Tully hanging around last night. Perhaps it was him, perhaps he had somehow got into the garden at the back.

On an impulse she ran through to the kitchen, turning the strong overhead light on as she entered, and checked the back door, although she knew for a certainty that she had locked it before going to bed. When she returned to the living-room she was tingling with unease. No one could get in – the house was secure – but still she couldn't dispel the awful feeling that she was overlooked.

If only the suggestion of light outside was true dawn. She knew she could not return to her bedroom and hope to sleep, now that these primal fears had been stirred up. She felt too vulnerable, too alone. Her gaze strayed to the telephone, and for a few moments she thought of ringing someone, just for the relief of hearing another human voice. But the only person who would conceivably forgive her for waking him at this hour in the morning was Mal. And she couldn't call Mal. For one thing, her fear of the unknown was not strong enough, yet, to overcome the embarrassment she would feel at confessing it. And for another, he would see it as a sign that she was coming to rely on him. That was something she couldn't acknowledge, even to herself. It was a step in a very dangerous direction.

Rowan decided that there was only one thing she could do. She must quash the creeping unease she felt, push it down before it could gain too strong a hold. And her best hope of achieving that lay in going back upstairs, dressing, and starting her day a good few hours earlier than usual. It would bring back some semblance of normality, and once dawn broke she would be able to laugh at the night.

It was when she stood at the foot of the stairs that she remembered her dream again. She had been so sure then that she was awake; the experience had seemed as real in its disjointed way as any waking moment. She knew now that if she went into her grandmother's old room it would be empty, but nonetheless she had to make quite certain.

She started up the stairs, aware that her pulse was quickening and not liking the sensation. Even with the staircase flooded with light, the landing had a disquieting atmosphere of its own, heightened no doubt by the dream. She gained the top of the flight and looked at the closed door that led to her grandmother's room. She would have to check now, before her courage failed and she ran straight to her own bedroom.

Rowan crossed the landing in four quick steps and pushed the door open as if about to challenge anything that might be on the other side. Light from the passage spilled in, illuminating the table, the closed curtains and the bed – bare and empty.

She leaned against the door-jamb, almost laughing in her relief. For the last few minutes she had been behaving like a child, afraid of nothing more than a simple and explicable dream, afraid almost of her own shadow. Closing the door, she left the room to its peacefulness and went on to her own bedroom to dress.

She felt safer on the upper floor of the house. Irrational perhaps, but the thought that there was a greater distance between herself and any unknown watcher was reassuring. It was easier, in this small, cosy room, to believe that the fears she had felt downstairs were products of her imagination and not real in any way. And yet, she thought as she brushed her hair in front of the old swing mirror on the dressing table, it was impossible to deny that there was something about the house itself that added fuel to those feelings. She would never allow herself to be so fanciful as to say that the house was *alive*, but she had so far been unable to shake off the impression that something that was a part of it, something vague and formless and not truly sentient, was aware of her presence in the shelter of its walls. She had had the feeling since the evening of her arrival, and time had not diminished it – if anything, it had grown stronger. It was that peculiar urge to look over her shoulder, or to pause in the act of crossing a room and wait, listening for a sound that wasn't there. At this very moment she knew that if she should release the firm hold she had on her thoughts she could imagine that there was someone, or an echo of someone, on the empty landing, observing her. It wasn't a pleasant feeling, but although it made her uneasy she was not truly frightened of it, for the sensations she had picked up – or thought she had picked up – bore no trace of malice. She recalled what Mal had said last night about her grandmother. But it wasn't that – that was too close to the realm of ghosts, and there were no ghosts here. It was more like living with the memory of a companion whom she had never met.

She lifted back the curtain at her window, crouching down to peer outside. Somewhere beyond the rising hills now there *was* a faint and barely discernible lightening of the sky; the first hint of the real dawn following the false. Rowan felt herself relax a little. By the time she had made tea and eaten something (now that she was fully awake she felt ravenously hungry), the outside world would be coming to visible life, and that would make her feel easier in her mind. If someone *had* been prowling around the house – although now she was beginning to doubt the possibility – they would not, surely, stay in the vicinity once dawn had broken; that would be courting discovery.

She let the curtain fall again and left the bedroom to return to the ground floor. The living-room greeted her ablaze with the lights she had switched on, its atmosphere cheerful and calming to her tautened nerves. She went through to the kitchen and set the kettle on to boil, then decided to cook herself a full-scale breakfast – eggs, tomatoes, fried bread, the lot. It was something she had not done since the days when she lived with her parents.

By the time she had cooked and eaten her meal, and savoured the childish feeling of guilty elation at the sheer self-indulgence of it, the sky was dove-grey with the first pink blush of sunlight filtering through a thin film of cloud. The hills with their morning mist showed vague and purple-tinged beyond the village, and somewhere in the distance a cockerel was announcing the day from someone's chicken-yard.

Putting her breakfast plate in the sink, Rowan unbolted the back door and opened it, letting in a cool rush of air that smelled damp and green. There had been a heavy dew, and the big, broad leaves of a clump of foxgloves near the door were weighed down with it, hanging limp and glistening. Rowan stepped outside, inhaling deeply and enjoying the tickle of wet grass on her ankles, then paused and looked carefully around the garden, seeking some sign that might give a clue to someone having recently been there. But there was nothing: no trampled patches of grass, no newly-broken stems on the crowding shrubs. The high stone wall, its surface green and slippery with moss and half-obscured by the withered brown tendrils of a long-dead creeper, would form an effective barrier to any but the most determined intruder.

So it must have been her imagination after all. Certainly no tramp of the ilk of old Cracky Tully would have been able to scale the wall, and who else would want to prowl this neglected garden in the depths of the night?

Reassured, she was about to turn back into the house when a glint of something metallic in the longer grass caught her eye. She moved towards it and, pushing her hands through the damp, browning tangle, picked up the object that lay half-buried in the dark earth.

It was a horseshoe. As she brushed away the clumps of soil that clung to it, Rowan saw that it was almost brand new. The bright sheen was only slightly tarnished, and although the two horns of the shoe looked worn it showed no other sign of ever having been used.

She turned it over in her hands, examining it more closely and wondering how it could have come to be in the garden. Perhaps it had been a good-luck piece that had once hung above the back door and had either fallen or been discarded. But in that case, how could it still shine so brightly? If it had been lying in that sodden grass for any length of time it would have been dull, rusted, ruined. Instead, it looked as though it had been dropped only a few hours before she found it.

Suddenly Rowan felt oppressed. The brightening day seemed to turn sour, as if the sky had curdled and cast a giant shadow over her. Quickly she looked up, scanning the garden once more, than gazed beyond the wall to the distant, brooding hills. There was something more to this small discovery than was apparent on the surface, she was sure. It *meant* something, and although she tried to hold her thoughts back they turned immediately to the Crown of Horn and Mal's story of the Wild Hunt. Baying dogs, invisible horses, and now a horseshoe that had seemingly materialised from nowhere. There had to be a connection. To believe otherwise would be to stretch coincidence too far.

Still holding the horseshoe, she went back into the kitchen and closed the door. The house felt suddenly claustrophobic, as if, no matter where she went, she could not escape from the lengthening string of peculiar events that dogged her. And following on the heels of that came the thought that she wanted to get away from the house for an hour or two. Maybe she could find a beach and walk for a while, or just sit and watch the sea and let its slow, ceaseless rhythm settle her mind. Anything, so long as it took her out of her immediate environment.

She fetched a coat, changed her slippers for boots, and snatched up her handbag, checking that the house keys were inside. Then she went out by the front door and walked to where her Mini was parked.

A distant whine and clatter announced the arrival of the morning milk as Rowan slid into the Mini's driving seat, and seconds later the float from the local dairy appeared round the bend. She could see the appeal of a job that meant rising with the dawn. There was something clean and untrammelled about the world at this time of day, an effect that could never hope to last long into the morning.

Rowan turned the key in the ignition and the car's engine coughed and spluttered damply. It started on the fourth try, and she drove towards the centre of the village, past the still-shuttered shops of the deserted high street. She took the narrow coast road, glancing quickly as she passed Coombe Cottage and seeing that its curtains were closed, and the car climbed gradually towards the height of Foreland Point with its huge vista.

Rowan drove for perhaps half an hour on roads that were as empty as anyone could have wished, seeing only the occasional cluster of sheep drifting across the landscape like stray, earthbound clouds. Then, leaving the high ground behind, she found a small bay that sheltered in the lee of a steep cliff, where the sea, flat and grey, licked sluggishly at a shingle beach. Leaving the car, she sat for a while on the broken stones of what had once been a complete harbour wall, but which now ended abruptly in a pile of seaweed-strewn rubble, cracked and pitted and eroded. A few small boats rocked sleepily at their moorings by the wall, and three stone cottages, all recently renovated, faced out from the lee of the cliff. But there was no sign of human activity, and the only sound to break the early quiet was the occasional harsh scream of the gulls that wheeled overhead.

Time passed, and the peace and solitude of the bay worked its own small magic on Rowan. There was still a fine veil of cloud over the sky, but the warmth of the sun, visible only as a smudge of light through the mist, filtered down and warmed her face as she sat. The tide was receding, leaving a swathe of dark and wet pebbles with strands of weed like long, long hair between them. At last she stood up, rubbing at the backs of her thighs to dispel the damp which had seeped through her clothing, and made her way slowly back along the little beach to her car.

The three cottages had come to life, she noticed; curtains were open and a trickle of smoke rose from one of the chimneys, hardly disturbed in the all but windless air. A door banged somewhere and a dog barked, and those homely sounds suddenly broke the quiet spell. Rowan's feet crunched on drier shingle, then she was back on the road, and moments later the cocoon of her car was wrapped around her again.

She reversed on to the shingle, turned around and drove back the way she had come. She felt as though the morning had cleansed her and driven out the taints of last night, replacing them with a new and welcome sense of well-being.

Wondering how long she had sat at the beach, she checked her watch and was astonished to see that it was almost ten o'clock. It must have been a good two hours since she arrived, and she felt suddenly guilty, as if there were something reprehensible in wasting so much time. But she was a free agent now, her time was her own. What did it matter if she wasted every hour of every day from now on?

A bad thought. She changed gear for a sharp bend, inwardly reprimanding herself for that piece of self-pity. Before long she would have to force herself to re-think her future, like it or not. This hiatus could not last for ever. However off-putting the real world might look to her at the moment, she would have to face up to it eventually.

But not today.

She had been driving more by instinct than anything else, following her nose to find the way back to Barton Tavey, and when a white van came round a bend ahead of her, travelling too fast, it shocked her out of her reverie. She swung the Mini's wheel to avoid the oncoming threat, and the van scraped by with inches to spare.

Doubly angry with herself now for that lapse of concentration, Rowan pushed all other thoughts out of her mind and attended to her driving. And it was then that she noticed how familiar this road seemed. She had travelled it before, and recently. But when . . . ? Idly curious, she tried to recall how it was that she knew the route, but memory failed her until, as she emerged from a long, blind curve in the road, she came upon a narrow belt of trees that lined the grass verge, with glimpses of an open field beyond. And there, unmistakably, was the half-concealed entrance to the rough track that led into the field – the field where the lightening-blasted oak tree stood.

Rowan lifted her foot from the accelerator without realising she had done so, and the Mini slowed until, as it passed the track, it was moving at no more than a crawl. Peering, she could see the tree in the distance through the network of nearer branches, and the sharp recollection of her previous visit came back. The atmosphere, so still and premonitory; the blazing sunset that had played tricks with the light; the watcher at the edge of the woods who might or might not have been there.

She hesitated, undecided whether to stop and get out. The unpleasantness of the place's aura was nothing more than a memory now. Broad daylight took away the sense of fear it had engendered before, and the sight of the oak tree, no longer unexpected, did not have the same power to shock. It might be as well to lay that ghost once and for all, to walk into the field and up to the tree and see them for what they really were, rather than what her nightmares had built them up to be.

But something made her decide against it. Not, she told herself, any lingering fear – simply the fact that she was no longer afraid, and therefore had no need to boost her confidence any further. She accelerated and left the turning behind as she headed on towards Barton Tavey. Perhaps on another occasion she would come back. But not today.

Reaching the village, Rowan realised that she did not want to go home yet. To go back indoors, to return to the oppressive atmosphere she had left behind, would be to break the pleasantly relaxed mood that had settled on her. Too many uneasy thoughts lurked in the house this morning, and it would be preferable to let them fade away of their own accord before she went back.

She got out of the car and strolled through the village, stopping at the grocer's to buy a few oddments which she didn't really need but which, she felt, gave her an excuse for being out. Then she walked on to the green and the pond, and spent a few minutes watching the ducks until she tired of their repetitive circling.

The church clock chimed the three-quarter hour, and Rowan wondered what to do next. Trudging back across the green, and noticing how the grass was churned and trampled from the previous day's festivities (though, miraculously, every other trace of the fête had been spirited away overnight) she passed the Oak and Ash and hesitated, looking across the road at its open door.

It would pass a half hour or so, just to pop in and sit down over a glass of something, and maybe chat with Rose Bastable, who wouldn't be busy this early on a weekday. Some lightweight company would complement her mood. Glancing left and right, Rowan crossed the street and walked in at the bar door.

Rose was polishing glasses with an air of burdened lethargy that quickened to relief and interest when she looked up and saw Rowan. Putting down her cloth she leaned her elbows on the bar and smiled a welcome.

'Well, this is a nice surprise! I didn't think you'd joined the ranks of the early-morning topers.'

'I haven't.' Rowan returned the smile. 'I've been up since before dawn, and I went out to the coast for a while. It's afternoon to me.' She pulled herself on to a high stool and surveyed the room. The pub had only one other customer – an old man who sat at a corner table over a tankard of thick, dark ale, and whose toothless mouth was set in what looked like a permanent grin. He nodded, and Rowan nodded back.

Rose's eyes flickered resentfully to the old man. 'Makes a change to see another face round here at this time of day,' she said in an undertone. 'I think if I have to spend another morning with no one but old Albert to look at, I'll go nuts. What are you going to have then, Rowan? Wine, is it?'

Rowan shook her head. 'Not this early, thanks! A half of something weak, perhaps.'

'Lager?' Rose suggested, and had opened a bottle almost before Rowan could assent. 'I'll have a lemonade myself, I think. With something medicinal in it to keep the boredom away.' She winked.

'Let me buy it.'

'Oh, thanks.' Rose poured the drinks, took the money, then resumed her leaning pose. 'Well, and what got you out of bed at an uncivilised hour?'

'Oh, nothing, really,' Rowan told her evasively. 'I just couldn't sleep.'

'And you've been exploring the coast?' The other girl pulled a face. 'What do you think of it?'

'The coast? It's beautiful, incredible. I found a tiny bay not far from Foreland Point, and I sat there for hours, just watching the sea.'

'Is that the place with the old harbour wall? Yes, I know it. Funny, I can never see anything in it myself. Just another bloody beach and a load of bloody shingle. Still, I suppose the gilt hasn't worn off the gingerbread for you yet.'

Rowan slightly resented her patronising tone and said, 'Oh, I don't think it will. It's so quiet and peaceful, I don't think I could ever get sick of it.'

'Want to bet?' Rose grinned wryly. 'Just give yourself a few more months, or maybe a whole winter here – that'll put it all in its right place.' She sighed. 'If I was going to live by the sea, I'd choose somewhere where the sea was worth having – the South of France, for instance! All that sun, and all those men! Have you ever been there?'

'No.'

'Me neither. Still, there's nothing to stop us dreaming. Here, how's that house of yours coming along? Are you doing anything with it?'

'Not much, as yet. I've found a few interesting bits of furniture, and Mal's renovating one of them for me. But apart from that, very little.'

Rose's expression wavered between acute disinterest in furniture and acute interest in Rowan's relationship with Mal. 'Ye-es,' she said at last, 'I've heard he's supposed to be quite good. He ought to be, the amount of time he spends working. Hasn't been in here for days.' Her tone verged on the resentful, as if Rowan's commission was responsible for keeping Mal out of circulation. 'Poor old Mal, he always was a sucker for punishment. He used to – oh, sod.' She glowered across the bar as a new customer walked in. 'Wouldn't you know it? This place is as dead as a doornail most mornings, then as soon as you turn up and I get the chance for a chat, half the world decides to come in as well. Hang on, I'll be as quick as I can.' And to the newcomer she uttered a belligerent, 'Yes?'

Rowan waited, idly studying the horse brasses that decorated the bar canopy and wondering who did all the work of polishing them. Not Rose, that was certain. Probably the landlord himself, who seemed to spend most of his time behind the scenes rather than actually serving. She knew him to nod to, but had never exchanged more than a half-dozen words.

'Right.' Rose came back, scowling at the customer who had interrupted her as he made his way to a table in a deserted corner. 'Where were we?' She stopped then, putting a hand up to her face. 'Damn it, I've got something in my eye. You haven't got a mirror on you, have you?'

'Yes, somewhere I think.' Rowan put her bag on the counter, noticing fleetingly that it felt slightly heavier than usual, and opened it, searching for her compact. Finding it, she pulled it out – and with it came something else, something bright and metallic which fell on the bar with a heavy thud. The horseshoe.

The eye that Rose's hand wasn't covering blinked in astonishment. 'What on earth's that – a horseshoe?' She glanced at Rowan, who was staring at the shoe in appalled silence, then back again. 'Whatever's one of those doing in your bag?' And, provoking no reaction, she laughed self-consciously. 'Your good-luck charm, is it?'

She must have dropped it into her bag without thinking, when she left the house in such a rush. What a crazy thing to do.

Wordlessly, Rowan passed the compact over to Rose and then picked up the horseshoe, letting it hang weightily over her palm and closing her fingers around the cold iron surface. Frowning, and still watching Rowan covertly, Rose held the mirror up to her face and flicked at the edge of her eye, then blinked, shut the compact and handed it back. Her face was alive with curiosity.

'Something funny about that?' she asked with the faintest touch of diffidence.

Rowan snapped out of the limbo she had been in, and gripped the horseshoe momentarily more tightly before setting it back on the counter. 'No. I just couldn't work out how it could possibly have got into my bag. I must be getting woolly-headed. I found it in the garden this morning.'

Rose made a move and picked the horseshoe up, holding it to the light so that a line of bright fire ran down the horns. 'You ought to hang it over the door, for luck. Here, it's in good condition, isn't it? Not tarnished. Looks brand new.'

'That's what I thought. That's why it puzzled me – the fact that it was in the garden, and it must have been there for some time, and yet, well, as you said yourself, it looks brand new.'

'Maybe you've had horses galloping through your garden in the middle of the night, then!' Rose grinned. 'Maybe that's why you can't sleep.' She started to laugh at her own joke, then stopped as she saw Rowan's face. 'Rowan? What's the matter, did I say something?'

Rowan reached out and took the horseshoe from her, pushing it down into the bottom of her bag and fastening the clasp so that it was out of sight. Rose's flippant remark had triggered off the very thoughts she had spent all morning avoiding, and suddenly she could not hold back. The fears had to find an outlet.

'Rose,' she said, 'Have you ever heard of the Wild Hunt?'

Rose frowned, and her gaze met Rowan's as if she were trying to assess the motive behind the question. 'Who on earth's been putting ideas in your head?' she asked.

'Have you heard of it?' Rowan persisted.

'Yes, course I have. Everyone born round here has.'

Rowan hesitated, then asked, 'Do you believe in it?'

To her chagrin, Rose burst out laughing, then suddenly realised that she was being tactless and suppressed her mirth, though with some difficulty. 'Believe in it?' she echoed. 'Christ, of course I don't! Ghosties and ghoulies and all that sort of thing went out with the Ark, didn't it?'

Rowan felt a flush burning her cheeks. She had made a

fool of herself, and when she looked at Rose's eyes she could detect the mockery in them.

Abruptly, Rose's attitude changed and she frowned again, then leaned closer over the bar. 'Here,' she said, 'who *have* you been talking to? I'm sorry, I didn't mean to laugh, but it struck me as so funny that anyone could believe in that sort of rubbish. But you're scared, aren't you? Something's put the wind up you, I can tell. What's it all about?'

Her initial reaction had been so off-putting that Rowan didn't know if she could bring herself to explain. But she had to tell someone, someone other than Mal, someone who might allay her fears rather than add fuel to their fire.

She stared down at the counter, embarrassed still. 'There've been a few odd things happening at the house,' she said, 'and I've been having some peculiar dreams lately, which isn't like me at all. Finding that horseshoe sort of tied in, you see.' And briefly she explained about the dreams, the hoofbeats, the sensation of being watched. She left out any reference to the Crown of Horn, though – somehow she felt that the fewer people who knew about that, the better. And if Rose in particular heard that there was a treasure of some kind connected with her grandmother's house, the news would be all round the village by evening.

When she finished, Rose raised her carefully-pencilled eyebrows. 'Weird!' she said, in a tone of voice that suggested she wasn't sure whether or not to believe a word of the story. 'So who told you about the Wild Hunt, then? Or had you heard about it before, and put two and two together?'

Rowan shook her head. 'No, I hadn't heard of it before, or at least, I didn't know what it was. It was Mal who told me, last night.'

Rose tried to mask the quick, sharp look before Rowan could see it, but she didn't quite succeed. Carefully, almost too casually, she said, 'Oh, Mal again. You've been seeing quite a lot of him, have you?'

It was a blatant probe, and Rowan didn't rise to the bait. When no answer was forthcoming, Rose rested her chin in her hands and appeared to be thinking deeply.

'It isn't any of my business, I know, and I've got no right to go giving you advice, Rowan, but if I were you, I wouldn't take anything Mal says too seriously.'

'What do you mean?'

'Well, Mal's a good-hearted bloke and all that, but he does like his little joke.' A note of patronage had crept into the barmaid's tone. 'I wouldn't be at all surprised if he was teasing you.'

'*Teasing* me?' Rowan's voice rose in anger, but whether the anger was directed at Rose or at Mal, she didn't know.

Rose shrugged. 'Oh, you know how it is. People love telling creepy stories, and if they get an eager listener . . . I'm not trying to put Mal down, but if he didn't realise how upset you really were, he was probably kidding you along. Men aren't very perceptive, are they?' Her look was innocent enough, but below the surface it was intended as a challenge, and Rowan knew it.

Quietly, she said, 'So what's your view about it all, Rose?'

Rose hesitated. 'Well, I don't really like to say.'

'Please.'

'I don't want to give any offence, but are you quite sure you didn't imagine all this stuff?' Rose smiled a little too sweetly. 'I mean, it all sounds a bit unlikely to me. I'm no head-shrinker, God knows, but it sounds more like there was something preying on your mind and it got to you through dreams, and then you imagined the rest. I've heard that it happens to a lot of people.' Her voice was gentle but, had Rowan been more on her guard, she might have detected the underlying trace of malice. Rose's jealousy over herself and Mal was something she had hardly thought about. As far as she was concerned, she was no threat to any ambitions Rose might have in that direction, and so she could see no reason why Rose should wish to drive a wedge between them.

Rose sipped her drink, eyeing Rowan sidelong and watching her reaction. Rowan's face tightened. Rose had succeeded – whether deliberately or not – in playing on her deepest fear: that she was becoming mentally unstable.

Thus far, everyone she had sounded out had been reassuring, but now Rose had thrown a spanner in the works with her subtle suggestion that Rowan had only herself to blame for the strange experiences.

And now Rose added her last, delicate knife-thrust. 'I think if that happened to me, I'd go and see the doctor,' she said. 'Get some Valium, or something. Maybe it wouldn't be a bad idea, particularly if you've been a bit nervy lately?' She made the last few words into a question.

'Yes,' said Rowan dully. 'Maybe I will.' Her fingers tapped edgily on her glass, and Rose asked, 'Like another one?' She had said her piece, made her point; now she could afford to be generous.

Rowan shook her head. 'No thanks. I think I'll go back to the house.'

Rose studied her, wondering momentarily if she had gone too far. She hadn't really meant to be bitchy. But after all, it was not in her own interest to see Rowan putting too much faith in Mal Lyndon. Then she dismissed her misgivings on the principle that all was fair in love and war, and if Rowan wasn't capable of standing up for herself, that was her bad luck. Besides, there *was* something odd about Rowan; she had thought it from the day they had first met. She didn't seem quite healthy, as if there were some skeleton in her cupboard that she could not shake off. But Rose wasn't overly curious about that. Her interest lay elsewhere – although she reflected that it might not be a bad idea to have a quiet word with Mal the next time he came into the pub, just to make sure he was fully in the picture.

Rowan finished her drink quickly and pushed the glass across the bar. 'Thanks for the chat, Rose,' she said with a hint of irony.

'Pleasure. I hope I haven't gone and upset you with what I said. It was just that I thought – '

'I know.' Rowan smiled bleakly. 'You spoke your mind. Everyone's got a right to do that, after all.' She rose, settling her bag-strap on her shoulder. 'I'll see you some time.'

'Yes, take care.'

Rose stared at the door for a few moments after Rowan

had gone, feeling just a little guilty. Maybe she should have been more careful in what she had said. But she couldn't help a small sense of elation in having scored a point or two. She would not have admitted to anyone that she was jealous of Rowan, but secretly she felt resentful that this stranger, who had had all the advantages which Rose craved for herself, should have walked into their midst and plucked the most attractive man in the district from under her nose. It didn't seem right, and Rose was glad to have redressed the balance just a little.

She smiled a tiny smile of satisfaction as she returned to the task of polishing glasses.

9

It was inevitable, in the light of the events of that morning, that Rowan would return to the puzzle of her grandmother's papers.

Once she had left the Oak and Ash there seemed little point in putting off going back to the house for her mood had been shattered beyond recall by Rose Bastable.

She was glad, however, to find that the atmosphere had changed for the better when she stepped through the front door and put her coat in the hall. The house was a familiar, welcoming friend once again, the last vestiges of the morning's uneasy hostility erased by the passage of a few hours. Yet Rowan was aware of the unease within herself, like a gnawing hunger-pang, and she knew that if she allowed it to continue unchecked it would soon begin to seep into the atmosphere again, and the vicious circle of oppressiveness would continue.

Rowan admitted to herself that she could not abandon this place, this house, until the conundrum that faced her was solved. In any case, surely to return to the city would be to turn tail and admit defeat yet again? Her stay in Somerset was an escape in itself. If she gave up and tried to 'escape' a second time, she would be damning herself as a feeble coward, and the last remnants of her self-respect would be lost.

When she sat down in her chair (strange how she was thinking of it automatically as 'her' chair) and opened the folder of papers on her lap, she did not feel too optimistic about the prospects of finding anything that she and Mal had previously overlooked. But she had at least to try. If she could discover anything, anything at all, that might give her a lead, however unlikely, then it would be a great boost both to her enthusiasm and to her flagging confidence.

Once again she stared at the small scraps from her grandmother's notepad, with their cryptic references. The Crown of Horn – that phrase had been orbiting in her brain for so long now that it seemed it had always been with her. So familiar, yet so oblique. And there had been so many hints – antlers, Wild Hunts, morris men . . .

She wondered, as she put the first batch of notes aside without having gleaned anything of help, if she were chasing a red herring. Or if the clues – assuming there were clues – lay elsewhere. Idly she began to thumb through the remaining sheets in the folder, putting the photograph of Geoffrey Fairfax out of sight, as something about its innocent optimism saddened her. And then she came across a scrap which she remembered having seen before, but had then discarded as being of no importance.

It was a list of what appeared to be book titles, the author's name noted alongside each. Rowan looked more closely, and one of the titles caught her attention.

Caversham, C. V. 'Exmoor Legends'.

It wasn't the title which was relevant; by itself it would have meant nothing to her. But at the very foot of the page her grandmother had scribbled the annotation, *'C of H'*.

Crown of Horn. It couldn't possibly refer to anything else. Rowan felt a stirring of intense excitement within herself, and though she tried to suppress it, half-afraid to trust this apparent lead in case it should prove futile, she knew, deep down, that she had stumbled upon something that could well be vital. Quickly she glanced over the list of books, and saw that each title was along similar lines. They all dealt with local history, tradition or folklore.

Hurriedly Rowan slipped the rest of the papers back into their folder. Her grandmother's books, she knew, were kept in a cabinet in the front room – not the antique bookcase, but another, more modest one wedged behind a jumble of furniture. If any or all of these titles should prove to be in there, she might at last find something of real value.

Ten minutes later, she closed the door of the front room behind her, feeling bitterly disappointed. She had been wrong. A thorough search of the bookshelves had revealed not one single volume that corresponded with the list. She had checked and double-checked, but there was nothing. Slowly she returned to the living-room, staring thoughtfully at the note in her hand. The only other possibility was that a library in one of the relatively local towns might have at least one or two of them, although, as she had no way of telling when the list was made, it was equally possible that the books were long out of print and that even the libraries had discarded them by now.

But it was her one and only lead, and Rowan was not about to abandon her search without thorough effort. Taunton, probably the nearest town of any size, was about twenty-five miles away, and she should have plenty of time to find the library and search for the books before the end of the afternoon, if she set out quickly.

The thought that she had something positive to do, something that might go at least some way towards solving the elusive mystery that dogged her, made her feel more enthusiastic and optimistic than she had done for a long time. Stopping only to change her shoes, retrieve her coat and – as an afterthought – remove the horseshoe from her handbag, she left the house to drive into Taunton.

The assistant at the Taunton library could not have been more helpful. The nature of Somerset people was something that Rowan still found both fascinating and gratifying, although by now she felt she should be growing accustomed to it. In London, few people would give a stranger so much as the time of day if they could avoid it; here, perhaps because the pace of life allowed time for old-fashioned courtesy, everyone seemed to feel it a pleasure to be of help.

When she saw the list, the girl at the desk nodded. 'Yes, I believe we do have these titles – or some of them, at least.' She smiled. 'We get a lot of people coming in during the summer who want to check up on local folklore before they tour round the countryside, and there's quite a demand for these books. If you'll come with me, I'll see if I can find them for you.'

And so, minutes later, Rowan was seated at a reading-table with four books at her elbow and a sheet of paper and pen spread out before her. All the books, she discovered, were quite old, the latest published in the 1940s, but the information she wanted was timeless.

The first volume she turned to was the Caversham *Exmoor Legends,* a heavyweight book with a distinctively Edwardian air. The text was dense and looked heavy-going, interspersed with pages of melodramatic drawings illustrating the various legends. The thought of ploughing through all this was daunting; it would have been a lot easier if she could have borrowed the books and taken them home but, as she was not a member of the library and could not join on the spot, that was out of the question. Perhaps the index would provide something; the problem would be knowing where to look.

She turned to the back of the book and checked the list for the Wild Hunt. That was of little use; there were a good twenty references and it would take too long to track down each one. Then it occurred to her that there might be some legend or story that was directly connected with the village itself, and flicked the pages back to the list of Bs.

Barton Tavey – it was in the index, and eagerly Rowan turned to the appropriate page. The text was opposite a line illustration, and as she looked at it she felt her heart stop and then start again at a more rapid pace.

The illustration depicted a man standing under the branches of a stylised oak tree. And sprouting from his forehead were two huge branches of antlers.

Almost feverish in her excitement, Rowan turned her attention to the facing page. There at the top was a headline: 'BARTON TAVEY – THE LEGEND OF DUIR AND NIAINN'.

Suddenly, nothing else seemed to matter to Rowan. All awareness of her surroundings, the quiet movements of other browsers, the passing minutes, faded away as she began to read.

'This strange and evocative tale tells of the adventures of Duir, the mythical Oak King and Master of the Wild Hunt (q.v.), who was said to inhabit the magnificent Exmoor hills that shroud and succour the small hamlet of Barton Tavey. Duir, as legend would have it, fell deeply in love with Niainn, a nymph whose name is linked with the ash tree. But Niainn was a powerful sorceress, and scorned the attentions of her suitor, declaring that, before he might hope to win her, he must first prove himself a fit lord for her. To that end, she set him to accomplish three tasks, and only by this could Duir hope to triumph in his ambition.

'His first task was to defend his beloved in battle. Accounts of this battle vary in the telling, but the author would suggest that in the original tale Duir was locked in combat with a great black boar, which he finally slew with an enchanted dagger. Second, Niainn commanded that he should undergo an ordeal for her sake, and to this he agreed. She therefore, by her sorcerous powers, transformed him into an oak tree (that from which his name is derived) and conjured a dire storm, in which the tree was struck thrice by lightning, inflicting terrible wounds upon the Oak King. From these wounds Duir nonetheless recovered, and bade Niainn tell him what his third and final task must be. At this she issued him a challenge, saying that if he could tame her own wild spirit, he would thus prove himself a fit lord for her, and she would consent to be his bride. With that she changed herself into a white hind, certain that her speed and cunning would be sufficient to outwit him. But she had reckoned without Duir's mastery over the Wild Hunt, that spectral and terrible pack of hounds which is said to haunt the Exmoor hills, roaming the windswept heights in search of their prey. Using his own supernatural powers, Duir summoned the Hunt and, mounted on a giant horse with eyes of fire and hooves that struck sparks from the very ground, set off in full cry to run his quarry to ground. The howling dogs, led by their Master with his hunting-horn and a great crown of stag's antlers upon his brow, pursued the fleeting Niainn through forest and over moorland, until, as the last vestiges of her strength deserted her, she fell exhausted to the ground, there to resume her own shape once more. Duir had triumphed, the three tasks were completed, and the Oak King at last claimed his bride.

'N.B. This particular legend, unlike the majority to be found in British folklore, would seem (but for its reference to the Wild Hunt) to be confined to the small area of which Barton Tavey is the hub, and the author's investigations have failed to produce any corresponding myth in other districts. It is also interesting to note that the village of Barton Tavey contains several features which would appear to lend weight to the veracity of this legend. The visitor will discern that the gargoyles which decorate the Norman church are, almost without exception, crowned with horns of one form or another, whilst the church door itself boasts as fine a pair of stag's antlers above its lintel as the author has yet found in any part of the country. The visitor may also note that the village's one public house bears the name of "The Oak and Ash", which has clearly discernible connection with the legend of Duir and Niainn.'

Pages fluttered in a draught from somewhere as Rowan released her hold on the book, sitting back in the hard library chair while gradually the world around her reformed into some sembance of life.

She had found it. She had found the one clue that could tie together all the loose ends of the conundrum. Suddenly her mind came back to earth as she realised that she still did not *know* how this legend of Duir and Niainn was connected with the strange jigsaw of her own experiences and the still-unsolved mystery of the Crown of Horn. But in her bones, like an ancestral memory, was the unshakable certainty that this was the key.

She glanced at her watch and saw that the library would be closing in ten minutes. She needed the details of this legend, needed to read them over and over again until they were rooted in her mind. Quickly she smoothed out the sheet of paper that the assistant had given her and began to make as accurate a transcription of the text as time would allow. The illustration, too, she copied in the form of a rough sketch, then closed the volume and stood up to put it and the others away.

The young assistant met her half way to the shelves. 'Shall I take these for you?'

'Oh yes, thank you.' Rowan was still a little bemused by her discovery.

'Did you find what you were looking for?' the girl asked.

Rowan smiled. 'Yes, I did. In fact I found a lot more than I'd hoped. Thank you, thank you very much for all your help. It's been invaluable.'

'Any time. Don't forget your list – you've left it on the table.'

'Oh, yes.' Rowan retrieved it, then walked out of the library into the comparatively bright light of the street, and turned towards the car park where she had left her Mini.

When evening closed in and the fire was burning, Rowan settled herself beside its glow and read the notes she had made. Her transcription from the book was as near perfect as made no difference; less flowery than Caversham's text, but all the essential details were there. As she read, she switched off the table lamp at her side, so that the only light in the room was that of the fire, moving and shifting across the page and forming its peculiar but familiar patterns of brightness and shadow.

Images formed in Rowan's mind as she took in the legend once again. They came unprompted, but they were strong; images of rivers and wild forests, trees that were not trees, deer that were not deer but could change at will and take on human form. She was lost in the story of Duir and Niainn, caught up in their mythical world, and the very atmosphere of the house seemed to play on that and enhance it, so that she could almost fancy that the wind whispering at the long window was the wind of the moors themselves, that time had slipped back and she was no longer in the twentieth century, but in a far older and more magical time that had existed even before the dawn of history.

She almost slept then, falling into a light doze in which the links of past and present became confused into a strange mutation. Something roused her at last, one of those half-waking mental jolts that are like a physical shock, and, shaking her head, she struggled upright in her armchair.

The house felt odd. It was an oddness Rowan had come to recognise, the sense of being watched, almost guarded, and the atmosphere was very intense. For perhaps a minute she listened to the sound of the wind and the hiss of the fire interspersed with an occasional lazy crackle. In a way she welcomed this feeling in the air and yet, perhaps because she had never been brought up to such stillness, such solitude, it had the power to make her just a little afraid. Turning, she switched on the lamp once more, and the intensity receded enough to allow her to relax.

The notes she had made lay in her lap, but she knew that she would gain nothing by reading them once more, beyond a sense of fascination. The legend, it seemed, had provided the key she had been seeking, but she still needed to find the door that it would unlock.

She wondered if she should talk to Mal again, show him what she had found and ask his help or advice. But what could Mal do? He had already admitted that he was as perplexed by the mystery as she was, and was in no better position to take up the search. Besides, Rowan believed that this was *her* mystery, her personal crusade. Mal already knew about the Crown of Horn and the dreams. To involve him further seemed to her somehow wrong. And anyway, to avoid Mal at this stage would be safer. She did not want to rely on him for anything, no matter how small.

Reluctantly she put the paper aside, aware that there was nothing more she could achieve now. Better if she put the whole matter out of her mind in the hours that were left before she went to bed, or she might trigger off the cycle of nightmares again. Tomorrow – well, tomorrow she would think about it afresh.

The next day broke with a fine, spindrift rain in the air and a mist of cloud that constantly promised to clear and yet never quite managed to disperse. Rowan woke late, surprised by the daylight and by the fact that she had slept soundly for nearly ten hours. She had not had a single dream that she could recall.

Agnes Teale pounced before Rowan could avoid her, catching her while she was bringing in the milk. Rowan invited her in for the obligatory cup of tea, and for an hour Agnes talked about the weather, the Harvest Festival (was it really so recent? Rowan wondered in astonishment), and the fact that someone called Jane was getting married in three weeks' time and moving out of the village. Cosy, insubstantial gossip. By the time Agnes left, Rowan was beginning to feel like a caged tiger. Time had suddenly become too precious to waste on village pleasantries. Every spare moment should be devoted to the mystery that was entangling her life like a spider's web.

Was she getting obsessive? She thought not; surely anyone in her situation would have felt the same? The Crown of Horn, whatever it was, whatever it meant, had become the focus of her existence, and until the puzzle was solved nothing else mattered.

Rowan did not stop to think about the other aspects of her life that until recently had seemed the most important things in the world. Upstairs, the framed photograph of Neil stood on her dressing table, but in the last few days she had barely given it so much as a glance, let alone a thought. The wounds were still there, as her attitude towards Mal Lyndon proved. But the knife-thrusts of pain which had constantly been re-opening the old scars had receded into an unreachable distance.

She had decided what she would do almost immediately

on waking. Although it was doubtful if she could learn anything concrete from it, she wanted to return to the field where the blasted oak tree stood. In her mind, since reading the legend, that tree had become synonymous with the story of Duir's ordeal; and the illogical thought had occurred to her that, if she returned to the site and explored it, another piece of the jigsaw might slip into place. Besides, it made her feel that she was doing something, pushing the mystery just a little further towards its solution.

The weather was still against her, but if she waited for the drizzle to stop and the sky to clear, she might wait for a week. Rowan didn't possess a pair of wellingtons, which were the only practical footwear in these conditions, but old leather boots and a coat should be sufficient to keep out the worst of the elements.

She felt faintly foolish as she left the house, her coat collar turned up and a scarf knotted under her chin. In London, she could never have dressed like this.

She put some petrol in her car at the local garage, which stood on the edge of the village and had hardly changed since the 1930s, then drove out on the coast road, taking the route she had followed the previous day. The change in the weather made the landscape seem grim and forbidding, turned by the cloud and the rain into a harsh taskmaster rather than a benefactor.

Rowan found the field she was seeking without much difficulty, and climbed out of the car into a flurry of drizzle that moved in from the distant grey sea and stung her face. Blinking, she thrust her hands into her coat pockets and trudged across to the farm track that led through the trees.

She knew as soon as she emerged from the woods that she should have picked a kinder day. The sight of the fallow field, so still and silent under the oppressive sky, made her shiver, and the branches of the oak tree, stripped of bark and as white as some giant skeleton hand, brought back her dreams so suddenly and vividly that she almost turned and ran back to the car. But she forced herself not to run. It was, after all, only a deserted field; there was nothing supernatural about it, however eerie it might look.

As if to prove that point to herself, she began to walk further along the track, which continued around the edge of the field, forming a border between the ploughed earth and the trees. She didn't want to approach the oak, but another vantage point might help to put the whole thing in perspective.

Sparrows were squabbling among the beeches that crowded the woods, and from a high branch somewhere a blackbird was singing enthusiastically, its voice carrying with odd clarity in the still air. And it *was* still today. There was not a breath of wind to disturb the leaves, only the faint susurration of the rain as it fell.

Rowan strolled on. She was beginning to enjoy the walk for its own sake. There was something about being alone in this deep country, with nothing to do other than whatever she wanted to do, that was like a balm to her soul. She had almost forgotten her original purpose in coming here, certainly it no longer seemed as urgent as it had done an hour ago. Bowing her head to keep the rain from her face, she allowed her thoughts to meander with her feet, savouring the atmosphere, the peace of it all.

And then something rustled in the undergrowth a few yards ahead.

Rowan stopped, startled by the sound, and as she looked up the noise came again, and she saw a small beech sapling sway violently, as though something had disturbed its roots.

And the birds had suddenly fallen totally silent. There was nothing now but the hiss of the rain.

Rowan felt her pulse quickening in apprehension. She could not have imagined the disturbance. There *was* something moving in the woods, and instinct told her that it was something far bigger than a bird or rabbit, or even a fox. She stood very still, wanting to turn and run back the way she had come, yet not daring to move, in case she attracted the attention of whatever stalked in those trees. She stayed where she was, not breathing, waiting.

The rustling came again, and with it a thumping sound, as if a horse moved invisibly through the wood. The rain was heavier, falling with cold, relentless force, and its soft hissing swelled to a patter that seemed to keep pace with Rowan's heartbeats.

She could not judge the moment when she first saw it. Somehow it seemed to take form from the shadow of the dense trees, like something in a dream, the leaves framing it.

It was a man, red-haired and laughing, or a horse, or a huge, red-eyed stag – or it was all three and yet none of those things at once; something out of nightmare, out of legend. And there were horns, tremendous antlers that rose like twin trees themselves from the head of the man, or the horse, or the stag. For one incredible moment the vision was a reality and it seemed to Rowan that she gazed straight into its eyes. And then in that same second it was gone, instantly absorbed into the leaves and branches from which it had been formed.

Rowan felt as though every part of her being had ceased to function. Her heart did not beat, her mind was locked, her muscles were immobilised. Dimly she became aware of the natural sounds of the day around her: the falling rain, the tiny movements of the now innocent woodland. But she couldn't think, couldn't feel for herself. Her only emotion was undiluted, primeval terror, and she had no defence against it.

And suddenly that terror reached her body and released her. She turned, her mouth opening but unable to make a sound, and ran blindly back in the direction she had come, slipping and stumbling on the track, hands clutching at the air before her as she raced to reach the car that waited for her on the road.

The Mini slewed to a halt in the lane opposite Coombe Cottage, and Rowan all but threw herself out of it, ran across the road without looking, raced to the front door and hammered the knocker until hurrying footsteps sounded on the other side.

'Mal – ' the word was half a sob, checked suddenly as the unfamiliar face of a boy of about eighteen stared anxiously at her from the doorway.

'Mal's not in,' he said. 'Is there something I can do?'

'Oh.' Rowan collected herself with a vast effort. She could feel her pulse pounding thickly in her ears. She was aware of the boy's surprise and aware, too, of how she must look to him – white, shaking and on the verge of tears. She tried to think straight, and managed to say, 'He – when will he be back?'

'Half an hour or so, I think. Can I help? I'm John Prior. I give Mal a hand here sometimes. Do you want to wait?'

She couldn't wait. It would mean sitting here with this boy, maybe having to talk to him, knowing he was well aware that she was upset and yet totally unable to explain to a stranger. Rowan shook her head.

'No, I don't think so. Could you – could you ask Mal to phone Rowan when he gets back, please? He knows the number.'

'Okay.' There was a painful silence while she stood still, too unco-ordinated to turn around and walk away, and he stayed too,-not liking to close the door on her.

'Are you sure you wouldn't rather wait?' he said at last.

'Yes, yes, I'm sure. Thank you.' Her muscles came to life at last and she was able to turn, leaving John Prior standing at the front door of the cottage and staring after her.

The shock was beginning to wear off by the time Rowan arrived, a little more sedately than at Coombe Cottage, outside her own house. As she locked the car and walked up the path she was aware that her whole body was shivering, her legs unsteady and her hands fumbling as she opened the front door. The image of what she had seen was seared on her mind as if by a branding-iron: the fiery eyes, the face that had been such a bizarre mingling of the human and the animal, the horns . . .

Savagely she took hold of her thoughts as they threatened to get out of control, knowing that if she allowed her grip to weaken she could give way to panic again. She was home now, safe; there were no visions and no nightmares here. She was suffering from shock, that was all, the shock of a hallucination, or – but she couldn't bring herself to think about the alternative.

If she had had a bottle of whisky or brandy in the house,

she would have poured herself at least three glasses in quick succession to blot out that relentless image.

She wished that Mal would ring. It occurred to her to go and look for Agnes, for the simple calming effect of human company, but she baulked at the prospect. Agnes, in her well-meaning way, would take one look at her and demand to know what was wrong, and that was something Rowan could not face, not from her neighbour. Agnes would never believe the truth. It was Mal she wanted. Only a day or two ago she had been resenting his involvement with her life and half afraid of him, but now he seemed like a rock of sanity in the midst of chaos, a single point of light in darkness. Rowan needed him, and at that moment she would have given a very great deal to see him arriving at her front door.

She knew that she had to do something mundane to set herself on an even keel again. Her clothes were damp from the rain, and she decided to go upstairs and change before making herself some tea and toast, in the hope that by the time she had done all that Mal would have returned home and would call her.

She started up the stairs, but halted half way to the top, certain that she had heard a noise. Wondering if it could, by some incredible chance, be Mal turning up at the house, she waited, listening, but there was no sound of footsteps on the path and no ring at the front door. Disappointed, she continued on her way, but paused again as she reached the top.

There was a smell in the air, a very faint smell that she did not like and could not place. Not roses this time, but something else a good deal less pleasant. Puzzled, she was about to start down the landing when she heard another sound, a kind of shuffling. It was not coming from outside, but from within the house – from one of the rooms on this very floor.

Rowan's skin crawled as she heard it, and all the horror of her experience at the field came back as though it were happening over again. There couldn't be something here, something that could haunt her even in the sanctuary of her own house.

And then she saw that the door to her grandmother's bedroom was ajar.

Very, very slowly, Rowan began to edge along the landing towards that room. All her instincts screamed at her not to do it, to stay where she was or run back downstairs, but she knew that she *had* to investigate and find out what was making that noise. It must be something totally ordinary, she tried to tell herself, like a loose window catch. There couldn't be anything in there. But if she reached the door and saw what she half-believed she might see, she would just stand there and shriek her head off.

She drew level with the part-open door, her back against the landing wall as she tried to peer through into the room. Then she saw the chair that lay overturned on the floor just inside, half-covered by what looked like a woman's blouse. Soft-footed, and afraid that her courage was on the point of failing her, she took two steps across the landing, reached out, and with a quick, jabbing gesture pushed the bedroom door wide open.

A grunt of surprise came from inside the room, and Rowan's astonished eyes met those of Cracky Tully, the village tramp.

He was crouched beside her grandmother's bed, his dirty hands rummaging through the contents of a tallboy drawer which he had upended on to the carpet. All around him the room was in chaos. Maud Fairfax's possessions lay scattered everywhere, one curtain hung half off its rail, and the cream-painted wall was daubed with finger marks. It was as if a demented child had been let loose in the room and run riot. As the tramp stared back at her, arrested in mid-movement, Rowan saw that his eyes were wide and unblinking, any intelligence they might have held replaced by an ugly kind of animal cunning, and saliva dribbled from his slack mouth. Cracky Tully was suddenly not the harmless old simpleton that both Mal and Tom Rushford had implied. Something had happened to him, changed him, and Rowan knew instinctively that she would have to tread very carefully indeed.

'Tully,' she said in a quiet but stern voice, like a schoolteacher addressing a miscreant, 'What are you doing in here?' There was no point in asking him how he had got in, why he had come, what he wanted. One simple question at a time was all she dared ask, in the hope that she might arouse some sense of shame and wrongdoing in the old man's feeble mind.

The tramp stared back at Rowan and his face twisted into an expression of anger. His shoulders hunched and he clutched the skirt of Maud Fairfax's he had been holding close to himself, as though to use it as a shield.

'Come on now, Tully,' Rowan said cajolingly. Her voice was shaking and she prayed that her nervousness didn't communicate itself to him. 'Come on. You know you're not supposed to go into other people's houses without being invited. You've been very bad, haven't you?'

The tramp made a gargling sound in the back of his throat, half aggressive and half frightened. A little encouraged, feeling that he had at least acknowledged her words if nothing else, Rowan advanced a couple of steps into the room. 'It's all right. No one's going to hurt you, but you must be good and go away, mustn't you?' She reached out a hand to beckon him, and he shuffled back, then grunted again and started to half-crawl slowly towards the door.

Rowan felt a wave of relief. She had succeeded; he was going to obey her. She walked carefully round behind him and shepherded him as he shuffled across the room. He started to rise fully to his feet, as if some small vestige of one-time dignity within him urged him to walk upright down the landing and the stairs. And then, as he turned round to face her, Rowan knew that she had made a very dangerous mistake indeed.

Tully was between her and the door. And in his hand, gripped in a way that suggested he might use it without any warning, was a long, sharp kitchen knife.

10

Downstairs, the phone was ringing. Rowan could hear it, insistent and shrill, but it had no effect whatever on the old tramp. He just stood staring at her with that same animal-like insensibility, the knife in his hand gleaming in the now leaden light from the window. At last the caller gave up and the phone bell stopped.

The silence then was thick, claustrophobic and ugly. Rowan looked from the knife to Tully and back to the knife, desperately willing her self-control not to snap. If she made one precipitate move, if she screamed, anything could happen. Certainly she would have little chance of getting past him and to the door unscathed. She had no doubt at all that, if provoked, he would use that knife.

Tully was insane. Something within him had snapped, a gear had slipped horribly out of place, and his normal placidity had been replaced by something alien and potentially deadly. She couldn't even cling to the hope that this was a dream. It was only too real. And unless she did something to break this hideous deadlock, she might well be dead within a few more minutes.

Summoning all her reserves of control she cautiously slid one foot forward a few inches and spoke to the tramp in a whisper.

'Come on, Tully. You don't want to hurt me, do you? You're a nice man; you don't want to hurt anyone, do you?' She put her weight on her forward foot, and Tully made an unpleasant barking sound which was obviously intended as a warning. The knife-blade flashed as he jerked it threateningly in her direction, and she shrank back again, the blood pounding in her head. Her gaze flicked quickly, briefly to the window. Could she jump out, if the worst came to the worst? She tried desperately to recall what lay directly below this room – was it the garden, or the village street? No, it was out of the question. She would first have to open the window and climb on to the sill, and by the time she had done that, no matter how fast she moved, the tramp could have stabbed her.

It was a hideous limbo. She did not know how long the two of them stood there, but to her it seemed like hours. Once or twice she tried again to make some small move, but each time Tully responded with one of his inhuman barks or gargles and a menacing jerk of the knife. It seemed that he too did not know what to do next. He made no effort to run away and escape from the house, and yet he showed no signs of attacking whilst she did not provoke him. He simply stood, alert as a fox, as if prepared to wait indefinitely for some obscure instruction from his warped brain.

The sound of a car engine did not register on Rowan's mind, nor the slam of a door as the vehicle stopped outside the house. She was too frightened, too intent on desperate efforts to anticipate the tramp's next move, to pay heed to anything else. But when the front door below her banged and a familiar voice shouted, '*Rowan?*' she was jolted from her mesmerised state.

'Mal – ' she started to call, but before the word was fully out Tully gave a high-pitched squeal of rage and shuffled towards her. Rowan cried out, '*No!*' and footsteps pounded heavily on the stairs. The tramp whirled round as Mal appeared in the doorway, and Rowan had time to shout, 'He's got a knife!' before Mal saw the situation for himself.

There was no sudden furore then, no dramatic struggle between Tully and Mal. Instead, everyone stayed motionless while Mal's eyes moved quickly from Tully to Rowan, asking an unspoken question.

She nodded, swallowing. 'I'm all right. But there's something wrong with him, Mal, he's gone crazed. I found him – '

Mal held up a hand, warning her not to say any more. Tully blocked his way to Rowan, and he suspected that any attempt to reach her would result in the old man attacking her. Maybe he could stop him in time, but Mal was not willing to take that risk.

'Tully.' He pitched his voice low, persuasive. 'Come on now, Tully, what's all this about? Has Rowan been frightening you?'

The tramp's small eyes darted to his face, and the drooling mouth opened and shut as if Tully were trying to speak.

'That's it, is it? Mal said, smiling at him. 'She frightened you? Well, I'm not surprised! After all, you're in her house, aren't you? I expect it was you who frightened her, really.'

Tully growled like a dog, uncertain, and the knife wavered in his hand.

'Come on, Tully,' Mal said. He had dropped his voice still further until his tone was hypnotic, drawing the old man's attention with a skill that Rowan had not dreamed he possessed. 'Give me the knife, old fellow. Give me the knife.'

Tully said, 'Ner!' which might or might not have meant No, and drew back, waving the knife wildly at Mal. Mal, however, did not flinch. It took courage to stay where he was, but he gambled that Tully did not truly want to hurt him. The knife was still again. But the tramp did not relinquish his hold on it.

Mal glanced again at Rowan, his look conveying both reassurance and a caution not to make a sound or a movement. Then he returned his attention to Tully.

The tramp was staring at him, obviously realising that Mal and not Rowan was the one to whom he should pay attention. His jaw moved and he smacked his lips together.

'That's right, Tully,' Mal said. His gaze was locked with the old man's now, and his voice became stronger, straddling the subtle border between cajolement and command. 'That's right. You don't want to hurt anyone. We don't want to hurt you. All I want is for you to give me that knife, so that I can put it away. Because if I don't put it away, you might hurt yourself, mightn't you?'

Tully whimpered, and Rowan could see that he was confused. There was an odd light in Mal's eyes, a look of such intense concentration that she herself could hardly keep watching without being drawn in. Like a mongoose using the cobra's own methods to hypnotise it before pouncing, he seemed to have Tully caught up in some kind of thrall, and when he spoke again his tone had crossed the borderline and was imperative.

'Give me the knife, Tully. Give me the knife, so that you won't hurt yourself.'

For an endless moment the tramp continued to stare back at him, drooling. Then, very slowly, the hand that held the knife moved towards Mal. But this time there was no menace in the gesture; it was submissive, childlike, the palm opening even as he stretched out his arm.

The blade slid from his hand and Mal caught it deftly before it could fall. His face was grey with tension, and without taking his eyes from Tully he said evenly, 'Rowan, go out of the room, very slowly, and go downstairs and phone the police.'

Rowan obeyed him almost as automatically as Tully had done. She held her breath as she sidled past the tramp, but it was obvious that he was no longer any threat to her. He stood passive and unresisting, like a machine which had been switched off, and did not even look at her as she passed. She gained the landing and ran downstairs to the telephone.

Somewhere at the back of her mind, as she dialled, was the knowledge that at some unspecified time in the future her veneer of calm was going to split wide open and give way to hysteria. But for the moment she was numbed, totally collected and controlled. She got through, calmly told the essential details of her story, thanked the anonymous voice at the other end of the line and replaced the receiver. There was not a sound from upstairs, and quickly she hurried back to the bedroom to help Mal keep vigil until the police arrived.

It wasn't Fred Dymock, the local constable, who turned up ten minutes later, but two young officers and a policewoman in a squad car. Tully made no protest as they led him away. If anything, he seemed bewildered by it all. The storm within him had blown itself out and he was as placid as a lamb.

One of the officers asked Rowan, 'Do you feel up to making a brief statement now, Miss Vosper? Just the details?'

Rowan's eyes were vague, but she nodded. 'Yes, of course.' She outlined what had happened since her arrival home, and Mal filled in the background about Tully himself. The constable noted down what they told him, then said that they would be in touch shortly, and would ask her to make a more detailed statement once she had had time to recover from the shock. The car drove away, and Rowan and Mal were alone.

Mal glanced speculatively up the stairs as he returned from seeing the officers out. 'That room's in one hell of a mess,' he said. 'Shall I give you a hand to clear it up?'

Rowan was in the sitting room, staring into the empty fireplace. 'What do you think made him do it?' she asked in a small voice.

Mal sighed. 'God alone knows. I can't even begin to understand it. Tully's been around this village for years, and there's never been so much as a hint of this kind of behaviour in all that time.' He watched her, seeing how calm she was and knowing it was a bad sign. She ought to react, let her feelings out rather then keeping them battened down like this.

She moved away from the fireplace, just a little closer to him. 'I was so frightened. I honestly thought that if I made a wrong move he'd kill me.'

Mal said, 'He might well have done.' It was a deliberate statement, intended to provoke her, and it had the desired effect. She said, 'Mal, *don't!*'

'It's the truth, Rowan. I don't know what happened to Tully, but he was dangerous.'

'I – ' her hands were beginning to shake. 'I can't think about that!'

'You should think about it. It's healthier.'

For a moment Rowan was silent. And then the tight strings of her nerves, stretched beyond the point of endurance, snapped. Her face crumpled and suddenly she was crying like a child, great, racking sobs as all the fear and strain of the last few hours broke through at once. Instinctively Mal moved forward, wanting to comfort, and this time, instead of flinching away from him as she had always done, she let his arms close round her shuddering body and leaned hard against him, hiding her face in the crook of his shoulder. He wanted to encourage her, to say, Go on, that's right, let yourself go and let all the tension come out. But he knew that if he did, she would move heaven and earth to bring herself under iron control once more. So he said nothing, just held her until at last the violent storm of her emotions began to subside.

And then she was calm again. For a few seconds she stood still in his arms, seeming only then to realise where she was, what she was doing, who was with her. Then abruptly she stepped back, putting a distance between them again. Her hand moved to her face a little confusedly, touched the tears on her cheeks and brushed them away, and she said, 'I'm sorry . . . '

'Don't be ridiculous.' Mal spoke sharply. He was determined that this time, unlike previous occasions, he was not going to allow her to put up her barriers again and shut him out of her private anguish. There was more to this reaction than the shock of the experience she had just undergone, no matter how harrowing that might have been, and Mal had made up his mind, as she cried on his shoulder, that he was going to get to the root of it. It would not be easy, but in her present state she would be more vulnerable than usual to determined persuasion.

'Sit down.' He propelled her towards a chair and made her subside into it. 'I'm going to make a pot of very strong tea, and then we're going to have a talk.'

She looked at him uncomprehendingly, still stunned. The first and worst squall was over, but it would be a long time before the effects wore off altogether. Then she nodded. 'Thanks. I could do with a cup.' She was trying to be matter-of-fact, a defence mechanism to hold back the aftermath of panic. 'The tea things are in the – '

'Don't worry about that – I'll find them.' He went out of the room, leaving her hunched in her chair and staring at the empty fireplace, and set about making tea, deliberately creating enough noise to let her know that she wasn't alone. Five minutes later, he returned with a precariously balanced tray.

'Right. I don't know if you take sugar, but I've put some in yours anyway.' He smiled at her. 'It's supposed to be a help in cases of shock.'

Rowan took the proffered cup with a grateful nod, her expression tight and miserable. Warming her hands on the cup's bowl she shivered, and wordlessly Mal reached down to switch on the electric fire. As the bar began to glow, and he waited for an opportune moment to launch into what he had to say, she suddenly spoke.

'How did you get in?'

'What?'

'Into the house. When I was – upstairs.'

'You'd left the front door wide open.'

She raised her eyes, giving him an anguished look. 'But I shut it when I went out – I *know* I did!'

'Quite probably. But when you came back, can you remember closing it then?'

Rowan hesitated, then shook her head. 'But that's not the point,' she insisted. 'What I mean is . . . ' her voice tailed off, and Mal, seeing what she was getting at, said gently,

'You mean how did Tully find his way inside? Frankly, God alone knows. I don't know whether the police checked, but you'll probably find that you left a window open somewhere.'

Rowan sipped at her tea, not noticing that it was hot enough to scald her tongue. 'That's another thing, isn't it?' she said hollowly. 'Everyone's been telling me that Tully's harmless, that he'd never hurt a fly and never interfere with anyone. So what made him suddenly want to get in here, Mal? Why did he do it, if he's as ineffectual as everyone says?'

That was a question that Mal had been asking himself, and he had no answer that made any sense. In all the years that he himself had lived here, Cracky Tully had been a permanent fixture of Barton Tavey, the friendly and simple-minded old tramp for whom everyone had a kind word. Something had happened to Tully, something that was as out of character as it was possible to be. It was almost as if some inexplicable force had driven him to do what he had done, and that if he ever regained his senses – poor as they were even under normal circumstances – he would be as baffled and distressed by his own behaviour as anyone.

He voiced his thoughts, and saw Rowan's face close up with disbelief. 'Why should he have picked on me?' she demanded.

Mal spread his hands helplessly. 'Again, how can we know? You were probably just unlucky, and he happened to be in the wrong place at the wrong time. It could have been anybody.'

'But it wasn't anybody. It was *me*. And after everything that's already happened – ' She stopped suddenly, realising that she had given away more than she intended. The ugly incident with Tully had all but put earlier events out of her mind; they had dimmed to insignificance by comparison. She did not know how she could explain her frantic message, but now she simply and perversely decided that she didn't want to tell him about the vision.

However, Mal was aware that she had unwittingly given him the chance he had been waiting for.

He said, 'What do you mean, "after everything that's happened"?'

'Oh.' She looked away from him. 'Nothing. Just a figure of speech.'

'Figure of speech, my foot! Rowan, listen,' he said, leaning forward. 'I had a message from John Prior, saying that you wanted me to get in touch with you urgently. He said you'd been round to the cottage, and that you were in one hell of a state. Now, that doesn't sound like you, Rowan. I tried to phone, and when there was no reply I got a bit worried, so I came round.' He smiled a little self-deprecatingly. 'Which was just as well, as it turned out. But even before the business with Tully, there was something else, wasn't there?'

The expression in Rowan's eyes changed, becoming almost furtive. 'No,' she told him, 'it wasn't anything important. Anyway, I wasn't in a state. Your assistant must have made a mistake.'

She knew deep down that she was being overly optimistic in expecting Mal to believe her, but she was taken aback by the vehemence of his reaction. He said, 'Rowan, for Christ's sake!' and before she could draw away from him he had reached out and taken hold of her free hand, gripping it so tightly that her fingers were numbed.

'Stop playing games!' There was an angry edge to his voice, an authority that to her suprise she was almost afraid of. 'I don't know what you think you'll achieve by being evasive, but it isn't going to work, Rowan. I know for a fact that something was very wrong long before you came face to face with Cracky Tully, and I want to find out what it is. No, don't try and pull away – you've done far too much of that since the day I first met you.'

Rowan stared at him like a half-mesmerised mouse in the face of a marauding cat. She had been caught off guard; this was a facet of Mal Lyndon that she had not expected to see, and she did not know how to respond.

Mal took advantage of her confusion to press his point. 'Look,' he said more gently, though there was still a trace of fire in his eyes, 'I don't want to pry into anything that isn't my concern. I know there's something in your past that you don't want to talk about. You haven't said as much, but it's pretty obvious. Frankly, I'm not interested in that right now. That's your business, and I have no right to interfere. But something else happened to you today. John said you drove in from the coast road, so you must have been out somewhere. And it wouldn't take a genius to guess that it has something to do with the Crown of Horn and your dreams. I want to know what it is, Rowan, and frankly, after the talk we had the other day, I think I've got a *right* to know.'

Instantly Rowan wanted to say that the fact that he'd told her a few stories about the Wild Hunt did not automatically bestow any privileges on him. She felt cornered, and that provoked her defences. But at the same time her sense of justice struggled to assert itself. Mal was, after all, involved in the mystery now, and it *was* unfair to turn her back on his help after he had taken so much trouble already.

She sighed, and her taut fingers relaxed in his grip. Slowly, aware that he had won this particular victory, he released her hand and sat back, waiting for her to speak. And by degrees, the story came out. Rowan told him about the list of books she had found, her visit to Taunton library, and then about her trip to the deserted field and what had taken place there. He listened without interrupting, saving his questions for later, and when Rowan finally fell silent he simply sat for a minute or two, staring at the glowing fire.

At last he said quietly, 'Tell me again what the creature you saw looked like. In detail.'

She hesitated, then said challengingly, 'Do you believe that I saw it at all?'

'Oh, yes. I believe it. I just want to have as clear a picture as possible in my own mind.' Carefully he took in each detail as she described her vision a second time. When she had finished, he nodded, but made no immediate comment.

'Well? Do you know what it might have been?' It was, she knew, a futile question; she anticipated Mal's answer before he gave it.

'No,' he said, 'I've got no idea at all; at least, not in any orthodox sense. But . . . '

'But what?'

He smiled wryly. 'Do I really need to say it? You must have been thinking along the same lines, or it wouldn't have affected you as drastically as it did.'

Rowan felt her skin chill. 'You mean it was something to do with the Wild Hunt?'

Mal shrugged, as if he were no more willing to admit the likelihood than she was. 'The Huntsman, this Duir figure from the legend – it doesn't really matter what we call it, does it? It all comes back to the same thing.'

It was what Rowan had known in her bones, the reason why she had been so frightened by what had happened to her in the field. Such an experience would have been bad enough under any circumstances, but added to the mystery of the Crown of Horn, the legend she had discovered at the library, the strange events that now seemed to be closing in on her and gathering her like a fisherman's net, its power to terrify her was increased threefold.

'I'd like to have a look at the copy you made of the legend,' Mal said. 'If you don't mind, that is.'

Now that he had broken the first barrier and was more sure of his ground, he was no longer pushing her too hard, but was prepared at least to sound a little more diffident.

Rowan nodded. 'Of course I don't mind.' She reached for the sheet of paper, which lay carefully folded on a small table beside her chair, and handed it to him.

As he read, she watched him, trying to interpret the expression on his face. A little of her battered confidence was beginning to seep back, and she was forced to admit that she had Mal to thank for it. The reassurance of having another human being to whom she could turn, whether to help her through a crisis or simply to sit down and puzzle out a problem with her, was worth a very great deal indeed. She had been a fool to think that she could handle the events of the last few days alone; she needed the support of a staunch ally.

And yet, at the back of her mind, the old fear still lurked, the fear that Mal would see this lowering of her defences as a sign of something more than a wish to be friends in adversity. However thankful she might be for Mal's guiding strength, she would have to tread more carefully now than ever before.

At length Mal lowered the paper and his eyes met Rowan's.

'What's the verdict?' she asked him. 'Does it tell you anything more?'

'Not directly, no. But it's made me realise that we've *got* to get to the bottom of all this, somehow.'

Rowan smiled faintly. 'I'd have thought that was obvious.'

'That's not what I meant. I know it's affecting you badly, and that's reason enough in itself for solving the whole mystery. But I've got a very strong feeling that there's more to it than that. You might think I'm crazy, and you might be right, but I'm certain that all of this – your vision, the legend, the notes, everything – is directly connected with *you*, and for a reason.'

She looked back at him. Something in what he had said rang bells in her mind that she could not interpret, and she frowned. 'What reason?'

Mal looked chagrined. 'That's where my brilliant theory breaks down. The fact is, I don't know. But I can't shake off the feeling that everything that's happening at the moment is happening to a purpose, as if there's some greater plan behind it all, and that whether you like it or not, you're in the middle of it because you have to be. You don't have any choice; it's something you've inherited.'

It made a bizarre kind of sense. These peculiar events had happened to *her* and no one else, and they were building up, as though Fate itself were steering matters towards an inevitable conclusion.

'Maybe,' she said slowly, 'that's what Gran was getting at in the notes she left. Do you remember what she said about something having been in the family for generations? And my mother not understanding the importance of it?'

'I remember it, yes. And didn't she write about finding the Crown of Horn, and that her own grandmother had done it before her?'

Recollection flooded back to Rowan. Mal's theory was beginning to look more and more plausible. She stared at the notes he still held, then said, 'Do you think she intended me to find those papers when she hid them in the bureau?'

'Did she know that you were in the antique furniture business?' Mal countered.

'Yes, I used to write to her now and again.'

He smiled. 'Then I'd say that she intended you to find them.'

Rowan nodded, allowing her own mouth to quirk in a smile that matched his. 'That would have been just like her. She loved mystery and she loved being cryptic.'

'Too cryptic this time, perhaps.'

'No. Whatever it is she was trying to convey, she didn't want to make it easy for me. But you're right, Mal, I'm sure of it. I *have* to solve this; it's, well, Fate if you like. If I don't, then it'll just go on dogging me and haunting me until I go out of my mind.'

'That's a harsh way of looking at it, but I can't disagree with you. So what's the next move to be?'

Rowan thought about that for some time. She felt that she was at an impasse. The clues were all there, but she still had no means of linking them together to find the vital answers. She needed time, she decided; time to let her mind recover, regain its foothold and clear away the confusion of the past few hours.

'I'm not sure, yet,' she said at length. 'I think for the time being I just want to settle a bit, give myself a chance to look at it afresh.'

Mal nodded agreement. 'In the meantime, then, would you mind if I did a little investigating of my own?' He saw the caution that crept into her expression, and added, 'Nothing drastic, but I've got one or two very vague ideas which I'd like to follow up. And if I could borrow your grandmother's notes for a day or so, that would be a great help.'

Illogically, Rowan felt dubious about that. The notes were private, personal. Then she reasoned that, after all, it was Mal who had found the notes in the first place. Without him, she would have made no progress at all.

'Okay,' she said, though a little reluctantly. 'If you think it might help.'

'I can't guarantee anything, but thanks. And I'll take great care of them.'

'I know. There's no need to . . . ' Her words tailed off and she shrugged. 'I took them upstairs. Hold on here, and I'll fetch them.'

She rose, and Mal rose too. 'What about your grandmother's room?' he said. 'I can't leave you with the responsibility of clearing up that mess alone.'

Rowan made a dismissive gesture. The scene with Tully had been all but forgotten in the last half hour. Once the danger was past, the tramp had become an isolated, ugly, but nonetheless minor incident.

'It doesn't matter,' she said. 'It isn't as bad as it looks on the surface, and I can get round to it later.'

'And then start brooding all over again when it reminds you of what just happened?' Mal smiled. 'Not a chance.

We'll do it together, and we'll do it now. That way, you can put it all out of your mind without having to face it again. Come on, I'm going to insist if you argue.'

Rowan didn't argue. The idea of anyone helping with the task of clearing up her grandmother's personal belongings made her feel a little guilty, but she was grateful for Mal's unequivocal offer. With a small, acquiescent gesture she led the way upstairs.

When they reached the room, she realised that to have tackled this chaos alone might well have caused her some unpleasant moments. With Mal, though, the onerous edge was soothed away and they found, as she had predicted, that Tully's assault on the room had done no real damage. Fastidiously, Rowan folded the clothes of Maud's that the tramp had mauled into a pile for washing, while Mal restored the disordered tallboy to its proper place and re-hung the fallen curtain.

Pushing a drawer back into its slot, he said suddenly, 'Have you ever thought of looking in here for some clue about the Crown of Horn?'

Rowan turned, staring at him with, he thought, a trace of censure. 'No,' she said. 'And I won't, I couldn't. It just wouldn't seem right. This is her room, the place where she stayed for the last few months of her life, and I'd feel like some kind of vandal if I started to search through her things.'

Mal shrugged. 'Fair enough. It just seemed a likely place.'

'I don't think it is.' Rowan glanced around her with a small, sad smile. 'Agnes told me that by the time Gran became bedridden her mind was starting to wander, so I very much doubt if she'd have deliberately left any clues for me here. Anyway, if she had, Agnes would have been sure to find them, and Gran wouldn't have wanted that at all.'

Mal decided to let the matter drop. He finished what he was doing, and straightened.

'I think we've done about as much as we can, apart from those fingermarks on the wall.'

Rowan looked at the paintwork. 'Leave them. They don't matter. It looks almost exactly the same as it was before, and that's what's important.' She started to move towards the door, casting a last critical eye over their handiwork. 'Yes,' she spoke half to herself, 'It's fine now.'

Mal followed her, closing the door behind him. Then, as she turned towards the stairs, he said, 'The notes. You said they were up here.'

'Oh, yes. In my room.' Rowan retraced her steps along the landing, and Mal followed more slowly. When he reached the door she was inside, opening a drawer of the small dressing table, and she looked up quickly and suspiciously.

'It's a bit of a mess,' she said, half defiant and half apologetic.

'You haven't seen mine. Anyway, I don't believe in being tidy.'

She smiled in response, but it was merely a courtesy, and Mal acknowledged wryly that her reserve, the familiar barriers, were beginning to creep back into her manner. He had made some progress today – although he wished wholeheartedly that it might have happened under more pleasant circumstances – but if he was not careful, the advantage would be eroded.

She straightened, holding the folder that contained her grandmother's notes, and for a moment Mal saw, behind her, the photograph that stood in its frame on the dressing table top. He had time to register the image of a young man's face before Rowan saw what he was looking at.

Two spots of colour flamed high in her cheeks, and she gave Mal an angry, challenging look.

'His name's Neil,' she said coldly, flatly. 'And he was my fiancé, until he jilted me for no apparent reason.'

Mal returned her glare calmly. 'I wasn't about to ask,' he told her in a quiet voice. 'It's none of my business. But I'm sorry.' An outright lie; she had explained a great deal in those few words, and, conscience or no conscience, he could not be sorry from a selfish point of view.

Rowan handed him the folder. She tried to smile, but her eyes were haunted.

'Here you are. I hope you can come up with something that makes sense, because I've tried time and again with no luck at all.'

He decided that a tactful exit would be the best policy. On one level he was dubious about the prospect of leaving her alone, but on another he didn't want to antagonise her by out-staying his welcome. Besides, she knew where the phone was. There was nothing to stop her from contacting him if she wanted to, or needed to.

'I'll take these back with me now,' he said as they walked towards the stairs. 'Although I'll have to do a bit more work today. I'm getting behind schedule on the bureau.'

'That doesn't matter.' Rowan was no longer remotely interested in the bureau as a piece of furniture; its only significance to her, now, was what it had yielded.

She wished that Mal had not seen the photograph. Mentioning Neil had stirred up thoughts and memories that she had lately managed to suppress. And made contrasts which she would have preferred not to think about at all.

The landing was unlit – she had not bothered to switch on the stairs light when they came up, feeling more sure of herself now that she was not alone – and as she reached the top of the flight and turned to go sideways down the steep steps, she glimpsed Mal's reflection in the tall, half-hidden mirror. And in that split second something in what she saw sent a sharp and unexpected nervous reaction through her. In the dimness Mal's hair looked far more red than usual, and some movement, some unconscious gesture as he passed the mirror, gave his reflected image an aura of . . . what? For a few moments Rowan could not put it in perspective, but as she started down the stairs it came to her.

Something about Mal reminded her of the man she had seen in her dream, the man who stood under the bare branches of the blasted oak – Duir.

She looked quickly over her shoulder at the real Mal as he descended behind her, but whatever it was that she had seen in the mirror was not there now. It had been a momentary illusion, a trick of light, nothing more. But suddenly Rowan was glad that he was leaving.

11

By noon of the next day, the news of what had happened to Rowan was all round Barton Tavey. The story had spread, each teller embellishing it in his or her own way, until the general picture started to assume something of the proportions of a national event. It was more than likely, Rowan decided, that the culprit for starting the tale on its way was Agnes. Even if her neighbour had missed the dramatic arrival of the police car and the shepherding away of Cracky Tully, she could hardly have failed to notice when the police made a return visit the following morning.

Rowan had had a bad night, worse than she had anticipated. She had had difficulty in sleeping. Every sound, every tiny creak of the old house settling or soft rustle of the wind, had seemed to her like the sound of someone moving along the landing, and she had spent half the night sitting up with the light ablaze in her bedroom, terrified of her own imagination.

The two police officers who visited her this time might well have noticed the paleness of her face, the dark crescents of shadow beneath her eyes, but they made no comment. They would like, they said, to check the house so that they could find out how the tramp had got in; and to ask her to answer a few more detailed questions, to save her the necessity of visiting the station to make a statement.

Rowan agreed reluctantly. She would have far preferred the whole ugly business to have been forgotten by all concerned. But now that the processes of law were under way she knew she could hardly expect to halt them on a whim. She would have to see it through.

'Will you be prosecuting him?' she asked.

One of the two men, older than his colleague and with

the wind-roughened skin and pronounced accent of the Exmoor-bred, looked a little surprised by the question. 'Old Tully? Well I doubt it, miss. To be frank with you, I don't think he's got enough sense to be worth taking through the courts. Unless, of course, you insist on an action. It is your right.'

Rowan shook her head. 'No, no – I don't want to insist on it. It was just that now I've had time to get over what happened, I almost feel sorry for him. Whatever he did, I don't think he could help it.'

'I think that's very likely.' He looked relieved, as if he had been anticipating that she might be out for legal vengeance. 'The best thing anyone can do for him, in my opinion, is to put him somewhere where he'll be looked after but kept in check, so to speak. Safer for the public, too, judging by this little lot. Now if you wouldn't mind just clearing up one or two points for me . . .'

Rowan went carefully over the details of the incident once again, and the officer noted down her comments, in shorthand she observed. Meanwhile, his companion checked through the ground floor of the house, and reported that it looked as though Tully had forced his way in through the window of the front room. There was some damage to the frame and the catch. These windows had not been designed for security, he pointed out, and it would have been a simple matter to force it open, if the intruder were determined enough.

Rowan shivered inwardly. She was still totally baffled by Tully's motivation, and said as much to the police officer.

He sucked air through his teeth, thinking that over. Then he said, 'I think it must be anyone's guess, mustn't it? I had a word or two with Fred Dymock, your local bloke, and he told me that the old man had never hurt a fly in his life before yesterday. He's been quiet as a mouse since we took him in, too. I don't think he's got the faintest idea what's happened to him. But perhaps that's how it is with people like that, when they're not quite right in the head to start with. They can go on for years never bothering a soul, and then suddenly, for no good reason . . .' he made a gesture intended to signify what words could not, and shrugged.

'That's the only explanation that makes sense to me, at any rate.'

Rowan was inclined to agree with him. It wouldn't have satisfied a conscientious psychiatrist, no doubt, but as long as she could believe that there had been no reason behind it, that it was just one of those things, she knew that it would cause her no nightmares.

Ponderously, the older man rose to his feet. 'Well, I think that's about it, then, unless there's anything else we can tell you?' He waited for an answer, and when none was forthcoming added, 'And if you want any more information, or think of anything that might be useful – '

'I'll phone you, yes. Thank you very much for all your help.' Rowan showed them to the door, feeling belatedly guilty that she had not offered them a cup of tea, which was probably the form in an area like this. But it was too late to rectify that now.

The car drove away, and she turned to go back indoors. But before she could close the front door, Agnes Teale, in a fast-moving blur of bright cotton print, was at her front gate.

'Rowan?' Agnes's voice was shrill with anxious curiosity, and her birdlike eyes darted from Rowan to the vanishing car and back to Rowan again. 'Is everything all right, dear? Whatever's going on?'

'Oh, Agnes . . .' She could not escape with some excuse, or Agnes would form her own, and doubtless very wrong, conclusions. Besides, she meant well. 'Come in.' Rowan waited for her elderly neighbour, then ushered her through to the living-room.

'I wondered what on earth could be up when I saw the police car,' Agnes said eagerly. 'Has something happened? What did they want? I hope it's nothing serious!'

The barrage of questions put Rowan on edge, but she forced herself to react calmly. 'I had a bit of trouble here yesterday,' she told her. 'Someone broke into the house while I was out.' And, as Agnes listened agog, she told the story yet again, as briefly as she could without prompting too many further queries. When she finished, Agnes shook her head with the wisdom of hindsight.

'Well, now! That grubby old tramp. And just think, he's been living around this village for twenty year or more, and never a bit of trouble before this! Mind, I always said it couldn't last. I knew something would have to happen sooner or later. That's always the way with people like him, isn't it? They're not all there like the rest of us, and it just isn't safe to trust them. They'll put him away now, though, I expect.'

'Yes, I expect they will.'

Agnes sighed. 'All poor Maud's things. What's the room like now, dear? Was there much damage? I'll give you a hand to clear up the mess if that would help.'

'That's very kind of you Agnes, but there's no need to worry,' Rowan assured her. 'Mal and I put it right last night.'

She knew even as she spoke that she had said the wrong thing, and Agnes pounced on the unintended information like a terrier. 'Mal Lyndon? Well, that's a good thing! Such a nice young man, I've always thought. I expect you and him get along very well?' Her eyes studied Rowan's face shrewdly.

Rowan gave her a bland smile. 'Yes. We're quite good friends. Would you like a cup of tea, Agnes?' She offered quickly, to turn Agnes's attention away from her relationship with Mal.

Agnes accepted eagerly, and for the next hour Rowan suffered further cross-questioning about the incident with Tully. Agnes's curiosity was insatiable; she would not be satisfied until she knew every small detail in its entirety, and by the time the grilling was over and she finally left, Rowan was exhausted.

She thought of calling Mal then, to let him know that all was well and to thank him again for what he had done, but decided against it. For the time being she wanted to put anything and everything to do with yesterday's crisis out of her mind. She would postpone ringing Mal until later in the day, when she felt stronger.

During the afternoon, Rowan had another, and unexpected, visitor. She had washed out her grandmother's crumpled clothes, which were now festooned on a rack in the bathroom to dry, and was just rolling down her sleeves when the doorbell rang. Surprised, and wondering if it might be Mal, she opened the door to see Tom Rushford standing outside.

He smiled his customary apologetic smile. 'Hello, Rowan. I hope I haven't interrupted anything vital?'

'No, not at all. It's nice to see you.' She stood back, a little confused, and he stepped into the hall.

'I hope you don't mind my dropping round on the off-chance,' Rushford said, 'But when I heard about you and Tully, I wanted to make sure that you were all right.'

'Oh, you know about that?'

'Well, yes. I'm afraid secrets don't survive for very long in a small village. Don't worry, I'm not going to start bombarding you with questions. I'm sure you've had more than enough of that already. But if there is anything I can do . . . '

Agnes had certainly gone to work fast, Rowan thought. It was strange how, the moment someone suffered an unpleasant experience, their neighbours and friends felt that they had to be treated as though they were invalids, or half-witted. What, after all, could Tom Rushford possibly do that would be of any concrete use?

She realised suddenly that she was being both uncharitable and unfair. Tom was neither a voyeur, nor patronising. He genuinely wanted to be of some assistance to her, and to reassure himself that she really was still in one piece. She smiled, and asked the unavoidable question. 'Would you like some tea?'

He shook his head. 'No thanks. I've been making parish calls, and I'm already awash with the stuff – one of the hazards of my job, I'm beginning to think.'

'Well, come into the living-room for a few minutes, anyway.'

'That I will do.' He followed her through and perched on the edge of an armchair.

'How's Jennifer?' Rowan asked.

'Oh, she's fine. We've just heard that one of our errant sons is descending on us this weekend, so she's turning the house upside down to make it look like a showpiece before he arrives. But that's by the by – I know I said I wasn't going to talk about it, Rowan, but I must ask you if you really are quite all right?'

Rowan smiled, more warmly than she might have done to anyone else under the circumstances. Despite not wanting to dwell on the subject of her ordeal, she was grateful for Tom's concern, and grateful, too, for the way he was trying to play the whole matter down for her sake, rather than turning it into a major issue as Agnes had done.

'I'm absolutely fine,' she told him. 'Really. I don't know what story you've heard, but the whole thing probably wasn't anything like as bad as you've been led to believe.'

Tom laughed. 'I dare say that's true. But all the same, I do want to get an apology off my chest. I feel rather responsible for all this – '

'Responsible?' She interrupted him, astonished. 'How can you be?'

'Well, maybe not responsible, but I've obviously been blind to the fact that there was more to old Tully than met the eye. I should have been more cautious, and I should have counselled caution to you.'

Rowan looked at him with affectionate exasperation. 'That's crazy,' she stated flatly. 'How on earth could you possibly have known, any more than the rest of us? Mal said exactly the same as you did – that Tully would never hurt a fly.' She smiled, unable to resist adding, 'Only Agnes was wise after the event.'

'Agnes would be! Well, I suppose I can comfort myself with the fact that even vicars aren't infallible. But I *am* sorry.'

'Thanks. It's all over now, though, and I think it's best forgotten.'

'Message understood!' Rushford eased himself a little more comfortably into the chair and clasped his hands together. 'Now, there is one other thing that brought me here to see you.'

'Oh?'

'Yes, it's about what we were discussing when you and Mal came for dinner at the vicarage. Your family legend, or whatever it is.'

'The Crown of Horn?' Rowan's interest quickened. 'Have you found something out?'

'Well, not exactly. But Mal came to see me this morning and asked if it would be possible to check through the parish records. He said he had a theory and wanted to see if he could verify it.'

'He did?' Rowan's surprise showed on her face, and Tom was clearly taken aback.

'Didn't you know? Oh, I naturally assumed that you were working on it together.'

'We are, in a sense. But I had no idea that he was making enquiries on his own.' Rowan did not know whether to feel angry with Mal or grateful to him for his interest. But either way, he should have at least told her if he was going to take matters any further.

'I wonder why he wants to do that?' she said aloud.

'He didn't tell me very much. But of course, your family has lived in this area for a very long time. Obviously Mal thinks that the records might turn up a few clues. I didn't realise that he was moonlighting, so to speak. I'm sorry, have I put my foot in it?'

She shook her head. 'No. I'm sure he'd have told me sooner or later.'

'Perhaps he wanted to spare you disappointment if nothing came of it.'

'Perhaps.' Rowan made a mental note to phone Mal the moment the vicar had left, and get the truth out of him.

'Anyway,' Tom said, 'I assumed that you were in it together, so I thought that as I was dropping round anyway I could tell you that I've persuaded the verger to get out as many of the old books as he can find, and that you're welcome to go through them whenever you like.'

'Well, I'll pass that message on to Mal, certainly. And thank you very much. It's good of you to go to so much trouble.'

'It's partly selfish, I assure you. I love a mystery, and I'm as keen as anyone else to see it solved. So I presume that when Mal comes to look at the records, you'll come along with him?'

Rowan grinned. 'I'd like to see him try and stop me!'

When Tom Rushford had gone, Rowan picked up the phone and dialled Mal's number. He took a long time to answer, but when he finally did, he sounded relieved to hear from her.

'I've been wondering if you were okay,' he said, 'but I didn't like to call you. I thought you'd be sick to death of neighbourly enquiries after your good health. Have you managed to fend off Agnes?'

'She's done her duty,' Rowan said. 'She came in this morning, grilled me, then spread the story like wildfire round the village.'

'I know. It's already come back to me twice. Have you been inundated with visitors?'

'Only Tom Rushford. He's just left, in fact.'

'Oh?' Was there a note of caution in Mal's voice? Rowan smiled mischievously to herself, then said, 'He told me about your discreet enquiries into the parish records.'

'Oh, that.' Guilt and amusement mingled in Mal's tone. 'So you've found me out, have you?'

'Yes, I have. Why didn't you tell me first?'

'Well, it was only a vague idea, and it probably won't lead to anything. I didn't want to depress you if it turned out to be useless.'

'That's what Tom said. He was very worried in case I decided to jump on you from a great height.'

She heard Mal laugh. 'And will you?'

'I don't know yet. It depends. But Tom left a message for you. He said that whenever *we* like to go along to the church, the records are ready for *us* to look at.'

There was a pause at the other end of the line, then Mal spoke with mock resignation. 'Round one to you. All right, name a time, and I'll meet you there.

As she walked towards the church, with the sun beginning to set over the hills towards the sea, Rowan realised that autumn was at last truly taking hold. There was a bite in the air that carried a frosty edge, and the whole atmosphere in the village had a look and a feel to it that made her think of woodsmoke. October now – there would be no more Indian summer days, no more hot afternoons to take the village by surprise. This was the season of bonfires, of carpets of leaves underfoot as the trees flamed and shed their burdens, of chilly nights and crisp days. She smiled at her own fancy. But October here was different indeed from October in London. Here, she could *feel* the world changing, the strength of the sun diminishing, the certain approach of winter.

She reached the lych-gate set into the bank of the narrow lane where the church stood, and started up the path. Ahead of her, light shone in a soft, diffused glow through the stained-glass windows below the bell-tower, and a single bulb glowed over the door, illuminating the great branch of antlers that adorned the lintel.

The oak door creaked as she opened it and her footsteps echoed on the flagged floor as she started to walk slowly along the aisle, uncertain of where she should go and whether or not anyone else was in the building.

From some hidden place came the sound of other and quicker footfalls, and the head of Cyril Thrace, the verger, whom Rowan knew by sight, appeared from behind the door that led to the vestry.

'Miss Vosper?' Thrace was a small, energetic man in his late sixties, with horn-rimmed glasses and a ruddy face. 'Ah, good day, I thought that must be you. Would you like to come in?'

Rowan followed him into the vestry and found Mal already waiting for her. He swung himself off the ledge where he had been sitting, and smiled a greeting.

Thrace, in the background, bobbed about like a lively robin. 'I've set all the record books I could find out on that table,' he said, pointing to a large and dusty pile of leather-bound volumes. 'So I'll leave you to it, unless there's anything else you need?'

'No, that'll be fine, Mr Thrace,' Mal told him. 'Thanks for all your help.'

'Any time.' Thrace nodded a farewell to each of them and hurried out, calling back over his shoulder, 'I'll be somewhere around if you want me.'

Mal watched until the door had closed behind him, then said, 'Thank God he's gone! He's a very pleasant old chap, but he wears me out – never stops talking, and never stops hopping from one foot to the other. It's exhausting just to watch him.' He turned to face Rowan. 'Well, how are you? You look a bit pale.'

She shrugged. 'Sleepless night. But never mind that. I want to know what all this is about, Mal. Tom Rushford said you had an idea about the Crown of Horn, and that was why you wanted to look at the parish records.'

'Yes.' Mal fished in his trousers pocket and brought out a single sheet of paper. 'It was this that started me thinking. Look, it's one of the notes your grandmother made, and it mentions something about your family history.'

Rowan studied the paper. It was a small scrap, and it read: *'Traditional attribute of the Crown of Horn – from Dwyer down – find out whether the hiding place has always been the same.'*

' "*From Dwyer down*"; I think I'm beginning to see what you're getting at.'

Mal shrugged. 'It seems worth a try. Your family have apparently been here for generations, in one form or another. And there's another thing. Has it occurred to you that there's a very strong similarity between the names Dwyer and Duir?'

Rowan stared at him. 'No,' she said, 'it hadn't occurred to me at all, but then I'd completely forgotten about this note.'

'It may be just a coincidence of course, but I think the records are well worth checking.'

'If there is a Dwyer,' Rowan frowned, 'it's going to take us hours to trace it back.'

'Well, maybe. But I think we might stand a better chance if we bear one point in mind. I'm certain that if the link *is* there, it'll be through the female line and not the male. Your grandmother's notes state as much. Whatever this legacy is, it's been handed down from woman to woman.'

'Yes, and that means that the name would change with every generation.' Rowan bit her lip. 'God, that's going to be difficult!'

'I know. But if we assume that the connection in each case is with the eldest grand-daughter, we might save ourselves a few headaches.' Mal held out an arm, indicating the two chairs that the verger had thought to set ready for them. 'Shall we take the plunge?'

For the next hour, they worked slowly and methodically through the record books. The task was less difficult than it was arduous. Beginning with Maud Fairfax, who had been born in Barton Tavey, they painstakingly traced the female lineage of Rowan's family. There were a number of red herrings to delay the search, particularly where branches of the family produced a large number of daughters, some of whom had died young, and in many instances the likely inheritor of the Crown of Horn was a matter of guesswork. But at last, in one of the earlier books, Mal came across a reference that riveted his attention.

The handwriting of the parson of the time was flowery and hard to decipher, the language and spelling archaic. But the entry in the 'Marriages' column was clear enough.

> '*On the Twelfth day of June in the Year of Our Lord 1620, Martha Jane Dwyer, spinster of this parish, to Edward Lacey Priske of The Gate House, Porlock Vale*.'

'Rowan!' He reached out and tapped her arm, making her start. 'I think I've found it.'

She leaned eagerly across, and he pointed to the page. 'Look. Martha Priske – she was the mother of Anne who became Anne Brand, and so forth. In 1620, Martha Priske wasn't Martha Priske, but Martha *Dwyer*. Your ancestor.'

Rowan stared at the ancient record. She felt excited, and yet at the same time disappointed, as if she had been expecting that the discovery of her long-dead multi-great-grandmother's identity would in itself provide some of the answers they were seeking. But in reality, it simply confirmed Maud Fairfax's notes and no more.

Mal, reading her expression and accurately guessing her thoughts, turned back another page in the record book. 'Let's see if we can find out who Martha's mother was, shall we?'

She nodded. It might produce something, no matter how small.

'Dwyer, Dwyer...' Mal bent closer to the book, his eyes scanning the faded leaf. Then, after a few minutes, he straightened, looking baffled.

'Well, that's peculiar. There's no mention whatsoever of a male Dwyer who might have been Martha's father.'

'Are you sure? How far back have you gone?'

'So far back that he must have been at least ninety when he fathered her. No, there's nothing here.'

'Perhaps they were married in another parish.'

'I suppose that must be it. Hang on, let me look in the christening records. There may be something there.'

She waited, trying to control her impatience, while he turned pages. Then he said, 'Wait a minute, what's this?'

'Where?' She looked over his shoulder to where his finger pointed.

The entry was for the year 1601, and it said:

> '*Baptised in this parish on the Nineteenth day of November, Martha Jane Dwyer, a foundling child and adopted daughter, by the mercy of Our Lord, of John and Elizabeth Wright, whom God may surely commend for their charity.*'

'There she is,' said Mal triumphantly. 'Our elusive Martha.'

Rowan chewed at her lower lip. 'I wonder why she didn't take her adoptive parents' name?' she mused.

'That's something we'll never know.' Mal leaned back in his chair, arching his back to ease the stiffness. 'And it means we've come to a dead end. Before Martha, the family tree is a complete mystery.'

'Maybe that doesn't matter,' Rowan murmured. The barest skeleton of an idea was in her mind, but she could not give it form or coherence. 'Maybe Martha herself is the beginning of it.'

'What do you mean?' Mal looked intrigued, but puzzled.

She shook her head. 'I don't know. It's just that it seems odd that a foundling with the name Dwyer should be the earliest ancestor that we can trace, and that, as you said, Dwyer and Duir are such similar names.'

If Mal felt the same premonitory stirring deep down inside him that Rowan felt, he was careful not to show it.

'That's something we can't even speculate about,' Mal said quietly. 'But if the mystery did begin with Martha, then I think we've at least pinpointed a date for the Crown of Horn – whatever it is.'

'Something nearly four hundred years old. But the legend – that's far older, it goes back long before Christianity if what Tom said about folklore is true. How can the Crown of Horn tie in with the story of Duir?'

'I don't know. Perhaps time, in this sense, isn't relevant. Or perhaps the answer lies somewhere right back in the past, and Martha Dwyer is the end of the chain rather than the beginning.' He sighed. 'What can I say? Whatever the real truth is, I don't think we'll ever be able to find it.'

Rowan looked down at the record book. So near, and yet so far. She felt frustrated, miserable. Mal's idea had been inspired, but it had produced nothing of any value, save confirmation of the family link with Dwyer. She began to wish that she had, after all, left him to make these investigations alone, and saved herself from being let down.

Mal started to close the books and return them to some sembance of order. 'Quite where we go from here I'm not sure,' he said. 'Maybe if – ' and he stopped, looking up. Rowan turned too, and saw the vestry door open to admit Tom Rushford. He was in what looked like gardening clothes – baggy trousers and a shapeless pullover – and he held a bulging carrier bag in the crook of his arm.

'Still hard at work?' He glanced at the books. 'How's it going?'

'Not too well, I'm afraid.' Mal moved two of the records so that Tom could sit on the edge of the table. 'The idea I had has been borne out, but unfortunately it doesn't tell us anything of any value.'

The vicar looked disappointed. He set the carrier bag down and opened it. 'How about some fortification? Compliments of Rushford Orchards Unlimited – the first of the autumn crop. We picked them this afternoon.' And he took out a handful of small russet-coloured apples. Thanking him, Rowan took one and bit into it. The flesh was crisp, sharp and firm, and the juice a welcome antidote to the dust of the vestry.

'Well,' said Rushford, 'what's the next move in this chess game? Mal told me about the legend you'd discovered – I hope you don't mind my letting on about that, Mal? – but I must admit I still don't see how the parish records could have helped.'

'It was just an outside chance,' Mal told him. 'In one sense it paid off, but ... ' And he explained about the family name, and the possible connection between Dwyer and Duir.

When he had heard the full details, Rushford raised his eyebrows. 'Intriguing. Certainly it seems to confirm the basic background of the story, but beyond that it's still anybody's guess as to what this Crown of Horn really is.'

'We're fairly sure that it's an heirloom,' Rowan said. 'In the sense that it's a physical object rather than something abstract.' She spoke a little diffidently; it seemed to her that in the race for answers she was beginning to be left behind. What had started out as a very personal conundrum was turning into something far more public, almost common property. She felt as though the reins were being taken out of her hands, firstly by Mal and now by Tom Rushford, and it created a degree of resentment within her. Not for the first time, she found herself half-wishing that she had not allowed Mal to become involved in the first place. She was tempted to stand up and walk out of the church right now, leaving the two men to think and do what they pleased.

'Well,' Mal said, 'Crown of Horn or no Crown of Horn, I don't see that there's anything more we can do here. If you'll tell me where these books live, vicar, I'll put them away.'

Rushford made a dismissive gesture. 'Oh, don't worry about that. Best leave it to Cyril; he knows the whereabouts of everything far better than I do, and he'll create if we put them all back in the wrong place. Just leave them in a pile; that's right. Now, can I offer you both a cup of coffee?'

Mal glanced at Rowan, as if he didn't intend to commit himself until she had spoken. 'No,' she said. 'Thanks, but I ought to get home. I've got one or two things to do.'

It was her favourite excuse. Rushford glanced enquiringly at Mal, and he shook his head. 'The same applies to me, too, I'm afraid.'

'Well, you can at least take a handful of apples each. Go on, Rowan, you'll be doing us a great favour; we've got a glut of them this year.'

Rowan accepted the apples with a slow smile. 'Thank you. And please give my thanks to Jennifer, too.'

'I will.' Rushford glanced round the vestry once more, then added, 'Don't wait for me, if you're in a hurry. It'll take me a few minutes to check that all the lights are off.'

Rowan and Mal made their farewells and left him to it. Dusk had turned to darkness outside, and as they stepped from the church they could only dimly make out the gravel path, with the headstones of the graveyard showing through the gloom like pale ghosts.

'Drink?' Mal suggested as they walked towards the lych-gate. 'Something stronger than coffee, that is?'

Rowan thought of Rose Bastable and her last visit to the Oak and Ash. 'I don't think I will, if you don't mind. I *have* got things to do.' She noticed how clearly her voice carried in the still air; another sign of the changing season.

Mal made no comment and no attempt to persuade her to change her mind. They walked slowly and in silence until they reached the gate, and then she said suddenly, 'I'd like those papers back, if you've got them.'

There was something odd in her tone, but Mal was beginning to lose patience with his own attempts to follow every twist and turn of her unpredictable mind.

'They're back at my house,' he said. 'I've only got that one note that I showed you earlier.'

'Oh, it doesn't matter. Some other time.' She stared into the middle distance, deciding that it wasn't worth the walk to Coombe Cottage simply to retrieve the folder. She wanted the papers back, wanted to keep them securely under her own wing where no one else could look at them.

But it would have to wait. She felt listless and depressed, anxious to put the day behind her.

'I'll walk to the end of the lane with you,' Mal said, 'then I think I'll call in at the pub anyway.'

'Okay.' Rowan thrust her hands into her coat pockets, head bowed as though against a wind. Mal watched her as she walked, feeling a mixture of concern and exasperation. She was drawing back again, returning to her private shell, and for once he was not in the mood to try and lure her out of it. The attempts he had made in the past had achieved next to nothing and it seemed pointless to waste further time and energy on fruitless effort. She'd come out of it soon enough, if she chose to, and in the meantime he had his own life to lead.

At the point where the church lane forked, one branch leading into the village, the other to Rowan's own unlit road, they said goodnight. For a brief moment Rowan was tempted by the glimpse of the village street: the comfortable, sleepy aura of it, the warm and welcoming lights of the pub that reflected distantly in the quiet water of the pond. But she was tired, hungry and a little confused. Better to go home.

She gazed after Mal for a few moments as he went on his way towards the green, not looking back. Then she turned and set her face homeward, her steps quickening unconsciously as the darkness of the narrow street engulfed her like a soft blanket. She had switched on the porch light before she left the house, and it glowed ahead of her like a tiny guiding beacon.

The last fading marigolds loomed like wan faces through the darkness as she opened the front gate and walked to the door. And inside the house, the scent of roses greeted her like an old friend. It was strong tonight, stronger, she thought, than it had ever been. And now that it had become so familiar, she was glad of it. It was as if the house itself were welcoming her back where she belonged.

12

Her dreams that night were full of roses: huge, pale and somehow threatening blooms that grew and hung in great clusters from the branches of a dead oak tree. And again she saw the half-human, half-animal face of her vision. This time it manifested from the bole of the tree itself, its outlines distorted by the gnarled bark. Once, for only a moment, the face took on a true semblance of life, and it was Mal, with red eyes and burning hair, who smiled and spoke to her – but all she could hear was a howling sound, like the baying of a pack of hounds.

When morning finally came, Rowan struggled into wakefulness and climbed out of bed, feeling as though she had not slept at all. Her eyes ached, her limbs were heavy, but she dared not even try to go back to sleep. The nightmares were too fresh and sharp in her memory.

Agnes, thankfully, did not make her customary call, and Rowan was able to settle her mind by completing a few tasks around the house that she had been putting off. It had a soothing effect on her, and by the time she had finished she had all but forgotten her disturbing dreams.

She was pulling on a coat in preparation for a leisurely walk to the local shops when the telephone rang. She lifted the receiver, and the voice at the other end said, 'Rowan? It's Mal.'

'Oh, hello.' She felt a sudden pang of guilt, recalling her feelings and her attitude of the previous evening. She felt she should make amends somehow; put matters right between them and ease her conscience.

She said, 'I think I owe you an apology.'

'Oh? For what?' He sounded surprised, which was encouraging.

'Last night. I was feeling scratchy and a bit sorry for myself, and I think I let it show.'

Mal paused, then she heard him laugh. 'Forget it. If I'd been in your shoes I think I'd have felt exactly the same. We were all disappointed, but it must have been worst for you. But listen, that's not important now. Are you busy?'

'Well, not really. I was just going out shopping.'

'Can you make a detour and come round to my house?'

There was something in his voice, something he was suppressing that sounded suspiciously like excitement. 'What's happened?' Rowan asked.

'I've found something.' Now the animation was unmistakable, and Rowan, feeling something respond at a primitive, intuitive level within herself, had no need to ask if it was important.

'What is it?' she demanded eagerly.

'It's too complicated to explain on the phone. I'll show you when you get here.'

Either that was the truth, or Mal was enjoying tantalising her with hints.

'I'll come straight round,' she told him. 'Five minutes?'

'Fine. The place is in chaos, but I'll just have to apologise for that in advance. See you shortly.' And he hung up.

The spindrift rain of two days ago had returned, and a flurry of tiny needles struck Rowan's face and stung her skin as she ran to her Mini and climbed inside. The wipers cut a swathe through the beads of water on the screen, and she drove down into the village and on towards the coast road and Coombe Cottage. As she turned right by the RAC sign, the village street gave way to dripping hedgerows and the sky opened out into a turbulent bowl of low, racing clouds that swept across the landscape like dark smoke. Coombe Cottage was a small oasis under that sky, a solitary outpost surrounded by dank, sodden vegetation. Rowan turned on to the patch of ground that fronted the house, avoiding a large puddle that spread across two-thirds of the surface, and pulled up as near to the door as she could.

The door opened before she could knock. Mal had obviously seen her arrive.

'Come on in.' He stood back to let her duck out of the

rain, and closed the door against a squall that tried to follow her. The room was much as she remembered it from her one and only previous visit, although today, with the weather as it was, the light that came in at the big front window was grey and gloomy. There were piles of newspaper everywhere, including one bundle that obscured the seat of an armchair, and in the middle of the floor, replacing the mahogany table which Mal had been working on when she paid her first call, was her own Queen Anne bureau.

In spite of her eagerness to know what was going on, Rowan could not help pausing to look at the work Mal had so far done on the writing-desk. The old, badly-applied varnish had been stripped away, revealing the natural grain of walnut beneath, and Mal had carefully removed the leather covering inside the lid.

'I've started rubbing down the wood where it's been scratched or chipped,' he said, crouching down on his haunches beside her as she studied his handiwork. 'It's a very slow job. The problem is to get it into as near perfect condition as possible without flawing the original line.' Critically he ran one hand down the curved front of the bureau where the damaged wood had been smoothed over. Then suddenly he straightened, looking down at her with a faint smile. 'And that's what I wanted to tell you about.'

Rowan frowned. 'The desk?'

'Yes. Your bureau is proving to be quite a little goldmine one way and another. Hold on. I'll put some lights on and then you can see what I mean.' He crossed the room and turned on a powerful overhead bulb which threw sharp shadows across the room. Then he reached inside the top section of the bureau and touched the wooden handle of a small inner drawer.

'See this? There's nothing peculiar about the drawer itself, except for the fact that when you pull it right out, it's shallower than it apparently should be. The outside of the compartment is quite a bit deeper than the inside. Do you see what I mean?'

Rowan nodded, the inklings of an idea occurring to her. 'It's almost as though it's been designed to hold something else behind it,' she said.

Mal didn't reply immediately, but felt about on the underside of the drawer slot. For a moment he could not find what he was seeking, then he said 'Ah!' and there was a faint click. Something moved at the back of the compartment, and Rowan peered inside to see that a false section had fallen back to reveal a second, smaller space beyond.

'Spring-loaded,' Mal told her. 'I discovered it completely by accident.'

'It must have been for love-letters, or secret documents.' Rowan was fascinated by the discovery, despite a slight frisson of disappointment. But then another thought struck her, and she turned to look at Mal, hardly daring to ask the question that formed in her mind.

At last she said, 'Was there anything inside it?'

There was laughter and triumph in Mal's eyes as he smiled. 'Oh yes. There was something in it all right.' And he crossed to the cluttered mantel, and took down a small blue envelope. 'Here.'

She took it from him and turned it over. The envelope was dusty and old. Clearly it had been hidden in the bureau for a good many years. Written on it was one single word: ROWAN.

Her fingers clenched round the envelope and she said, 'That's Gran's writing. And it's addressed to me.'

'Then you'd better open it, hadn't you?'

She gave him an anguished look. 'I don't know if I dare, Mal. It might be so important, and yet it might be nothing.'

'I hate to state the obvious, but there's only one way to find that out. Here – ' He bent to lift aside the newspapers on the armchair. 'Sit down. I'll go and make some coffee and leave you to read it in private.'

She sank into the chair as he left the room, and her fingers were unsteady as they fumbled with the flap of the envelope. Vaguely she was aware of the sound of a kettle being filled in the adjacent kitchen, and of Mal's ginger cat who, disturbed from sleep, abandoned his basket under the kitchen table and came to investigate. He jumped elegantly on to the arm of Rowan's chair, tail raised questioningly, and stared over the crook of her arm as she drew out the single piece of paper that was folded inside the envelope.

The first thing that caught her eye was the date at the top of the page. The letter had been written nearly twenty years ago – at almost the same time, she realised, as the quarrel between her grandmother and her mother, which had never been resolved.

She felt a hard little lump form in her throat and swallowed it back as she began to read.

'My dear grand-daughter,

I hope that this letter one day finds its way to you. By the time you read it, if you do, I expect that I shall be dead, and my house will have come to you as I have stated in my Will.

When you read this letter, I must ask that you don't show it to your mother, or even tell her that you have it, as what I have to say to you concerns you alone, and not her. I don't know if she will have told you the reasons why she and I fell out; knowing Margery, I doubt it. You may know by now that in addition to the house there is another legacy which I have to leave to you; one which must be passed down through our family, as it has been for a long time, from grandmother to grand-daughter...'

The Crown of Horn. Rowan bit her lip, and read on.

'Your mother could never understand the significance of this legacy, and I was unable to convince her that it was you, and not she, who was the rightful heir to it. That was the reason why we quarrelled, and I have the feeling that that quarrel will never be made up. Certainly it's up to Margery to make the first move, and without a promise from me to hand the legacy on to her – which I'll never do – I doubt if she will be willing to patch up the argument. I regret that deeply, but even though Margery is my daughter, you are my grand-daughter, and that is the most important thing of all.

Rowan, I think that by the time you read this letter you will already be in possession of at least some of the facts. I have hidden certain notes and papers in this bureau which are meant for you, and from them I think you'll have pieced together some of the story. You may be hoping that this letter will tell you the rest. Well, my dear, I'm afraid I must disappoint you. I am sure you have guessed by now that you are the rightful possessor of the Crown of Horn. But the nature of it, and the way in which it will come into your hands, is something that I can't tell you. You must find it, as I did, by your own efforts, and I have complete faith in your success. There are just two things I can tell you – when you find the Crown of Horn, you will know it for what it is, and when it passes into your hands, the real meaning of the legend of Duir and Niainn will become clear. I'm sorry to be so cryptic, my dear, but one day you will understand.

I hope that you and I will meet again before I die. Perhaps when you are older, and if I am spared, you will come and stay with me again, as you used to with your mother and father. If not, then I send my love to you for always.

Your Grandmother'

Mal came in from the kitchen to find Rowan sitting in the chair with one hand over her face, the letter clutched tightly in her other hand.

'Rowan?' He set the two mugs he carried down and crossed over to her. 'Rowan, what's wrong?'

She looked up at him, and he saw the misery in her eyes, the tears glittering on her cheeks. 'Hey, come on! What is it?'

She sniffed, wiping her eyes and blinking. 'It's this letter. I'm sorry, but it really brought home to me how lonely Gran must have been.' She smoothed the crumpled page out, staring sadly down at it. 'It's something she said at the end. It made me feel so awful, so guilty.'

Mal crouched down, reaching out absently to stroke the head of the ginger cat, who started to purr. He didn't like to ask what was in the letter, but after a moment, without any prompting, Rowan held it out.

'I'd like you to read it,' she said.

He looked dubious, but he took the letter. 'Are you sure?'

'Yes. Please, Mal.'

Rowan settled back in the chair, half-watching him as he sat cross-legged on the floor with the letter before him. The cat, curious, sprang down from the chair arm and sniffed at his hand, its tail curling across his line of vision.

'Tigger! Get out of the way.' Mal pushed the cat aside, and with a piqued twitch of his long whiskers Tigger returned to his former perch and nudged his head against Rowan's arm for attention. She rubbed him under the chin, waiting as Mal read through her grandmother's letter.

At length he looked up and handed the sheet of paper back to her. 'I see why it upset you,' he said quietly.

She shrugged. 'It's far too late to put things right now. I suppose that's the worst thing of all.'

'Were you an only child?'

'Yes. So in a sense the whole responsibility devolves upon me, or I feel that it does, anyway. It must have been very hard for her to break the links like that.'

Mal nodded. 'But the reasons must have been very important indeed to her, or she wouldn't have done it. It seems to me that you can still put things right, by finding the Crown of Horn.'

Rowan stared at the letter again. 'She's guessed how much I'd have found out by the time I came across this letter, and she's precisely right. It's almost uncanny, isn't it?'

He smiled. 'I think where this is concerned we're just going to have to accept the uncanny as normal.'

Rowan looked back at the paper. 'Yet again, this is full of clues, but there's nothing *concrete* in it.'

'Except for what she says about the legend of Duir and Niainn,' Mal pointed out. 'Okay, it's not exactly concrete in the sense that you mean, but it at least tells us that there is a definite connection.'

'Yes. "*The real meaning will become clear*." I wonder what she could have been getting at?'

'It looks as though you'll only find that out when you get the Crown of Horn.' Mal picked up his mug and took a gulp from it, then grimaced. 'Hell, this coffee's gone cold! Would you like some fresh?'

'No, don't bother. I can drink it as it is. Well, obviously that's got to be the next step. Finding the Crown of Horn, I mean. Whatever it might be.' Rowan looked up, her expression troubled. 'Mal, I'm completely at a loss. Where do I go from here? How *can* I find it?'

After a few moments Mal replied: 'There are two possibilities, as far as I can see. We can go on playing detective, although frankly we're at a bit of an impasse because there aren't any leads left that we can follow. On the other hand, I've got a sneaking suspicion that there may be no need actually to *do* anything.'

Baffled, Rowan frowned at him. 'What's that supposed to mean?'

'Hasn't it occurred to you that everything seems to be gradually slotting into place just a little too neatly? One thing happens, then another follows it unprompted. Think of the way you came across the list of books just when you thought you'd run into a dead end. Then there was the legend, closely followed by the discovery of this letter. What I'm trying to say is, I have the feeling that if finding the Crown of Horn is the next stage in the game, you'll find it apparently by accident, whether you're trying or not.'

It was a very tempting theory, as it offered the encouraging prospect of success without too much effort. But somehow it all sounded too easy. Her grandmother had implied in her letter that the discovery of the heirloom was a task which must be undertaken with determination, and the idea that she could accomplish it by sitting back and doing nothing seemed too simple to be true.

But what other choice did she have? she asked herself. Mal had been right when he said that the clues had run out. Maybe, she thought, maybe with a little patience, and an alert eye, it *would* come of its own accord.

'I hope you're right,' she told him ruefully.

'So do I. Because if I'm not, we're right back to square one. Look, you can't possibly drink that coffee, and I'm going to make myself some more anyway. Give me your cup.'

She handed it to him not because she wanted coffee but because she needed an excuse to stay for a while, to avoid the rain and the isolation which would make her brood about this disappointment that could so easily have been the answer she had been hoping for.

When he came back with the two mugs refilled, she said, 'Mal, could we try and forget about being detectives for a while? I'm beginning to get sick of the whole thing. I've twisted myself into knots trying to find the answers to this puzzle, and right now I need a break from it.' She smiled. 'I don't doubt you do, too.'

Mal sat down opposite her, on a smaller and more dilapidated chair. 'You're right. Okay then, so what shall we talk about instead? The weather? Television? Farming?' He was grinning at her, making a joke of his words, but she knew that there could well be something more pertinent underlying them. Her involvement with Mal had become inextricably tied up with the search for the Crown of Horn, and she was being careful to keep it that way. But now, at a time when she felt she needed company and yet wanted to steer away from the mystery, she was dismayed to find that she had nothing to say to him. Was it, she asked herself, that beyond the one subject that held them temporarily together they had nothing at all in common? Or was it something in herself, something that was growing into such an obsession that she was no longer able to focus her mind on anything beyond those narrow limits? She wasn't sure which was the answer, or whether the truth lay somewhere between the two.

In the last few months she knew she had lost the technique of making light, easy conversation. Living here had forced some of it back, but the likes of Agnes Teale and Rose Bastable didn't demand much beyond the gossip of the day. Yet with Mal, it was different. She wanted to be able to talk with him as easily as with her neighbours; but to try and do so would, she felt, show herself up as shallow and inconsequential. Mal was too intelligent and too shrewd to be interested in trivial niceties, and her self-esteem would suffer a severe blow if she found that was all she could offer him.

During the awkward silence that had followed his last remark Mal had been observing Rowan, judging her reaction to that slight sting and judging it accurately. He raised his coffee mug and held it to his face, watching her assessingly over the rim.

'Tell me something,' he said. 'When this is all over, what are you going to do?'

Rowan glanced at him with sudden appreciation. It was the first time anyone, barring Agnes, whose interest had been short-lived, had asked her about her future plans. Everyone else, from Tom Rushford onwards, had seemed to assume that she would stay in Barton Tavey as a matter of course, and she was gratified that Mal had enough wisdom not to make the same mistake.

'I don't know,' she told him. 'It's something I've thought about, of course, but I haven't made any decisions yet.' She smiled, looking down at Tigger, who had fallen asleep in a precarious sprawl on the arm of her chair. 'I certainly can't go on living the life of ease for more than a few months. I'll have to start thinking about a job before next spring.'

'Do you think you'll go back to London?'

She hesitated for some while before replying, then: 'No. When I first came down here I thought I would go back, but now I couldn't. I've been away for long enough to realise that London was slowly strangling me. Anyway, there are too many bad memories there.'

Mal didn't ask what she meant by that; he already knew enough to let it pass.

'I'll have to make the journey back there, obviously,' Rowan added. 'All the belongings I didn't bring to Somerset are in store with a friend.' She felt a sudden sharp pang of memory, recalling her hurried departure and, after a week in Exmoor, the phone calls that had finally broken the old links with her London home. By now strangers would be in her flat, changing it, probably paying a higher rent than she had done. And yet she didn't really miss it.

'It must be like tearing up your roots,' Mal said gently.

She shook her head, emphatic. 'No, it isn't. I've only realised lately that I didn't really have any roots in London. It was a place to live and a place to work, but not much more. If I *have* got any roots, they're more likely to be here.'

He smiled. 'It's funny, but I could never visualise you in London. You're not hard enough for the city.'

Rowan met his eyes, and there was an air of challenge in her look. 'Maybe, but don't run away with the idea that I was cut out to sit in a country cottage making daisy-chains for the rest of my life, either!'

'Of course you weren't. You'd go crazy if you tried to live like Agnes. The real you lies somewhere between those two extremes.'

'That's right. The trouble is though, the perfect lifestyle isn't as easy to find as it is to imagine.' Her mouth quirked in self-mockery. 'I'll probably end up working in an antique shop in Bath, as the best possible compromise. Anyway, whatever happens in the end, I'll have to go back to London in the meantime. I'm getting sick of washing the same clothes to stop myself running out!'

Mal nodded sympathetically, then said, 'Look, in all seriousness – if you do have to make a return visit, and if you've got a lot of things to bring down, I'll gladly come with you and give you a hand. It'd be a lot easier with the van.'

She gave him an odd look – a mingling of surprise and gratitude with a little pain, too. 'That's kind of you, Mal. I appreciate it. But I don't want to say yes at this stage. It's hard to explain, but I think it might be better if I did it on my own. Could I think about it?'

'Of course. But bear the offer in mind.'

'I will.' It might be easier with him, she thought. His presence would support her, take away the harsh edges and make the task less hard to face. But at the same time, if she went with him she would have to maintain a mask; there could be no giving way to emotion. And the pretence would be very hard to keep up in the face of the memories London held for her. But she would think about it.

Finishing her coffee, she stood up. 'I'd better go,' she said. 'I've already wasted enough of your time. I'm getting to the stage where I forget that other people have to work for a living.'

'Take my advice – make the most of it while you can!' Mal smiled broadly. 'Have you got your letter?'

'Yes.' She stared at the folded sheet for a few moments, then tucked it into her handbag. 'I'll think about what you said, Mal. About finding the Crown of Horn.'

'Good. And you'll let me know if you have any revelations?'

'Oh yes, but don't count on it. Thanks for the coffee. I'll see you soon.'

Mal watched her run through the rain to her Mini, and a minute later the car turned out into the lane and headed for the village. Closing the front door, he stood for a few moments debating what to do. He had work to complete and he was already behind schedule, but right now that had to take second place. He needed to think. Something had occurred to him and was nagging at the back of his mind, and he knew he wouldn't be able to concentrate on anything else until he had taken time to chew it over.

He went through to the kitchen, followed after a few moments by Tigger, sensing a chance of food. With the cat winding ingratiatingly around his shins, Mal made himself a sandwich and took it back to his living-room. The cat stayed at his feet waiting for titbits of ham while he sat staring at the bureau as the idea that had come to him gradually took form.

The most cryptic passage of all in the letter from Maud Fairfax to Rowan had been the one in which she spoke of a connection between the old legend of Duir and Niainn, and Rowan's legacy. Rowan, he knew, had been totally nonplussed by it, but Mal believed that he had at least the germ of a clue to what it might mean. And it presented him with a very big problem. If he were to explain his theory to Rowan, she would reject it out of hand because she would be too afraid to admit that it could possibly be true. If the facts should bear out his theory, then a time would come when Rowan would have to accept it, but for now it was better – safer – that she did not know.

Mal suspected that if he was right, then his own part in the whole affair might soon come to mean a lot more to both of them than it did at present. That thought discomfited him, and he had to admit to himself that he was half-afraid of its implications. His role would be difficult, in fact, the biggest challenge he had ever faced in his life.

He gave the last piece of ham to Tigger, who showed his appreciation with staccato purring. Then he stood up, put the plate to one side, rolled up his shirtsleeves and turned his attention to the comparatively soothing demands of his work.

13

During the next two days, the weather continued to deteriorate. The flying drizzle had become a cold, ceaseless rain, and the atmosphere grew heavier and more oppressive as the clouds began to build up.

From her living-room window Rowan could see the lowering banks that seemed almost to touch the tops of the hills, weighing down on them and draining them of colour so that they became gaunt and grey and hostile. Her senses told her that there would be a storm before long; something she preferred not to think about. Since childhood she had had a deep-rooted fear of thunder. Living in London had helped to reduce the fear; its enclosed urban environment had cushioned the effects of storms and kept them one degree removed. But here it would be different. Here, there would be nothing between her and the elements. Still, if the worst came to the worst there was always Agnes to go to.

She felt restless and frustrated. The weather had virtually confined her to the house, and the constant unease at the back of her mind about a thunderstorm kept her on edge. She had heard nothing from Mal since her visit to his house, and although she had spent a lot of time thinking about her grandmother's letter, re-reading it and trying to interpret the meaning behind it, there had been no sudden inspiration to resolve the puzzle.

On the second day after her last meeting with Mal, Agnes called round, a little later than was usual for her. She had, it transpired, been making bramble jelly from the blackberries that grew in profusion in the hedgerows around the village, and she brought a large pot for Rowan. Agnes, Rowan decided, was not an easy woman to fathom. She veered between meanness of tongue and generosity of spirit. Underneath her bland exterior she was, perhaps, more complex than she seemed.

Today she gave Rowan a long, penetrating look, then said assertively, 'You don't look too well, dear. Are you getting a cold?'

Rowan was surprised by the question, but after a moment she realised that Agnes's guess might be right. Since the previous evening she had been feeling slightly out of sorts. Her head was heavy and her mind not functioning sharply.

'I don't know,' she said, 'I might have one coming.'

Agnes nodded sagely. 'Hardly surprising, with all this weather, is it? It's hard to believe that only a week ago we had all that sunshine. But there you are, that's England for you. George was saying this morning that there'd be a big storm soon, and he's not usually wrong.'

George, Rowan recalled, was the milkman. She suppressed a shiver. 'Well, I hope he's wrong this time.'

'You don't like storms?' Agnes sat down with all the comfortable ease of someone who felt equally at home in her neighbour's house as in her own. 'Well, I don't blame you. And when we get them round here, they can be quite frightening.'

'Can they?' Rowan glanced at her, not wanting to hear any more and yet unable to hold back a morbid interest.

'Oh, yes. Every time we get one, I start thinking about that disaster that happened in Lynton and Lynmouth some years back, and I tell myself, you never know, if something like that can happen once there's nothing to say it can't happen again. Horrible, that was.'

Rowan's eyes widened. She would have liked to ask Agnes not to pursue the story any further, but didn't know how to put her off without giving offence. But Agnes, once started, was warming to her theme.

'I don't suppose you ever heard about that, did you? No, you'd have been too young. Well, you know Lynton and Lynmouth, down the coast a bit? Two villages together, built on the side of the cliff just about, very steep. There was a dreadful storm over the moors one night – they said the sky turned sulphur-coloured and you couldn't see a yard in front of your face and there was lightning crackling in the air right down to ground level.' Agnes's eyes took on a faraway look, and she seemed to be savouring the memory ghoulishly. 'Well, they'd diverted one of the rivers thereabouts, and when the torrential rain started, the water just built up and built up until the river broke its banks. What happened was, it returned to its old course, just like that, and the whole lot was swept straight through the villages and down into the sea. They didn't have any warning at all. One minute there was just the rain, and the next, a great wall of water came thundering down the cliffs like an avalanche. It picked up everything that was in its way – trees, cars, and all. They said you could hear the noise of it for miles.'

A flash-flood. Rowan had never seen anything of that kind in her life, but imagination and memories of disaster newsfilms on TV gave her a clear enough picture. With the darkness and the lightning, it must have been terrifying.

'Was anyone killed?' she asked.

Agnes looked at her pityingly. 'Killed? I should just say so! Near on quarter of the people who lived there, so I heard. Just picked up and swept away, out of their sitting rooms, some of them.'

Even if she was exaggerating, it was a horrifying picture. And for those who had survived it, the memories must be appalling.

'They found great elm trees floating half a mile out to sea,' Agnes went on. 'And it cost a fortune to clear up all the mess.'

Rowan shuddered. She would have given anything, at that moment, to have looked outside and seen the clouds miraculously vanish and the sun appear.

'But nothing like that could ever happen here,' she said, trying to reassure herself. 'There aren't any rivers of any size, to start with.'

'No, of course not,' Agnes agreed complacently. Then she glanced speculatively at the window and added, 'Mind, we're in a valley where we are. And with them hills all around, if there was a lot of rain . . . '

She succeeded in shattering Rowan's cautious confidence. 'But it's never happened, has it?' Rowan persisted.

'Oh, no! But you never know, do you?'

You never know. The phrase preyed on Rowan's mind long after Agnes had gone. She could hardly blame her neighbour. Agnes simply enjoyed telling tales of woe – to her it was a form of entertainment – and she certainly hadn't meant any harm. But the story of the Lynton-Lynmouth disaster had awoken all Rowan's deepest fears about the danger of a really big storm, to the extent where she closed all the curtains at the ground floor windows so that she need not look out at the threatening sky.

During the afternoon, she rang Mal, reasoning that in her current state the last thing she could face was the prospect of an evening alone in the house. If the storm broke, she would feel a good deal happier if she was out of the house and in congenial company. Maybe Mal would agree to meet her for a drink at the Oak and Ash.

But the telephone was answered by John Prior, who told her that Mal had gone out and was not expected back until eight.

'He's gone into Bridgwater,' John said. 'Needed to get some solvents or varnish or something for a desk he's working on.'

Her own bureau, Rowan surmised ironically. 'Oh, okay, not to worry. Could you give him a message when he comes in, please?'

'Well, I won't be here. I'm going home in a minute. I'll leave him a note though, if you like.'

'Yes, if you would. Ask him to phone Rowan.'

'Rowan. Right.' Judging from the tone of his voice he remembered their last encounter, and Rowan was suddenly glad that they were not talking face to face. She thanked him and hung up, then went to fetch some more logs for the fire.

There was an element of Murphy's Law about the way that Mal was never in when she really needed him and yet at other times was always available. Eight o'clock, the boy had said. It would be dark by then. Perhaps, if she felt she really couldn't stand staying in the house, she would drive down to the pub and call him from there. Meanwhile, she would find something to keep her busy, and the curtains would stay closed.

The storm broke over Exmoor at dusk. Mal saw the huge, purple bank of cloud building up from the south-west as he drove through the Quantock Hills on his homeward route. A vast, anvil-shaped head was forming in the sky, blotting out the last of the evening light, and he switched on the van's headlamps, aware that he stood little chance of reaching Barton Tavey before he ran into it. Unconsciously he accelerated a little. If he could get home before the storm reached its full force, maybe the journey wouldn't be too bad.

Darkness came down quickly, hurried by the approaching cloud-bank, which gave the fading twilight an unnatural and unnerving quality. Thunderstorms never worried Mal as a rule – in fact he rather enjoyed them, provided he was under cover – but in the comparatively high cab of the Transit with its big windows, the scenery was a little too visible for comfort. It made him feel vulnerable.

For the past two hours or so it had not been raining, a suspicious sign in itself, but the roads were still wet from the earlier downpour, and the hiss of the tyres was almost hypnotic. The road was virtually deserted; people whose journeys weren't imperative had wisely decided to stay at home, and Mal found himself wishing that he had picked a different day for his Bridgwater trip. He had another ten, perhaps fifteen miles to go. With luck he would be back in the village within half an hour.

Minutes later the first heavy drops of rain fell on the windscreen, and within seconds sheets of water were hammering against the van and streaming across the glass like rivers as the wipers cut a swathe through them. Mal slowed down as visibility deteriorated, silently cursing because he hadn't left the town just a few minutes earlier, and leaned forward over the wheel, trying to see through the hurtling rain. He knew what would come at any second, but when it did it still made him start, for it was closer and more violent than he had expected. A single fork of lightning flared above the road ahead, cutting through the blackness in a shocking split second, and an instant later thunder exploded almost directly above him, drowning out the engine noise and rolling across the sky.

Mal sucked air in through his teeth as his nervous system slowly settled after the jolt it had received. This was going to be a big one, and if he had judged the position of the lightning accurately, Barton Tavey would be right in the centre of it.

A second flash of lightning, a savage electric-blue bolt, sheared through the clouds and struck groundwards even as the thunder bawled again. Another followed almost immediately. The storm was building very rapidly towards its full force, and Mal found himself beginning to feel distinctly uneasy. A lonely Exmoor road was not, after all, the ideal place to be in weather conditions such as these, and the idea that the van, which was unreliable at the best of times, might break down did nothing to improve his misgivings.

He thought of Rowan, wondered how she was faring in the storm, and told himself that it might be worthwhile stopping off at her house when he reached the village, just to make certain that she was all right.

He was nearing the edge of the Exmoor forest by this time, and the comparative openness of the hills gave way to a denser, closer landscape of trees. Overhead, the storm's fury was building up. Lightning spat and crackled across the sky like nightmarish flak, and the noise of the thunder was a ceaseless battering in his ears. Mal concentrated all his attention on the road, following the cold white glitter of the cat's-eyes in his headlamps, trying not to start as the lightning showed violently sudden images of trees and hedges that seemed to leap out of the blackness ahead.

When the thunderbolt came, it was directly over his head and so low that he jolted and almost lost control of the van. There was a tremendous crack, as though a vast capacitor had discharged its load, and the entire road lit up momentarily with a white-hot glare. The crack became an echoing boom, and following on its heels came another, more muffled bang. Dazed by the light and by the explosion, Mal could not have hoped to see the tree as it gave a lurch, then, shattered and uprooted by the lightning bolt which had struck it, keeled over and fell like a Titan across the road. He had time only for an instantaneous, horrifying glimpse of the monstrous trunk and clawing branches as they plunged towards him, then the van was skidding and spinning, its tyres shrieking on the wet surface as the full weight of the blasted tree came crashing down on the roof.

It seemed to Rowan that the full power of the storm was centred over Barton Tavey, over the house itself. She had watched the anvil-headed clouds as they moved up slowly and inexorably from the south-west and had wanted to get out, to go to the Oak and Ash, where she would at least have some company to alleviate her fear. But instead of leaving immediately she had waited, hoping that Mal would return, until it was too late and the storm had begun to break.

Now she sat hunched in a chair in the living-room, every light ablaze. The bulbs dimmed and dipped alarmingly with each onslaught of the lightning outside, but that was better than the prospect of staying in a dark room, where each bolt would flash through the house as though the storm were under her very roof. There was an ugly, uncontrollable sickness in her stomach: the sickness of helpless terror.

She didn't dare to switch on the television because of the outside aerial, and the radio, when she tried it, crackled with so much static interference that the programmes were unintelligible. She would have given almost anything for some homely and comforting sounds, music or even conversation, that would shut out the noise of the rolling, bellowing thunder and the furious lash of the rain against the window. But there was nothing to take away the terror that the storm inflicted on her.

She tried three more times to call Mal, her hand shaking on each occasion for fear that, somehow, the lightning would home in on her down the phone line. But the bell at the other end kept on ringing and ringing, and no one answered. Uneasy, she looked at her watch after the third try. It was almost nine, and John Prior had said that Mal would be back by eight. Something cold and constricting clutched at her, a horrible sense of foreboding. Even allowing for delays, he should have been back long ago if he had left Bridgwater on time. Perhaps, she told herself, the telephone lines were down. But no, that was one straw she could not clutch at; if the lightning had damaged the lines, then Mal's phone couldn't possibly be ringing. Just to be certain, she picked up the receiver again, and heard the familiar buzz of the dialling tone. Still working. Perhaps she should call the pub and see if Mal might by some chance be there?

Quickly, she went into the hall to fetch the local directory to look up the number of the Oak and Ash. She stopped suddenly, her spine prickling with a preternatural chill. For a split second she had the distinct feeling that someone was standing behind her . . .

She turned swiftly, and at the same moment the lights dipped as a tremendous thunderbolt crashed seemingly only yards above the roof. Rowan screamed aloud with shock as the rectangle of the window flashed with brilliance. For a few moments the atmosphere was quiet again, the room normal, the strange feeling gone. The air shivered, seeming to wait for something, and then there was another, lesser flash and the thunder rolled again.

Her heart hammering with sick terror, Rowan ran to the phone and scrabbled for the receiver. Clasping it to her ear, she put out her hand to dial –

It was as if some malevolent force had read her mind and decided to play the cruellest trick of all on her. The last thunderbolt had turned her fear into reality, and the telephone line was totally dead. At first she wouldn't let herself believe it, and her fist hammered on the receiver rest, trying to bring the line back to life. But there was not so much as a click – just the hollow emptiness of disconnection.

The receiver fell into her lap and she looked wildly round the room. She was effectively imprisoned: too afraid to go outside, even to run the short distance to her car or to Agnes's house, and now cut off from any communication. And it was after nine o'clock, and Mal was an hour late and she had no way of knowing what could have happened to him.

Her self-control broke then and she felt tears of anguish and fright brimming in her eyes. There was nothing she could do other than give way to them; and she sank to the floor by the phone, covering her ears with cupped hands and biting her lip like a child struggling to keep nightmares at bay, while the storm cracked and thundered overhead.

It took Mal some seconds to realise that he was still conscious. His shoulder was wedged hard against the van's door, and the door seemed to be jammed shut. He blinked, shaking his head slowly and drawing air into his lungs, as though he had just surfaced from deep water. And as his spinning mind cleared, he realised why the door would not open.

The force of the falling tree had not only spun the van wildly off course, it had also taken the nearside wheels off the ground. When the tree crashed down, the vehicle had gone over with it. Now it lay on its right side, and as the lightning crackled overhead again, with a simultaneous and deafening shout of thunder, Mal could see by the searing blue glare that the tree had struck the cab directly. Half the nearside window was smashed away, and branches clawed in through the gaping hole, with more boughs forming a mad tracework across the screen.

He shut his eyes tightly, trying to hold back a wave of sickness that rushed into his stomach and clutched at him with cramping pain. It was a reaction of shock, fear and, most of all, the realisation that he had escaped death by the narrowest of margins. If the tree had been that few feet taller, then the entire weight of the trunk itself, rather than simply the boughs, would have come hurtling down on him, and the cab would have been crushed under the onslaught.

He did not know how much time had passed since the impact, whether he had been knocked out or whether it had only happened a few seconds ago. And there was no way of telling what damage had been done to the van. Fuel might be leaking from somewhere; the ignition was still switched on although the engine had cut out in the crash, and at any second the petrol tank might catch and explode . . .

He took hold of himself, forcing back the feeling of panic. The chances of such a thing happening were remote; he had been watching too many television thrillers. But nonetheless he thanked whatever gods were listening tonight that the tree hadn't caught fire when the lightning struck it, or the van would have been an inferno.

A triple flash of lightning forked down less than half a mile away and made him jolt with fear. Rain was coming in through the shattered window, cold and stinging, and he could smell ozone, a kind of menacing, electric smell that made his nerves crawl.

He had to get out of this, but slowly, gently, carefully. By a miracle he didn't seem to be hurt, or at least not seriously. His legs were wedged under the steering-wheel, which was cutting into his thighs, but he thought that he could ease himself forward just a little. Flexing his toes he found that he could still feel them, without pain. Nothing broken there. His right arm hurt like hell where it had taken his body weight as the van went over, but that was probably no more than bruising. He was lying on his side, still, incongruously, in a driving posture. Taking his weight on the bruised elbow with a wince, he struggled to raise his head and body a few inches.

Another savage flash of lightning outside showed a dark smear on the window beneath him, and as the thunder roared above him he managed awkwardly to wipe his finger across it. Blood, probably from the side of his head, he thought. He put his right palm to his temple and found more. Well, at least it hadn't knocked him out, and as yet it had given him no more than a dull ache in his skull.

Suddenly remembering the ignition, he groped for the

key and turned it off. The effort made him sick and dizzy. The thunder had died away and the sound of the pelting rain and the branches of the fallen tree scratching on the windscreen seemed like silence by comparison. Mal used the respite to calm himself, taking several very deep breaths until the dizziness receded. Then he tried to clear his mind and think what to do.

Someone was sure to come along this road eventually. But would the driver be able to see this accident in time to avoid another? The idea of a lorry coming round the bend ahead and ploughing into his van brought back the terror. He *had* to get out.

Very carefully, he tried to draw up his legs and wriggle out from under the steering wheel. But there was not enough clearance; he needed to slide sideways to do it, and that was impossible – what would normally be sideways was now upwards, and he didn't have sufficient leverage. He fumbled under the seat, trying to find the catch that would enable him to slide it back on its runners, but it was jammed somehow and would not budge.

After a few minutes he lay back against the cold glass of the window, panting like a dog. The exertion had exhausted him and for a moment or two he thought he would pass out as the ache in his skull swelled to a pounding, pulsing agony. He knew deep down that there was no point in any further effort. He was wedged, and would not be able to escape from the van without help.

Maybe he could turn the lights on. If they were still working, they might give enough warning to any oncoming driver to prevent a disaster. His hand moved towards the switch, but hesitated as he thought that lights meant electricity, and if anything had gone wrong, if there was a short-circuit, one spark could set off the tank. It was an unpleasant dilemma.

His mind was beginning to spin again, and he felt foggy and confused. *Make a decision*, he told himself angrily, *just do one thing or the other*. On an impulse he reached out and activated the van's sidelights. A branch beyond the windscreen and a little above his head suddenly shone chilly white, casting a stark shadow over the glass, and he knew that the lights were still working. He held his breath, half-waiting for disaster to strike, but nothing more happened. The thunder was grumbling in the sky, but there had been no lightning for several minutes. Maybe the storm was abating.

He jumped as a terrific flash lit up the landscape, flinging up one arm in an instinctive gesture to protect himself. His hand grazed against something sharp and woody, and reflexively his fingers closed round the branch they had touched. It broke, and his startled jolt brought his temple hard against the window again. He felt as though a knife had seared through his head. His face twisted and a blanket of darkness obscured both his vision and his thoughts as he slumped limply into a huddle and passed out.

When he woke, the night was still pitch-black outside and he could hear thunder growling and grumbling somewhere in the distance. It seemed the storm was diminishing. But the rain wasn't. Mal's clothes on his left side were saturated, and he could feel spots of water pricking his face as the rain found its way in through the smashed window.

He tried to move and found that his muscles had stiffened agonisingly with cramp. His head still hurt, too, as though someone had fetched him a blow with a sledge-hammer, and his mind was woolly.

He wondered how long he had been out. Five minutes? Five hours? It was impossible to guess. The van's side-lights were still on, but dimmer now, casting only a thin and sickly glow on the silhouette of the fallen tree. The battery must be running flat, which meant that he had been unconscious for some while.

He tried to shift from his painful position and manoeuvre himself into a drier and less confined space, but his limbs responded sluggishly and he found he hadn't the strength. For a few moments he shut his eyes, asking himself why it was that no one had come to help him. Admittedly this was a quiet road at the best of times, but surely at least one car would have come this way by now?

The thought was futile. It only started him worrying, and he pushed it away, trying to concentrate his mind on something else. He became aware of an itch in the palm of his left hand, and realised that his fist was clenched tightly and that he seemed to be holding something. Gingerly he shifted the angle of his body an inch or two, until he could bring the hand towards his face and, stiffly, open his fingers.

A twig. He couldn't remember how or why he had grasped it, but he must have broken it from one of the branches that was protruding through the window. A single leaf still clung pathetically to the dead wood, half crushed but still recognisable. Mal stared at it, uncertain at first whether or not the darkness was deceiving him, but after a minute or two it was unmistakable. The tree that had fallen on his van was an oak.

Mal's theory was suddenly confirmed. Maud Fairfax had said in her letter that the meaning of the legend of Duir and Niainn would become clear before too long. For Mal, at least, that prophecy had now been fulfilled.

Subtly, but undeniably, the legend of Duir and Niainn was being re-enacted, and he and Rowan had taken the place of the original figures. Neither of them had been aware of it until very recently – and indeed, he reminded himself, Rowan was not aware of it at all yet – but in its own way, and its own time, the story was unfolding all over again.

He recalled the three tasks that Duir had been set in order to win the woman he loved. Firstly he had to defend her from an attacker. And in the here and now that attacker had been Cracky Tully, who had turned, for no apparent reason, from his normal harmless self into something alien and dangerous. Mal knew that if it hadn't been for his own intervention, Tully could well have killed Rowan, without the least idea of what he was doing. Even the knife was suspiciously coincidental; according to the legend, Duir had used a dagger to overcome his adversary in battle.

That was all very well, but it had needed more than one incident, which could have been put down to pure chance, to convince Mal beyond any reasonable doubt. Now, though, he had all the evidence he needed. The ordeal, which had been the second of Duir's tasks, had come about – he was going through it at this very moment. All right, he told himself, it *was* possible that this accident was another coincidence. Like Tully's attack, it could, after all, have happened to anyone. But Duir's trial had also been in the form of an oak tree which was struck by lightning.

Mal closed his eyes, aware that his mind was beginning to cloud again. There was something gnawing at the back of his brain, something important that he should consider and think about, but he was too shaken and confused to bring it into focus. The third task. To tame Niann's wild spirit and prove himself a fit lord for her, that had been it. But how could that piece of the legend possibly be woven into a twentieth-century setting?

He frowned, trying to concentrate, but his thoughts were growing blurred. And then, on the verge of lapsing into vague semi-consciousness, he started as a beam of light stabbed through the cabin of the van.

At first he thought it was lightning, but instead of flashing momentarily and then vanishing, the light swung in an arc that made stark shadows jump across his line of vision. And, mingled with the fierce hissing of the rain, he heard the lower-pitched throb of a car engine.

Mal's mind raced with terror that the driver would not see the obstruction in time, and convulsively he tried to struggle upright. But the first light was joined by another, blue and flashing rhythmically, and he could hear not one but two engines, both slowing down and coming to a halt.

Then came voices, the metallic slam of doors and the faint crackle of a radio. A few seconds later a torch-beam thrust down through the broken window, shining directly on to his face, and a disembodied voice said, 'Christ almighty!'

Mal's head swam with relief and he wanted to laugh. But he held the laughter back and forced himself to speak in as matter-of-fact a tone as he could muster.

'It's all right,' he said. 'I'm okay, not hurt at all apart from a bang on the head. I've just been stuck here.'

Voices clashed and swirled somewhere beyond the van's cramped confines, instructions were shouted, and the voice behind the torch-beam told Mal reassuringly that all he had to do was hang on, and they'd soon have him out.

The next few minutes were something of a jumble to

Mal. In retrospect, he could recall the confusion of lights and voices increasing, the breaking of glass and the tearing of branches as his rescuers cleared a space around the van, then the presence of three strongly built men who helped him at last to raise himself from his cramped, trapped position. Whether they pulled him out through the window or through the hole they had made in the windscreen he didn't know, but suddenly the rain was falling full on him in an icy rush, and his feet touched the tarmac of the wet road.

Mal's legs gave way beneath him, too stiff and numb to hold his weight. Hands supported him, and he shook his head to clear it, feeling peculiarly agoraphobic in the open air after so long in a confined space.

A rich Somerset voice said, 'All right now. Take it gently,' and someone else cut in, in less accented tones, 'Get him into the car, and I'll have a look at that head injury.' Mal smiled, recognising the voice of Bernard Craven, the doctor who looked after most of the surrounding villages, including Barton Tavey. Craven was an ex-military man, and used to being obeyed.

Mal was helped into the back seat of what he now realised was a police car, and he closed his eyes again as expert fingers probed at the wound on his temple.

'Not serious by the look of it,' he heard Craven say. 'Just as well – we'd have a fine time getting him to the hospital at Taunton with this road blocked! As it is, I can patch him up in my surgery. All right, sergeant, thank you.'

Mal leaned back against the car seat as the driver started the engine and Craven climbed in beside him, slamming the door with a force that sent daggers of pain through his skull. He didn't want to talk to anyone; he felt too dazed and now the sickness was beginning to return. He made a pretence of being only half-conscious, allowing his head to slump as the car began to move.

The doctor leaned forward to speak to the driver, giving brisk instructions. 'Turn round if you can, and drive back the way we came. I'll direct you from the crossroads.'

The engine revved as the vehicle reversed, then they were moving away towards Barton Tavey, and within a few minutes the steady hum of the wheels on the road lulled

Mal into a semi-comatose sleep from which he hoped he would not wake for a good long time.

14

Rowan started out of her chair with a sudden jolt. She was on her feet before she was aware of what had happened, and swayed unsteadily before regaining her balance. For a moment she stared at her surroundings in bewilderment, then her senses righted themselves as she realised where she was.

She had fallen asleep, extraordinary though it seemed under the circumstances. After her bout of panic, she had curled up in the armchair once more and somehow, despite the thunder and her fear, she had drifted off. She had been dreaming, and she thought that it was something about her dream which had finally woken her, although she couldn't now recall what it was.

The room was still brightly lit, but the fire had died down to a hummock of dully glowing embers with little heat emanating from them. She crouched to put more logs on, hoping that they would catch, then straightened, and glanced around the room again. There was something in the atmosphere that she didn't entirely like, a kind of unnaturally empty space as though someone or something had departed hurriedly in the few seconds before she awoke. And again she felt as though she were being watched.

For a minute or so Rowan stood still, listening, but although the feeling remained with her, there were no odd sounds to break the quiet. She realised suddenly that the storm had stopped. The rain continued to pour, hammering against the window, but there were no sudden dimmings of the lights, and no crack and rumble of thunder overhead.

Rowan let out her breath in a long, thankful sigh. Perhaps that was why the room felt so peculiar. Certainly there was something peaceful about that sense of emptiness, a relief after the tension of the storm. Now, perhaps, she could relax and think about how she was going to spend the rest of the evening.

And then she remembered Mal.

A cold, invisible hand clutched at her, and she turned to look at the mantel clock. The hands read a quarter to eleven.

Mal hadn't come back. Rowan knew it for a certainty. A small, hopeful voice tried to tell her that he couldn't have received her message and phoned, because the lines were down, but she dismissed it without a second thought. No logical argument could overcome the intuitive and absolute knowledge that Mal had not arrived at his home.

She began to feel very sick as fear churned at her already empty stomach. For more than an hour she had slept, and in that time anything could have happened to him. *Anything*. The roads were lethal in this weather, and on a night like this there were other dangers.

Her first instinct was to snatch up the phone, and as she did so she prayed that by a miracle the lines would have been restored. But the receiver was dead, and she let it fall back into place with an unsteady hand. She wanted to cry, but refused to give way to the urge. What she needed now was strength and commonsense, not weakness.

She had to find out where Mal was and what had happened to him. And the only way to do that was to brave the weather and drive out to Coombe Cottage.

As she slipped on her coat, she did not stop to question just why she was so desperately concerned about Mal. If it had been Agnes or anyone else who was missing, she would have been worried, but there would have been none of this frantic fear that welled in her like a physical pain. And perhaps if she *had* stopped to question herself, she might have thought twice before leaving, simply because she would have been afraid of what her reaction implied. But her only thought was to get to Mal's house as quickly as possible.

She left all the lights ablaze – they would make a more welcoming sight on her return – and opened the front door, to be confronted by a vertical wall of falling water. The ferocity of the rain shocked her. The noise of it was tremendous, and the road had become a river as the drains struggled and failed to cope with the torrent. For a moment Rowan remembered Lynton and Lynmouth, and her courage all but failed her; then she took a grip on herself and pulled the door shut behind her. There was nothing dangerous about this. It was simply a downpour, the sort of thing that happened often. Provided the thunder didn't begin again, she had nothing to worry about.

Turning up her collar and bowing her head, she ran down the path and splashed out into the road. Her car stood forlornly a few yards from the gate, and as she slid into the driver's seat and shook water from her eyes, Rowan prayed that the engine would start. It did. Bent forward over the wheel in an effort to see through the teeming rain, she drove off towards Coombe Cottage.

The village looked like a tiny, half-drowned haven in the wild sea of the hills. The street was deserted, but many of the windows were still lit, and the Oak and Ash, with its illuminated sign and the amber glow shining from within, looked alluringly warm and comfortable. Rowan drove on past, beyond the reach of the lights and back into darkness, and turned right at the coast road fork.

Lightning shivered in the distance ahead of her, but it was too far away now to be alarming, and there was no answering rumble of thunder. The storm was passing over the sea, heading northwards. Nonetheless, Rowan did not look up again, but kept her gaze firmly within the limits of the headlight beams.

She knew that Coombe Cottage was deserted even before she swung into the patch of ground in front of the house. There was nothing to see but blackness; no lights shone from any of the windows, and until she turned off the headlamps and stared for some minutes into the dark void, she could not even make out the silhouette of the cottage against its background of trees.

Her heart began to thump painfully as she sat, unmoving, her arms resting on the steering wheel. Mal had not come home, and she could achieve nothing by sitting here and waiting for some sign that her eyes were deceiving her.

What now? she asked herself. The most sensible thing to do would be to return home, try and sleep, and hope that the phones would have been restored by morning. Then she could start looking for him in earnest – ring the local hospitals, the police.

But until she knew what had happened to Mal, she could not bear to be alone with her thoughts.

She switched on the car's interior light and checked her watch. Five to eleven. If she hurried, she might just get to the Oak and Ash before it closed. And if anyone had any news of Mal, it would surely have reached the ears of the local publican by now, if it had reached anyone at all.

She turned the Mini round, returned to the road and drove back towards the village.

The bar of the Oak and Ash was more crowded than it had been since the height of the summer season. The press of people had brought Jack Davies, the landlord, out from his usual behind-scenes role. He kept a watchful eye on the clock, but tonight he had the feeling that it would do no harm to stretch the licensing laws by a half hour or so, particularly considering the fact that the village's one local policeman, Fred Dymock, was comfortable by the fire with a pint of Guinness and showed no signs of leaving yet. The pub was a haven in weather like this, somewhere where people could huddle together in a fug of warm air and smoke, and forget about the storm.

It was Rose who first saw Rowan as she eased her way towards the bar across the crowded floor.

'Hello, stranger!' Rose said brightly. 'You're a late one tonight. What's it to be, then?'

She ought to have a drink. It would warm her, and perhaps calm her, too. 'Scotch and water, please,' Rowan said.

Rose brought it, and as she handed over a fistful of small change Rowan added, 'Rose, I'm really worried. I think something's happened to Mal – '

Rose stopped in her tracks, looking surprised. 'Mal?' she echoed.

Rowan looked miserably back at her. 'He should have been back in the village at eight o'clock and there's no sign of him. And the phone lines are down, so I can't – '

'Had a date, did you?' Now there was a tiny trace of a smile playing at the corners of Rose's mouth, which took Rowan aback. Surely she couldn't find Mal's disappearance *amusing*? Her eyes darkened with unhappy anger, and she said sharply, 'Something's *happened* to him, Rose, I'm certain of it! And I thought that if anyone knew anything, the news would have got back here.'

Rose's smile broadened and she nodded. 'Oh, yes.'

'Rose – ' Suddenly Rowan knew what it was that Rose found so funny, and she could have knifed her for it. 'You *do* know something, don't you?'

Rose glanced at her. For a brief moment her eyes were full of resentment, then suddenly she relaxed and her expression became slightly bleak and a little ashamed.

'I'm sorry,' she said, 'It's not something to tease about, is it? Yes, we do know something. Someone came in here about – oh, I don't know, more than an hour ago, anyway. Said he'd been driving towards Bridgwater, and there was a tree down, blocking the road. Nearly ran into it, he said, and then he saw that it had fallen on a van.'

The colour drained from Rowan's cheeks and she set down the glass from which she had been about to drink. 'Mal's van?' she said in a whisper.

Rose nodded. 'The bloke didn't know what to do, so he came back to the village. Luckily, old Dr Craven was drinking in here – do you know him?'

'No.'

'Oh. Well anyway, he was here, and he took over. He's an ex-lieutenant-colonel or something. Army, anyway. And he organised a police car and the lot, and they all went back to sort it out.'

She sounded so calm, so matter-of-fact. Rowan hated her for her indifference, and hated herself, too, for being weak. She took her glass and drank, and felt the whisky soothing and warming its way to her stomach. Then, more evenly, she said, 'Is that the end of the story?'

'No.' Rose examined a chipped fingernail. 'About half an hour ago the bloke who'd found the van came back here and told us that everything was all right. Apparently Mal wasn't injured; he'd just been stuck in the van.'

Her words took a few seconds to sink in, and when they did Rowan thought that she might cry with sheer relief. 'Where is he now?' she asked.

'Well, they couldn't get to the hospital without making a detour, so I gather Dr Craven took him back to patch him up at his surgery. He'll probably be home before long.'

Rowan felt the tension in her muscles begin to ebb, as though she were waking from a nightmare. And following closely behind that came a desire to go to Mal, to see for herself that he really was unharmed. She drained her glass, and said, 'Maybe I should go back to his house, then – '

'I wouldn't.' Rose smiled, sweetly but without humour. 'It's probably best to leave him alone for a bit, until he's had a chance to recover from the shock. Anyway, I wouldn't be surprised if old Craven keeps him at his place overnight. He's very thorough, and I expect he'll want to make sure that there isn't any concussion, or anything like that.'

Rowan looked back at her. What Rose had said made sense, but Rowan was well aware that by pretending greater wisdom and counselling caution Rose was trying to score a point over her.

She returned Rose's smile and said aloud, 'Well, I'll see. Anyway, thanks for telling me what happened. Goodnight, Rose.' And before the barmaid could speak again, Rowan had turned and was making her way towards the door.

The rain came swirling to meet her when she stepped out of the pub, and she could hear it hammering on the roof of her car as she unlocked it and climbed in. There were fewer lights in the village now, and the road shimmered like molten glass under the cold white gleam of the street lamp. Rowan shivered from the sudden drop in temperature after the warm bar and, as she switched on the Mini's ignition, wondered fleetingly if she should, after all, drive past Coombe Cottage once more, just to see if Mal had returned yet. But she knew if she did that, and there *were* lights in the cottage, she would not be able to resist calling in.

She turned the car towards her own house.

Rowan dreamed of Duir again that night. She thought she was back in the field by the blasted oak tree, reliving her walk. But this time, when the vision appeared from the crowding branches of the wood, it was no momentary glimpse of something unnameable that sent her screaming back to her car and safety. It was simply the figure of a man, crowned with quite brilliant red hair, from whose brow the familiar antlers rose like twin trees in their own right. His face was like Mal's yet subtly different, less human, and even as she stared at him he raised one hand and held it out towards her, and his lips moved in a strange, phased way, like a jerky film reel.

It was that, she thought afterwards, that had caused the dream to break, waking her to the chilly half-light of dawn. Something in the gesture had reminded her subconsciously of the previous nightmare she had had, about her grandmother, in which the old lady too had reached out to her, as though trying to convey something in both words and movement which Rowan had been unable to interpret.

She lay back against the pillow, feeling her pulse beating over-rapidly inside her rib-cage. The dream hadn't upset her in the way that many previous dreams had done, but nevertheless she felt disturbed by it. She could not shake off the conviction that someone – or perhaps more accurately some*thing* – was trying to get a message across to her, a vital piece of information, and that the barriers of her own mind were preventing her from understanding what it was. Mal had suggested something similar a few days ago, when he said that perhaps the echoes of the past were filtering through to the present. But how could she break down the wall between then and now? And did she truly want to break it, or was she too afraid of the possible consequences to allow it to happen?

Rowan sighed, then opened her half-closed eyes, surprised by the way that one small sound carried. The room seemed almost unnaturally silent, as though something that should have been there was suddenly and unexpectedly missing. The rain. Of course. She had fallen asleep with the sound of it in her mind, the ceaseless, steady drumming as the downpour continued. But now it had stopped, and the void of quiet that it had left behind felt alien.

She turned over on to her other side and pulled up the blankets, wrapping them around her like a cocoon. She still felt tired, not in the mood for early rising, and so she closed her eyes again, welcoming the return of sleep. As the reality of the room began to merge with the first vague fantasies of dreams, she thought she heard the faraway echoes of a faint, eerie howling, a pack of dogs giving tongue beyond the surrounding hills. But she was too close to sleep for it to disturb her, and merely murmured wordlessly to herself, huddling down in her bed and hiding her face in the softness of her pillow.

By the time Rowan woke again and got up, not only the rain but also the clouds that had brought it had cleared. The sky was a high, pale blue, and the watery light of the sun glistened on trees and rooftops, and lent the surrounding hills a kindlier aspect reminiscent of summer.

Yawning, still heavy-eyed and warm from sleep, Rowan brought in the milk. The village was quiet, peaceful and cool, the air incredibly fresh after the ravages of the night. She made breakfast, and afterwards, when she judged that it was late enough to avoid the risk of waking him, went to ring Mal. She picked up the phone receiver, then smiled ruefully and replaced it. She had assumed that by now the lines would have been restored, but she was wrong; the slow ways of the country would be stirred no faster than usual to repair the damage. Maybe the lines would be working again by evening, maybe not. In the meantime, if she wanted to find out how Mal was, she would have to make a personal visit.

On a morning like this the car seemed superfluous and Rowan decided to walk to Coombe Cottage. She left the house before Agnes could waylay her and hold her up, and strolled through the village, past the pond which seemed fuller than normal, almost overflowing its banks, and on along the coast road. The light was vivid, the coast clear almost to Foreland Point so that the sea was visible like a flat, blue mirror. Rowan picked a handful of late blackberries and ate them on the way, licking the purple juice from her fingers.

When she reached Coombe Cottage, the first thing she saw was Tigger sitting on the doorstep in a patch of sunlight. He rose to meet her, stretching and arching his tail, and wound himself round her legs as she knocked on the door.

A minute later it opened, and Mal smiled at her.

He looked different. She couldn't tell what the difference was; certainly nothing physical. Considering what had happened to him, she might have expected outward changes in his appearance, but apart from a piece of sticking plaster on his right temple he looked the same as ever. Yet there was something about him, perhaps in his manner, perhaps more tenuous even than that, that she had not seen before. It disturbed her, but she didn't know why.

'Come in.' Mal indicated the living-room, which was in its usual state of disarray.

She smiled at him, closing the door behind her. 'Am I glad to see you! How are you, Mal? Is everything all right?'

He waved her to a chair, and sat down himself. 'I'm fine. But I was getting worried about you. I found your note when I got back here, and I realised that you must be wondering what the hell was going on.'

That, Rowan thought, was an understatement. 'I did get pretty worried,' she admitted. 'And I was scared stiff of the storm, too. In the end I went to the Oak and Ash, and Rose told me what had happened.' She was tempted to say how grudging Rose had been about giving the information, but thought better of it.

'Ah, yes. I gather that the guy who first found my van went back there to get help. Funny, isn't it, the way a pub is the first place people think of when they're not sure where to turn.'

'I'm glad he did,' Rowan said. 'Otherwise I'd have had a sleepless night.' She settled herself more comfortably and patted her knee, inviting Tigger to jump on to her lap. 'So, are you going to tell me the whole story?'

She was behaving very coolly and calmly, she realised; a very far cry indeed from how she really felt underneath. Relief and anxiety were combining together within her and making her nervous behind the smooth mask, but she didn't want Mal to get any idea of her true feelings.

Mal stretched out his legs, and yawned. 'It's not all that exciting. A tree fell on the van, and I was stuck in the damned thing for hours until someone came along and hauled me out. They called out our local doctor, old Craven. He thought I wasn't serious enough to be worth taking to hospital, so he drove me back to his place and did a quick patch-up in his surgery.'

'Your head – '

'Oh, that's nothing to worry about. Craven doesn't even think I'm concussed. All I've got is a graze and a headache. And barring a few bruises, I got away with that.'

Rowan shook her head in a kind of uneasy wonder. The thought of just how narrow an escape Mal had had made her turn cold inside. 'I can hardly believe that you're safe,' she said, her voice more serious. 'The chances of your getting out of something like that in one piece, it's – '

'Uncanny?' Mal lifted his eyebrows. 'Our favourite word. I know.'

She shivered. 'If it had happened half a second later, or – '

'Don't say it!' He held up a hand quickly. 'If I start thinking along those lines, I'll have nightmares.'

'Sorry.' Rowan backed the apology with a smile, and tried to think of something more mundane to talk about. At length she asked, 'What about the van?'

'A write-off, I'm afraid. Mind you, I suppose it's a blessing in disguise in one sense. The damned thing was on its last legs anyway, and I can just about afford to buy something else. I'm quite friendly with Bill at the garage in the village, and he's usually got a bargain or two on offer, so I'll have a word with him in a few days.' He eased himself forward, starting to rise. 'Hey, I'm being a bad host. How about a cup of coffee?'

Rowan forestalled him. 'Let me make it,' she said. 'I don't know what the doctor said, but I wouldn't mind betting he told you to rest.'

Mal grinned. 'He did. Two or three days sitting around doing nothing, then I can return to normal providing I don't start seeing flashing lights. You'll find coffee on the lower shelf and sugar in the cupboard next to the fridge. Thanks.'

Rowan headed into the kitchen. 'Until you're mobile again,' she called back over her shoulder, 'is there anything I can get in for you? Food, or whatever?'

'Well, I'd be grateful, just for the next day or so. Once I'm pronounced fit it isn't going to kill me to walk to the village for once, but I'd appreciate it if you could get me a few bits and pieces in the meantime.'

'Make a list,' she suggested. 'I'll bring them round this afternoon.'

They sat drinking coffee for half an hour, talking idly and avoiding the subject of both the Crown of Horn and Mal's accident. In fact it seemed to Rowan that it was Mal rather than herself who was deliberately keeping the conversation on a light level, as if trying to hide some facet of himself that he did not want her to see.

At last she rose to leave, and as he saw her towards the door, after handing her a hastily scrawled shopping list, Mal said, 'Oh, hang on a moment – there's something I forgot.' He fished in his pocket, and brought out what looked like a crumpled leaf. He was smiling oddly as he held it out. 'Souvenir,' he said.

She stared at him, bewildered. 'Souvenir of what?'

'What happened last night. I pulled this off the tree that fell on me. Don't ask me why. It was just a reflex action.'

The drying leaf lay in Rowan's palm, and she said slowly, 'It was an oak, then.'

'Yes.'

'Do you think that's significant?'

Mal shrugged. 'Your guess is as good as mine. But I think it's worth bearing in mind.' He took the leaf back, studied it for a moment, then threw it carelessly into the empty fireplace. 'Anyway, I'll see you again later, I expect.'

His eyes were masking something, and Rowan didn't entirely like what she thought she saw behind his expression. She nodded. 'Yes. Look after yourself, Mal. See you this afternoon.'

She had to force herself not to run to her car as he closed the front door behind her.

When the Mini had gone, Mal felt angry with himself, aware that he had handled the last few minutes very badly. He had equivocated, dropping vague hints and allowing her to see a glimpse of what was going on in his mind, yet baulking at the idea of being bluntly forthcoming. And as a result he had unnerved her. She had known that there was something odd afoot, and had reacted like any animal confronted with an unfamiliar and therefore potentially threatening situation. He should either have told her everything, or kept totally quiet.

He slumped into his chair, leaning his head back against the padded cushion as the pulse in his temples began to thump painfully. Right now, he could have done without any added complications in his life. He would have preferred to forget everything to do with Rowan and with the Crown of Horn at least until he had fully recovered from the accident, and thinking didn't hurt so much. But that was impossible. There was too much to think about.

Mal was more certain than ever that the ancient web had caught himself and Rowan up in its threads. Neither of them could escape it. Rowan would try, of course, once she realised the truth. She would fight tooth and nail against the web, out of fear. And as for himself –

How was it possible to tell, Mal asked himself, if he truly loved her? In some ways she was becoming as familiar to him as if he had known her all his life. Yet in others, she was a virtual stranger, cussed, irritating, distancing herself deliberately from any close contact. He could not imagine a future that did not include Rowan. And yet reason counselled caution.

But, even if – as he knew in his bones – he wanted her, did she want him? At the moment, the answer to that question was no, and had been since they first met. But was that a genuine feeling on her part, or was it caused by the wounds of the past which had made her put up so many barriers? Until those barriers came down, the truth could not be known. And that was where Duir's third task came into play.

It was the thought of that third task which gave Mal his worst moments of doubt. As with the first two, it had to be interpreted in a twentieth-century context: there would be no wild flights across the moorland at dead of night. But the parallel between Rowan and the legendary Niainn was quite clear. As Duir had had to prove himself fit to be Niainn's lord, so Mal had to prove to Rowan that he would not hurt or abandon her, and so win her trust. If that was what he wanted to do.

Mal had the deepest suspicion that, no matter what he might or might not want, he would have very little choice in the matter. Whatever force had put the wheels into motion, he doubted if it could be stopped now.

The thought alarmed him, for it placed a responsibility on his shoulders that he was unsure whether he could handle. Rowan needed to be released from her self-made prison, but was he capable of turning the key that would unlock the door? And, what was more important, how could it be done? Whenever he thought about that, it sent a cold chill through him, like a premonition of something he could neither name nor recognise.

He had a feeling, deep in the back of his mind, that before too long events were going to take a startling and maybe even frightening turn. He had no idea what it would be; anticipating it was like waiting for another storm to break. It made him tense and restless, and vulnerable to the power of something a great deal bigger than himself.

He sighed and made an effort to relax. The room was very quiet, and the sound of Tigger purring on his knee was hypnotically peaceful. Mal closed his eyes. And within five minutes, he had drifted into sleep.

15

Mal's recovery was a matter of some debate between himself and Dr Craven. Craven, in his conscientious way, took the attitude that the longer his patient rested, the more certain he could be of recovering fully. But by the time his headache had finally worn off and he had spent some thirty-six hours being idle, Mal felt that another moment's inactivity would be more than he could tolerate. By the afternoon of the next day, the doctor gave in and pronounced him fit.

Even after only two days confined to the house, walking into the village was an unfamiliar activity, and Mal had something of the feeling of a prisoner unexpectedly released. His leg-muscles protested, but only mildly, and by the time he reached the village centre his mood had improved and the restlessness that had been nagging at him was appeased.

He considered going on to Rowan's house and calling in, but decided against it. Since their last meeting she seemed to have taken a retrograde step where he was concerned. He had phoned her, once the lines were restored, to give her a progress report, but her attitude had been both cautious and evasive, and she had been all too eager to keep conversation to a minimum. He had the impression that she was half-afraid of something, and again cursed himself for having handled the incident with the oak leaf so clumsily. He had put her on her guard – although the chances were she didn't even know what she was guarding herself against – and he had the distinct feeling that if he should try to press her for a reason she would, metaphorically, bite his hand.

Nonetheless, as he strolled through the village, Mal found himself keeping a lookout for any sign of her. If they ran into each other by coincidence, she could hardly accuse him of forcing his presence on her uninvited. But Rowan's was not among the faces he passed, and finally, feeling bored and a little piqued, he went into the Oak and Ash for a lunchtime drink.

The pub was quiet, as usual on a weekday, with only one or two of the regulars to keep Rose occupied. Her face lit up with pleasure when she saw him.

'Mal! You're up and about again. This calls for a celebration!' Without waiting for him to say anything she began to pull a pint of draught cider. 'On the house,' she said as she pushed the glass in his direction.

Mal wasn't sure what the landlord would have said to that piece of generosity, but neither was he about to argue. He sat down, leaning his elbows on the bar. 'Thanks, Rose. And thanks too for what you did the other night, helping out the chap who found me.'

Rose shrugged. 'Couldn't do any less, could we? How are you, then, all right?'

'Yes, a hundred per cent.' He glanced briefly around the bar, putting names to faces, then asked, 'Has Rowan been in lately?'

Rose's eyes narrowed, catlike. 'Not since the night of your accident,' she told him, her voice careless. 'She came in asking if we knew where you were.'

Mal smiled. 'Was she worried?'

'Not particularly.' Rose paused to let that barb sink home, then added, 'Anyway, she doesn't show her face round here much. Not the pub type, I suppose. Funny sort, really.'

'Oh, I don't know.' Mal's instinct was to defend Rowan, but in another sense he was amused by Rose's transparent efforts to put her down.

Rose was giving him an old-fashioned look now. 'Well, you wouldn't know, would you?' she said. 'About things like that, I mean. Men don't notice what women notice, after all.'

He grinned at her, aware that she could not discern the irony in the smile. 'Okay, so tell me what you can see that I can't!'

'Well, she's just a bit funny, that's all. I don't want to be unkind, because I like her, I really do, but she just isn't very friendly, when it comes down to it. I try, but I don't seem to get anywhere, and I'm beginning to think that she's a bit odd.'

'Eccentric, you mean?' Mal said, straight-faced.

She agreed eagerly. 'That's it exactly! I get the feeling she could end up a bit like old Mrs Fairfax. You know – a sort of recluse.'

Despite her motivation for saying so, Mal had to admit to himself that Rose probably had a point.

'Anyway,' Rose finished bluntly, 'if you've got any ideas in that direction, I'd forget 'em. I don't think you'll ever get anywhere with her.'

'Who says I want to?' Mal asked gently.

'Nobody.' Again she gave her self-conscious shrug. 'It was just a thought. And I think Rowan's convinced you're after her.'

If she had hoped for any categorical denials from Mal, Rose was disappointed. He simply said, 'Well, even if she is, I doubt if anything I did or said would make any difference.'

Rose stared at him in irritation and decided that he was being cryptic on principle. She was sure that Mal was well on the way to being besotted with Rowan, and she felt that he was making a fool of himself, as well as putting obstacles in the way of her own ambitions.

She was almost thankful to see one of her regular customers making his way towards the bar with an empty glass, and went to serve him, leaving Mal sitting and gazing at nothing in particular. When she had taken the regular's money, Rose watched Mal for a moment or two, trying unsuccessfully to interpret the thoughtful expression on his face. He wasn't aware of her scrutiny. Probably, she thought, he wasn't even aware that she had moved away to the other end of the counter.

Rowan had not ventured out of the house at all that day. The weather was tantalisingly good: cold (it seemed to grow colder with every dawn now), but bright and clear. There were a hundred things she could have done, a hundred places she could have visited. But instead she had spent the morning sitting by the log fire, trying desperately to involve herself in a book that she had rooted out from her grandmother's shelves, and yet failing to banish the one subject that was preying on her mind.

She knew that something as simple as a dream should not have the power to affect her. Dreams were no more than the products of imagination, and although a bad dream might reflect an equally bad state of mind, by themselves they had no deeper significance. Or shouldn't have. But this one had been like nothing she had ever experienced before, and when she woke from it she had been terrified.

Angrily, she slammed the book shut, realising that to try and concentrate on it was a useless exercise. The dream had too strong a hold, and it would not let go. She rose, pacing across the room. She felt restless and unhappy, yet incapable of doing anything about it. Going out would not help her to escape from her own thoughts; she would merely carry them with her wherever she went. And added to that was the fear that, if she got into her car and just drove, she would not be able to stop herself from going to the one place that at this moment she wanted to avoid.

It seemed that since her arrival in Barton Tavey her whole life had been ruled by dreams, oppressed by them, something that had never happened to her before. And the worst thing was, each nightmare carried a terrible significance that even the staunchest sceptic wouldn't have been able to deny. And now this one was the most powerful of all, the most graphic and, she felt instinctively, the most important.

It had begun as one of those strange blends of fantasy and reality, in which she had been quite certain that she was in fact lying awake in her bed listening to the soft sounds of the night outside. She had not thought it odd that she could see every detail of the room with clarity; the moonlight filtered greyly through her drawn curtains. But then, very slowly, the bedroom door started to open, and she felt the unmistakable presence of someone just outside on the landing.

At first, when she saw him on the threshold, she thought

that he was Mal, and she sat up, wanting to ask him why he had come at this hour, what he wanted. But then she stopped, as she saw him more clearly. *He wasn't Mal – he was Duir.*

The room shivered about her, its outlines warping and changing as a mist that seemed to emanate from the walls themselves formed in the air. Duir did not move; he stood just inside the room, statue-like, and suddenly Rowan wasn't sure if he was really there at all, or if he was an image, an echo, a ghostly imprint on her memory. She tried to speak but could not. It was as though time had stopped, or no longer had any meaning, and all she could do was stare back at the dark, not quite human eyes that met her own.

Then, without warning, he raised his right hand, and Rowan felt an ice-cold shudder run through her, as though she had been plunged into freezing water. He held something, something dark and curved. She could not see what it was, but thought it must be a knife. And in that same moment he stepped forward, as if lunging at her, and a burst of wild laughter erupted in her ears.

She remembered screaming then at the full pitch of her voice, twisting and turning among blankets that snatched at her limbs and held her down. For an instant she was trapped in the grip of the chaotic nightmare, and then, abruptly, she was awake and there was no moonlight, no open door, no Duir.

When she tried to rationalise the dream, as she made tea and drank it in the kitchen, she knew that there was no logical reason why the fear she had felt should have remained with her. But it was still there, lodged somewhere in the pit of her stomach, and nothing she could do would shake it off. It was fuelled by the conviction that there had been something premonitory about the nightmare, something that had its parallel – or would have before long – in her own real world. Perhaps if the dream had been an isolated incident she would have felt less threatened by it. But there had been other things, and in the past two days, since she had last seen Mal, they had been getting progressively worse.

The sensation that she was being watched had come back the previous evening, and this time, instead of being a brief half-hour of unease that wore off once she had reasoned it out in her mind, it had stayed. Wherever she went in the house, she felt that unseen eyes were following her, overlooking everything she did. It had started when dusk fell, and by the time she ventured upstairs to bed, Rowan was so unsettled that she could have screamed. Then, of course, there had been the nightmare; and this morning the feeling had been with her again, so that every few minutes she would turn her head quickly and look over her shoulder, as if expecting to catch a glimpse of her watcher before it could conceal itself. And each time she looked, the space where her gaze fell had appeared *abnormally* empty.

Once, feeling that she was on the brink of cracking under the tension within her, she stood in the middle of the living-room and called out, like a child giving up in a game of hide-and-seek, *'What are you? What do you want?'*

An intense silence followed, and suddenly Rowan felt small and foolish. How in hell, she asked herself, could anyone answer her, when there was no one but herself in the house? There was nothing there, nothing watching her. It was only her imagination.

But despite her angry self-reproach, the uneasy sensation stayed, and by the time the afternoon waned and the shadows began to merge with encroaching darkness, she was at a low ebb, drained of her ability to fight the unknown with logic. She heated up a prepacked lasagne and mechanically ate the bland result without tasting it, as she sat in front of the television, latching on to the programmes with the shallow part of her mind, while the deeper recesses gnawed and worried and feared.

She thought about Mal, remembering the strange incident with the oak leaf. He had expected it to mean something to her, and when it didn't he had dismissed it too casually for comfort. The trouble was, it *had* meant something, but she had been unable to say precisely what. Even now the significance of it was no clearer to her, but she recalled the intuitive voice inside her that had told her to be careful, to shy away from whatever it was that Mal was trying to convey.

The thread of that thought ran through her brain as she pushed her empty plate aside and curled up in the commodious chair, her eyes focused on the small screen before her. Time moved on, and all too soon the TV stations closed down for the night, abandoning her to solitude. She switched the set off and, reluctantly, decided that there was nothing more she could do other than go to bed.

She made the ritual nightly round to check that all the doors and windows were secure, then, resisting the urge to do it again to make doubly certain, climbed the stairs to her bedroom. She undressed by the glow of the electric fire and slipped between the sheets. She switched the lamp off but left the fire glowing, both to warm the room and to give it some relief from the total darkness that would otherwise have closed around her. Its light bathed walls and ceiling with a dim, comforting wash of red, soothing her mind so that she was able to fall asleep without the difficulty she had feared.

And then the dream happened again.

It began as it had done before, with Rowan waking and not knowing whether what she saw and felt was reality or illusion. The room was grey – but surely she had left the fire on? Where was the warm red glow now? The wind murmured outside the window, seeming almost to speak to her in a language which she could not quite understand. A draught blew in under the door, lifting the edge of the carpet and making it flap against the floor, like the wing of a trapped bird. Then, over that small sound she heard another – the sound of soft, slow footfalls on the landing beyond her door.

Rowan wasn't afraid. She knew what was about to happen, and it no longer frightened her, for it was all familiar. She watched, breathing quietly and evenly, as the door-handle turned and the door began to open. It swung wide, letting in a warm crimson glow, and with it a shadowy figure that moved across the room until it was standing at the foot of her bed.

She couldn't see him clearly; the rich glow behind him

was too strong and he was only a silhouette. But she knew who he was. Rowan waited, resigned. She could do nothing, say nothing. If they were to communicate, it would be Duir who made the first move.

The voice that spoke her name seemed to come from far, far away, and it was oddly phased, the volume rising and falling as though her mind were attuned only enough to catch the fading edge of it.

'Row . . . annn . . .'

She tried to answer, but when she spoke there was no sound at all.

'Row . . . annn . . . '

The red glow was fading; very slowly the silhouette before her was becoming three-dimensional, the features gradually emerging from shadow. As the room darkened, so, it seemed, Duir's shape grew brighter, illuminated by its own faint radiance. Suddenly she could see him as clearly as if they had met in daylight, and his red hair and wind-browned skin were as real as her own flesh.

Fascination and fear mingled in Rowan's mind. She wanted to twist away, to wake from this dream, yet at the same moment she wanted to reach out to him, draw him to her and be drawn in her turn. A brief image of the storm-withered oak tree in its empty field flashed across her mind. It made her flinch momentarily, and her involuntary movement broke the spell of stillness. Duir's form swam back into focus and he took a step towards her.

This time, she did not panic when he raised his right hand, for her instinct told her that there was no danger. How could there be danger in a dream? Again he was holding something, and as he moved closer, now seeming to glide rather than walk towards the head of her bed, Rowan leaned forward to meet him. She felt a warmth spread over and through her, and when the oak-man's fingers touched her face they seemed to burn, but without pain. He traced a line down to her jaw, and her gaze was held by the inhuman eyes that looked into hers as if reading every crevice of her numbed mind.

She found her voice at last. It seemed wrong to speak, but she had to. There were so many unanswered questions.

'*What is it you want?*' Her voice was a whisper which seemed to mingle with the sigh of the wind outside. For a few moments she waited, breathless, not knowing if he could hear or if he would respond. Then he lifted his other hand, and she saw for the first time what he held.

It was a horn, hollow and polished until it shone like dull jet, a drinking-horn such as might have been used in mediaeval days. Its rim was chased with a broad band of gold, and where it narrowed and curved was another gold band.

As she stared at it, Rowan suddenly felt that she was no longer in her bedroom, nor even in the house or the village. The air was the air of the moorland, blowing cool against her skin, rustling the long grass. They were out among the elements, under the moon, she and Duir; far away from anything that was familiar. The sensation lasted only a moment before the walls closed in once more, but there was still a sharpness in the air, a wind-carried taste of the sea on her tongue.

He was holding the horn out to her, and she knew if only she could grasp it, take it, she would know the truth at last. Her hand reached towards it, but as she did so it seemed that the horn receded, or was drawn away.

'*No*!' She needed to touch the drinking vessel, but her fingers closed on empty air. And suddenly Duir was no longer a human figure, but had reverted to the eerie silhouette she had first seen. And he too was receding, fading back into the darkness, taking the precious horn with him.

Rowan climbed out of bed, trying to follow him, but before she could even find her feet on the suddenly uneven floor, he was gone. Laughter echoed in her mind, wild, strident laughter that resolved into a harsh cacophony of barking. There was a thud – and Rowan found herself sitting on the floor at the end of her bed, one arm gripping the brass footrail, suddenly and shockingly awake.

The room was bathed in a livid red light, and for one awful moment she was sure she must still be dreaming, for although the room looked normal, the barking had not stopped. She could hear it now, not too far away, high-pitched and hysterical. She gasped, pulling herself to her feet, and half-fell back on to the bed. That terrible noise – it was an echo of her dream; but she was awake now, and it *must* stop.

But it continued, and gradually Rowan realised what it was. Not the spectral hounds of the Wild Hunt, but something far more prosaic. There was a house further along the lane whose owner kept a spaniel. The animal was quiet as a mouse normally, but tonight something had disturbed it and it was barking as though its very life depended on it. The monotonous yapping carried only too clearly in the quiet night; a desperate sound somehow, as though the dog realised that its quarry was unpursuable, yet still kept up its show of bravado. The poor creature had seen something, or heard something, or sensed something. And dogs did not have imaginations. Whatever had disturbed the spaniel had been real enough.

Rowan crawled back under her blankets, the dog's cries setting her teeth on edge. She wanted to cry too, not through fear but through frustration. The dream was coming back to her in every detail and she knew that if she *had* been able to touch that drinking horn for even a moment, she would have found the answers that had been eluding her for so long. Now the chance was lost, and she did not know if it would ever be presented to her again.

She felt miserable, despairing. And as if in sympathy with her, the spaniel's barking fell away to a whimper, a last defiant *yap*, and then a howl which faded into silence.

In her red-lit room Rowan lay motionless, staring up at the ceiling with empty eyes. And little more than a mile away, in Coombe Cottage, Mal Lyndon tossed and twisted in his sleep, shaking his head from side to side as though struggling to wake himself from something he could not bear to face.

The following day, the weather and Rowan's mood were equally disturbed. A strong north-westerly wind had risen in the small hours before dawn, and it blustered restlessly across the hills, funnelling into Barton Tavey's small valley, where it blew with a force that tore browning leaves from the trees and bowled them like scurrying mice through the village.

Rowan could hear the wind rattling doors and windows in the house as she prepared herself for the day. Curtains flapped and the ever-present draught under the kitchen door was savage. She lit the fire, listening to the hollow booming noise the wind made in the chimney, and was relieved when only a little smoke blew back into the room.

This was real October weather – not mists and mellow fruitfulness, but gales, wild skies and high, scudding clouds. Rowan felt as though the wind were in her head today, making her restless and edgy. She wanted to be active, to find something that would release her pent-up nervous energy and put her in a calmer frame of mind. She knew that she couldn't lay all the blame for her state at the weather's door; the dream that had come to her for the second night running was largely responsible, for it had awakened in her a desperate need to resolve her own personal mystery. She felt that she had been as close as it was possible to be to the answer, yet it had escaped her by a hair's-breadth, leaving a void of frustration that screamed out to be fulfilled. Now she could concentrate on nothing for more than five minutes at a time.

She decided at last to go into the village so that the gusty air could clear her head. She went out by the front door into a wind that whipped her hair in stinging strands across her cheeks and tried to tear her shopping-bag from her hand. Leaves were racing like dervishes along the lane – a long dune of them was already building up against the garden wall – and the marigolds, their heads now gone to seed, flapped and shuddered madly under the gale's onslaught. Someone was making a valiant attempt to keep a bonfire going; she could see the blue woodsmoke rising from a hedge only to be shredded away on the wind, and the autumnal smell of it carried to her nostrils as she turned out of the gate.

Walking was like being drunk, a cautious swaying progress while the wind buffeted and pounced from all directions. Rowan staggered along the high street and ducked into the general store, thinking wryly that the more shopping she bought the better; it would weigh her down on the return journey and stop her from being whisked away. She made her purchases, and on an impulse added a large bottle of Italian wine which was on a special offer. A glass or two with her evening meal might help her to sleep better tonight.

Coming out of the shop, the wind caught her again with all the energy of a boisterous dog that didn't know its own strength. Regaining her footing, she started back towards her house. The sea would be an impressive sight on a day like this, and she considered the idea of driving to the cove she had found before, to sit watching the fury. But the day was turning decidedly cold and there were fine spindles of rain in the air. It would be warmer and more comfortable indoors, and this short walk had achieved its goal. She felt calmer, better, and more in the mood for some home comforts than for a Spartan vigil by the sea.

The gale bowled her back home, and she arrived pink-cheeked and breathless, pushing the front door shut against the onslaught. She was momentarily surprised by the comparative silence which followed. The fire in the living-room was hissing sluggishly. She built it up, then made a lunch of toast, generously spread with Agnes's jam, and sat down cross-legged on the hearthrug, savouring the comfort of the warm room.

Her relaxation, however, did not last long. Whether it was the muffled voice of the wind, which kept up an eerie, incessant moaning and shook the window-frames as if it would rattle them from their surrounds, or whether it was the memory of the dream still lodged in her mind that caused it, she did not know. But within an hour of her return she was like an uneasy cat again, unable to sit still, itching to do something, yet finding nothing that could occupy her to her own satisfaction.

In her restless pacing, she came across something that she had completely forgotten: the cardboard box which – weeks ago now, it must be – she had brought in from the front room and then had abruptly pushed away out of sight. At the time, she had been alarmed by her discovery of the old scent bottle with its familiar fragrance; now, after so much had happened, those fears had receded into the dimmest distance. She decided to pull the box out again. At least it might hold her attention for a while and stop her from brooding.

As she had done before, she dragged the box from its hiding place and manoeuvred it across to the hearthrug. The ornaments which she had hastily put back inside were still dust-free, but underneath the top layer was an unexplored treasury, filthy from long disuse. Rowan carefully set aside the pieces she had already examined – including the scent bottle, which still gave off a faint, reminiscent perfume – and began to sort carefully through the remainder.

If she had expected to unearth anything of fabulous value or even interest, it seemed that she was to be disappointed. Her grandmother had apparently put the worst examples of this little collection at the bottom of the box, perhaps wanting them as far out of sight as possible. Rowan lifted out a small and sadly ugly mock-Dresden statuette of a shepherd-boy, grimaced and put it to one side without even bothering to wipe away the accumulated dust. There was nothing here that even appealed to her, let alone –

She stopped then in mid-thought as, peering into the box, she saw what lay among the last few pieces. At a glance it might have been taken for a chunk of dark wood that someone had started to carve and then lost interest in. But it wasn't that. Rowan recognised it instantly, and for a moment, unable to believe the evidence of her own eyes, she was almost too afraid to reach into the box and pick it up. But at last, very slowly, she stretched out her hand.

The object lay in her palm, smooth and heavy and somehow warm, and as she looked at it Rowan unconsciously bit her lip until pain startled her back to reality. She knew that by all the laws of logic this was not possible, but at the same time everything within her cried out that it could not be coincidence. What she had found was a very old but beautifully-preserved animal's horn, its dark surface gleaming like satin in the firelight. And around the rim was a wide band of gold.

It was a drinking-horn – the very same drinking-horn that Duir had offered to her in her dream last night.

She gazed at the horn, her expression awed. For the moment she could think of nothing beyond the fact that she had found it, and that the find was perhaps the most significant thing that had ever happened to her in her life. As yet she could not begin to consider what it might mean, how it fitted with the strange jigsaw of events that had been taking shape around her. All that mattered was that it was here, in her hand.

She stroked a tentative finger down the horn's curving length, marvelling at its smoothness. It must be so old, and yet it had been so perfectly preserved that it might have been made only yesterday. She frowned in surprise as her tracing finger suddenly found an obstruction, and she noticed that a second and much smaller band had been fitted around the horn just short of its curling point. It was as black as the rest of the horn, and for a moment she thought it must be some natural flaw. But as she touched it, it came free and fell on to the hearth with a tiny, chiming metallic sound.

Rowan picked the small object up. It seemed to be nothing more than a black ring, perhaps lead, which seemed incongruous beside the wide band of gold circling the horn's rim. Her thumbnail scratched gingerly at it, and her eyes widened as a scrap of the dark coating flaked away, revealing the glint of gold beneath. For a moment the meaning of her discovery did not register, then Rowan drew in a sharp breath which seemed to echo in the quiet room, and scrambled to her feet.

She hunted for cleaning materials – anything that would remove the black disguise – and bent over the ring, working at the surface of it until after half an hour of painstaking work, the black-leading with which some unknown person had concealed its true nature was completely stripped away and she held in her hand a small, untarnished ring of pure gold.

She had to fight against the intuition that hammered in her mind, telling her the answer, for she could not allow herself to believe it. But when she examined the ring still more closely and saw the pattern that, centuries ago perhaps, had been engraved around its circumference, there could no longer be any doubt. Criss-crossing, interlocking together, were the carefully etched shapes of stag's antlers.

Rowan crossed the room as dazedly as a sleepwalker, the ring clasped in her tightly-clenched fist as though she dared not let go of it for a single instant. She was hardly aware that she had lifted the phone receiver and was dialling, but when a voice at the other end of the line answered, it shook her out of her trance. She opened her mouth to speak, but the words would not come.

'Hello?' The voice in her ear sounded perplexed. 'Hello? Is anyone there?'

'Mal – '

'Oh, Rowan – hey, is everything all right?'

'Yes, everything's fine,' she answered mechanically, then, 'Mal, I've found it.' There was no other way to explain, no detail she could give. 'I've found the Crown of Horn.'

16

Mal gazed at the ring that lay in his hand, seeming to wink at him as the flickering light from the fire caught it. He was aware of Rowan's close presence, hovering and anxious as if she were half-afraid to let him touch the small treasure in case it was somehow lost to her. And he felt some of the reverence that he knew she was feeling, the sense of awe and of achievement now that the mystery of the Crown of Horn had at last been solved.

In his wildest imaginings he would never have dreamed that Maud Fairfax's greatest legacy would prove to be a simple gold ring. But now, with the wisdom of hindsight, he could see that it was perhaps the most apt symbol of all for the legend of Duir and Niainn.

He gave it back to her, noting the way her fist closed quickly and protectively around it. Suddenly he felt out of his depth, and to save himself he had to say something matter-of-fact.

'You're the expert.' He spoke quietly. 'How old do you think it is?'

Rowan shook her head. 'I don't know. I only know about furniture, not jewellery. It could be fifty years old, or it could be five thousand. I just don't know.' She raised her head, looking at him. 'But I want to think it was hers, once.'

'Niainn's?'

She nodded. 'I know that she probably never even existed, but . . . '

'Oh, I wouldn't be too sure of that. You know the old saying – "There's no smoke without fire". Even if Niainn didn't exist in the way that the legend suggests, I'm sure there was once a real person who was very much like her.'

She gave him a warm, grateful smile, knowing that he felt as she felt. 'I'd like to believe that this was her wedding ring.'

'Maybe it was; or maybe it belonged to a woman who embodied her qualities in a more human form. Martha Dwyer, perhaps.'

'My ancestor, yes. And ever since then, it's been handed down from grandmother to grand-daughter, until – me.' She blinked, her eyes suddenly moist, and turned her face towards the fire so that its heat might dry the tears before they could fall. 'I wish Gran could have known that I've succeeded.'

'She probably does know.' Mal's voice was gentle, but deep within himself he was aware of an undercurrent that counselled caution. Rowan believed that her search was over, that with the finding of the ring, all the disparate pieces of the puzzle had at last come together in a complete whole. But she was wrong. The final mystery – and the most important one of all – was only just beginning.

He recalled the terrible excitement that had struck at the pit of his stomach when Rowan had told him her news over the phone. It had been the thrill of triumph, mingled with the stark realisation that now there could be no turning back. The finding of the Crown of Horn had set an obligation on him that he had no choice but to face, and as he walked from Coombe Cottage with the rumbustious wind snatching at him, he had felt the stirrings of a deep-rooted and primeval fear. He could not even guess at what was going to happen now that the ring had been discovered, but he knew that it was the focus for the final fulfilment of the ancient legend.

He looked at Rowan, watching her as she pushed a strand of hair back behind her ear with a self-conscious gesture. She was so anxious not to show weakness, to be self-possessed and independent, and suddenly Mal felt that if the barriers between them were to be broken, then the remedy must surely lie in his hands. She would not change of her own accord; she had retreated too far. Not an easy task for anyone – but it had an undeniable parallel with Duir's taming of Niainn. If the legacy were to bear its full fruit – as Mal believed it must – then he would have to win Rowan, as his legendary counterpart had done.

She saw him looking at her and frowned, a trace of mistrust in her eyes. 'You've got something on your mind,' she said abruptly, almost accusingly.

Mal smiled. 'Sort of. I was just wondering what you're going to do with the ring, now you've found it.'

'I – ' she hesitated, surprised by the question. 'I don't know. I'll keep it, of course – there's no question of that. But as to what I can *do* with it – '

'Keep it for your own grand-daughter?' Mal suggested mildly.

Rowan's expression tightened painfully. 'I don't think I'm ever likely to have a grand-daughter.'

He had got through the first of her defences; she had dropped the indifferent mask and her underlying feelings were beginning to show. Mal's sense of propriety told him to be careful, but he ignored it. Sometimes it *was* kinder, in the long run, to be blunt. He said, 'Why not?'

She drew in a sharp breath. 'I don't think that's something I want to go into. I've had one bad experience. I don't want any more, thanks very much!'

'So instead you'll go through the rest of your life alone? You'll allow yourself to end up bitter and lonely, simply because of one "bad experience", as you put it?'

Rowan flared up. 'If I do, I don't see why it should concern you!'

'Maybe not. But don't you think that that ring you're holding so tightly has some purpose, other than to be just a pretty object for you to keep in a box, Rowan?' He was treading on increasingly thin ice, but now that he had begun, he would not back down.

She stared at him, and he could tell that she was trying to stay calm and be reasonable. By the look in her eyes, it was a losing battle. Then she demanded, 'What's that supposed to mean?'

'As I see it, it's quite straightforward.' He hadn't intended to tell her about his beliefs concerning the legend, but nothing could be gained by keeping them hidden any longer. 'Rowan, has it ever occurred to you that there may be a great deal more to the legend than is apparent on the surface? Haven't you ever seen it as an allegory for something?'

'I don't know what you're getting at.' She was defensive.

'Think about your grandmother's letter to you. She said that when you found the Crown of Horn, the meaning of the legend would become clear. Well, now you've found it.' He paused, waiting for a reaction. She looked at him blankly.

'Mal, you're talking double-Dutch. I don't understand.'

Mal clasped his hands together and studied them. 'Don't you think that there might be a link between the legend and all the things that have been happening to us?'

'I – '

He interrupted before she could say any more. 'To put it quite baldly, Rowan, I think that you and I have unwittingly been re-enacting the story of Duir and Niainn, in some kind of twentieth-century parallel.'

'*What?*'

'Think about if for a minute. Duir saved Niainn from attack – that was his first task. And then I saved you, when Tully got into this house. Then he was changed into an oak tree, and the tree was struck by lightning. And just a few days ago my van was crushed when a lightning-struck oak fell on it, and if that wasn't an ordeal I'd like to know what is. Can you call that coincidence?'

Rowan didn't speak. She only continued to stare at Mal, her eyes wide with a realisation that she didn't want to acknowledge. Suddenly the strange incident of the oak leaf was clear to her, why he had behaved so oddly, and why she had felt so disturbed by it. And the dreams she had had, in which Mal and Duir had become confused: her subconscious had been trying to tell her the very same thing.

She knew it, and she fought against it with all the resources she possessed, finding her voice so suddenly that he was startled: '*No!* Mal that's crazy, impossible – I don't believe it!'

'Don't you?' His eyes met hers, and to her they were like Duir's eyes. 'Are you quite sure?'

'*Yes!* It isn't true, it can't be, because if it is, it means that, that – ' Unable to find the words she put her hands to her face in distress.

Mal leaned forward. 'The fact is, Rowan, you don't *want* to believe it, because it upsets your comfortably ordered idea of what your life's all about! But you can't go on hiding from the truth forever, even if it does hurt – you can't go on living in a shell!'

She lowered her hands, which were shaking, and looked at him with an intensity of cold, frightened anger that took him aback. Her voice was savage. 'What are you trying to do, Mal? Is this your idea of a game? Because if it is, if you're deliberately trying to goad me for some twisted reason of your own, then I'll – '

Mal's own temper got the better of him. 'A *game*? What the hell do you think I am? I'm telling you the truth, Rowan – or I'm trying to. But you're too stubborn and too self-obsessed to see it! Two of Duir's three tasks have been completed, and nothing you can say will make me believe otherwise. Now you've found the Crown of Horn, and now it's time for the third task to be finished. For God's sake, woman, are you completely *blind*?'

Rowan sprang to her feet. 'No! I'm not blind, Mal

Lyndon, but I'm not stupid either! You're trying to twist me, work me round to your way of thinking so that you can – '

'Can what? What do you think I want from you, Rowan?'

She hesitated, and when she spoke her voice was quieter, although it still carried the dangerous edge. 'I don't know. And I don't want to know.'

He rose and moved towards her. She backed away, but a table in her path stopped her progress.

'Rowan,' Mal said, 'I'm trying to get through to you. I'm trying to make you understand that we're both caught up in something that we can't run away from. The third task has to be completed. Your grandmother knew that, and she tried to tell you in her letter.' Stepping another pace forward he laid his hands on her shoulders, gripping them. 'I'm trying to tell you that I love you.'

For a few seconds there was silence. He could feel the tension in her muscles, saw her jaw tightening. And then, suddenly and violently, she flung up her arms and threw him off, twisting away from him with the strength of panic.

'You *bastard*!' She was almost screaming. 'Go away, just get out!'

Mal was astounded. He had expected nothing like this; she was on the verge of hysteria, and he felt that if she had had a knife in her hands at that moment she would have killed him.

'Rowan – '

'No! I don't want to listen to you!' Her voice dropped to a sneer. 'You start talking about *love* – what the hell do you think I am? God, I thought you had some *integrity*, but you haven't. You're just like everyone else! It doesn't matter what *my* feelings are, does it? Just so long as you get what *you* want. God, I hate you for that! But you're not going to play with my feelings, Mal, I'm not that stupid!'

Mal's suppressed fury now broke through with full force. '*Stupid?*' he echoed furiously. 'Jesus Christ, you're more stupid than I ever believed possible! You're so paranoid and so prejudiced that you can't recognise the truth when it walks up and *slaps* you! Do you honestly think that I'd waste my time *playing* with someone who behaves like a spoilt child? If you don't know sincerity when you see it, you must be pretty sick, Rowan! But all you can do is compare me with your precious Neil. Okay, you go your own sweet way, you stick in your safe little cage, but if you end up a bitter old maid, you'll only have yourself to blame. Everyone has to take chances in life, everyone has to get hurt some time, but most of us have the guts to fight back and give the wounds a chance to heal! If you want to wrap yourself in cotton-wool for the rest of your life, fine. But one of these days, you're going to run out of friends!'

The atmosphere in the room was like ice and almost physically crackling with tension. Rowan's eyes narrowed to slits, and she said hoarsely, 'Get out, Mal. Get out of my house. I don't want you here. Ever.'

'My pleasure!' He strode past her, virtually knocking her out of the way as he went. And the whole house rattled with the crash of the front door as he slammed it behind him.

With the onset of darkness, the wind began to strengthen. Rowan could hear it as she sat motionless in her chair near the fire; a deep, gusty moaning sound that grew louder and more insistent as the evening went on. Sometimes, above the moaning, came a high, thin wail, like a banshee-scream, that made her shudder where she sat. And now and again the chimney would roar like a lion as the gale funnelled across it.

The logs in the fire-basket were burning away to white ash, hissing as they crumbled, but Rowan made no effort to replenish them. She stared dully into the grate, neither seeing nor caring that the fire was almost out, her face as withdrawn and immobile as a wax image. Beside her, the large bottle of Italian wine stood half empty, and her fingers moved spasmodically on the stem of her glass. She was beginning to get drunk, but the sooner her thoughts faded into an alcoholic haze, the better as far as she was concerned.

In just a few words, Mal had destroyed everything that they had worked on together over the past weeks. He had brought back to the surface all the old pains and fears that

Rowan had thought she might escape, and had opened the wounds again until they bled. She could never forgive him for that.

Her last sight of his furious face was imprinted on her inner vision now. But what right had he to be angry? If anyone had been wronged, surely it was herself and not Mal? When he had gone, she had given way to a storm of tears that brought out all the bitter anger and frustration that had been pent up inside her. And when the storm abated and she was dry-eyed again, she had launched into a silent tirade of grievances in which Mal was the central culprit.

Part of her knew that it was wrong to blame him for all her unhappiness, but his words had mocked her, and he should have had the sensitivity to realise that. She wasn't like other women – she couldn't be persuaded by warm smiles and warm words and apparent sincerity. She had fallen into that trap once before, with Neil, and it would not happen again. And if Mal thought he could win her, he was mistaken. She was not such an easy target as that.

And yet, deep down inside a small, secret part of herself, she knew that the break with him had hit her hard. Small incidents came back into her memory: his excitement over the writing-desk, the hours they had spent poring together over the parish records, the day of the village fête . . . Yes, they were the things that hurt, and she could not push them conveniently aside and forget them.

She listened to the wind, and its voice reflected her feelings. Cold, isolated, lonely. And so tense that she felt at breaking point. The wine was not relaxing her at all; it was only making her light-headed and slightly queasy. Nonetheless she picked up her glass again and drained it, feeling that the solace of getting drunk was better than nothing. And that was her alternative. *Nothing*.

She almost wished that she had the courage to phone Mal. Not that she wanted to apologise, just to phone him. But if she did, she would not know what to say, and then she might say something she didn't mean, and they would argue again, and . . . She sighed, putting the glass down once more. What was the point of even thinking about it?

He was out of her life now, and that was probably the best thing for both of them. She wanted to trust him; she had known that, even as she screamed at him to get out, but it wasn't possible. She couldn't let herself believe that in the end he wouldn't turn out like Neil, and rejection was safer, easier.

Rowan refilled her glass again, and as she did so saw the small, shining object that lay on the table beside the bottle. There was the real perpetrator of it all: the ancient gold ring around which all the mystery of the last weeks had revolved. She wondered what her grandmother would have said, had she known what would result from its discovery.

Idly she picked the ring up and twisted it in her fingers. The dying glow from the fire made it glint and sparkle – there was no other illumination in the room – and she could only just make out the pattern of crossed antlers engraved on the ring's surface. It would have been a wedding ring, originally. Perhaps her grandmother had worn it when she married Geoffrey Fairfax, although Rowan couldn't remember having seen it on her finger.

Toying with it, she tried it on. It was a little large, but it slipped over the third finger of her left hand and it felt comfortable, as though it were back in its familiar setting after a long absence. She felt tears start in her eyes as she looked at her own hand, outstretched in the firelight, but didn't understand why it was that she wanted to cry. Whatever good luck the Crown of Horn might have brought to her ancestors, it seemed that the pattern was not to hold true for herself.

Suddenly railing against something she couldn't define – fate, chance, luck or her own misery – she made to pull the ring off, but before she could twist it over her knuckle something made her pause. For a moment she was still, then she turned her head towards the window, alert and listening.

The wind howled dismally from the hills, but its voice had been joined by others, far away, almost at the very edge of perception. But she knew after a few seconds that it was not her imagination. Somewhere on the distant moors, the hounds were baying again.

The room wavered before her eyes, whether from the effect of the wine of from something less identifiable she didn't know. The high shriek of the gale vibrated through the house and brought the belling, baying sounds closer. Rowan felt as though an invisible web were closing around her, drawing her into its entangling grasp, so that she was no longer her own mistress. The howling dogs called to her and she felt compelled to answer that call. She could not stay where she was – she had to follow the eldritch summons of the hound-pack.

She rose without realising it, knocking over the glass and spilling wine in a spreading stain across the carpet. The faraway cries, carried on the wind, swelled inside her head until she thought her mind would burst with their urgency, and she turned, stumbling across the dark room towards the door. Her vision blurred, but it wasn't the wine – it was the desperate need to get outside, to listen, to hear, to follow.

She ran into the hall, pulled open the front door and, wild-eyed, stared out into the gale-swept darkness, looking not to the village, but to the towering silhouettes of the hills that rose against the cloudy sky. Cold air filled her throat and her nostrils; she breathed it in with a gasp, every sense straining for some sight, some sound that would tell her what to do and where to go, how to answer the summons that tore at her mind.

For a few moments there was nothing but the hooting laughter of the wind, but then, when she felt she could have screamed aloud, Rowan heard them again – the hounds, baying, demanding, calling. Something surged up within her and she ran down the path to the gate, not caring that she wore only slippers and the thinnest of clothes. In a reflex action she had snatched her car key from its place on the mantel, but beyond that she had made no preparations, taken no care. She knew where she must go, and that was all that mattered to her.

She was almost sobbing with frantic impatience as she started the car engine, then stamped down on the accelerator and drove westwards.

At the empty house, the front door gaped open like a

shocked mouth, and in the living-room the last embers of the fire were dying slowly away to nothing.

It was the right place. Rowan knew it even before the Mini screeched to a halt at the point where the farm track met the narrow road. She had driven there by pure instinct, unaware of where she was going until she reached her destination, and unaware of how she had arrived there. She had a vague memory of the car's lights cutting through blackness, showing the stark shapes of trees leaning against the gale, of fighting with the steering-wheel as the howling wind cut like a tornado across the high, open stretches of the road. But beyond that she had been conscious only of the sounds that still echoed in her head: the insistent call of the pack. And now she was here.

She cut the engine and stepped out of the car into the teeth of the gale. Her hair streamed straight out behind her, mimicking the racing clouds high overhead. Black holes gaped in the sky, showing a chilly scatter of stars, and the waxing moon spilled its light like a flashing heliograph as the clouds tore across its face. Rowan swayed, finding her balance against the wind's onslaught. She felt drunk, but it was nothing to do with the alcohol. This was a wild, elemental kind of drunkenness, a drunkenness of the spirit and not the body.

Running, she plunged along the track and into the woods, her way lit by the intermittent moon, and now the sound in her ears was of leaves hissing and clashing as their branches tossed. Leaves were falling, torn from their moorings and fluttering like mad moths against her face as she ran. She struck at them with unco-ordinated hands, wanting only to reach her goal, her fate.

She came out of the belt of trees, tripped as her foot wedged in a rut, and fell forward on to ridged earth. Gasping, she struggled to her knees and raised her head, looking out from the woodland's edge at the expanse of the field before her.

Just for a few seconds the sky cleared and the full power of the moon shone down on the scene. The field was a black waste, the woodland that bordered it no more than a turbulent, chaotic silhouette. But there, in the very centre of that emptiness, the great dead oak tree rose like a gigantic, twisted hand, its whole form turned to stark silver by the icy moonlight, its high branches bending and straining in the gale.

Rowan stayed motionless, like some awed pagan worshipper from another time. Every sense within her was alive and crackling with intensity, each sound and sight and sensation magnified tenfold. A feeling of tremendous power was building up in her head, a knowledge that *something* must come.

Clouds roiled across the moon, and the landscape was plunged into darkness. Suddenly unable to see, Rowan could only listen as the keening voice of the wind brought with it other sounds – the eerily distant boom of the sea and the thin wailing of the gale in the upper air. But now there was no far-off howling of the hounds. Wherever they were – whatever they were – they had fallen silent.

They were waiting. With an illogical, dreamlike certainty Rowan knew it. Slowly she rose to her feet, not pausing to brush earth and crushed grass from her body, and forged forward into the screaming wind. She moved unsteadily at first, like a child taking its first faltering steps, and then her confidence grew stronger and she began to run, slipping and stumbling towards the gaunt oak that drew closer, a nightmare hand reaching out towards her –

And then, as she came within range of the tree's moonshadow, she saw him.

Just for a moment, the gale seemed to cease altogether, and the field was utterly silent but for the far-off growl of the sea. He was there beneath the blasted oak, the Duir of the legend, not a true man but something beyond that, his hair the red of autumn leaves, his face an unnerving blend of the animal and the human, and the great antlers that rose from his brow shimmering under the stars.

Time slowed down for Rowan, and she might have stood where she was for an hour, gazing, hypnotised, at the motionless figure before her. She hadn't felt afraid before, but now her nerves began to crawl with the first sensations of approaching terror. For a brief moment her disorientated mind righted itself, so that she was suddenly shocked by where she was, what she had done, what was happening. But then the web enmeshed her again and she was held in the spell that had summoned her.

And it was at that moment that the hounds began to give tongue.

They were in the woods that bordered the field on the Eastern side, an entire pack of them, baying and belling, their voices echoing eerily from the trees. And they were coming closer.

She heard her own breath rasp in her throat, and then the figure of Duir raised its hand in a sharp, commanding gesture as though giving a signal.

Suddenly freed from the thrall that had held her, Rowan turned her head. And by the flashing moonlight she saw the black wave of small, racing bodies that erupted from the woodland, spreading out like flood-water and rushing towards her. Their yelping cries swelled in pitch and volume as they came hurtling on, and above them, mingled with the shriek of the gale, rang Duir's high, wild laughter.

The Hunt! In one hideous instant, realisation slammed into Rowan's mind. Reality or a terrible illusion, it made no difference – the Wild Hunt was in full cry, and she was its quarry!

Her senses exploded into chaos as she spun round. The huge oak seemed to fall out of the sky at her, branches clawing, and as the moon rode out from the clouds again, lighting the field with cold brilliance, she ran. Buffeted by the gale, stumbling across the rutted field, she knew instinctively that she had to reach the trees before the pack caught up with her. She had to escape, had to find safety.

At her back the voices of the hounds howled their challenge, and over them sounded the wailing note of a hunting-horn and a sudden thundering, pounding beat of a gigantic horse galloping in their midst. Rowan plunged on, the line of the forest ahead swaying crazily as she raced towards it, until the trees were around her, engulfing her in darkness. The horn wailed again. She stumbled and fell, brambles tearing at her legs and ripping her skirt, then was up again and fighting through branches that clutched and snatched. It was a dream, a nightmare, not real, and she cried out, pleading to awake and find herself in her bed at home. But there was no awakening.

Now she could hear the dogs crashing through the undergrowth, and the thumping of vast hooves, and when in a frantic moment she turned her head and looked back, her eyes caught a glimpse of the inhuman Hunt-Master, mounted on a monstrous horse with blazing eyes, pursuing her through the woodland.

Sobbing in terror, Rowan ran still faster, until the ground beneath her feet pitched downwards in a steep slope. Wildly she grabbed at branches to stop herself from falling, but she lost her footing, and suddenly the trees and the sky whirled and twisted as she pitched down the treacherous incline in a chaotic shower of stones and loose earth.

She landed at the foot of the slope, winded and bruised but otherwise unhurt. As she raised her head, she realised that a strange quiet had fallen, broken only by the muted sound of the wind that could not reach down into this sheltered valley. She stayed still for some seconds, listening, but there was no baying, no pounding of hooves. Very slowly and cautiously she climbed to her feet, her battered senses beginning to creep back towards some semblance of sanity.

And then, with a suddenness that shocked her into panic, a tremendous howling split the air, and the entire hound-pack came spilling over the lip of the incline and bore down on her, even as she screamed aloud with horror, like a mad black torrent.

17

Long before he arrived at Rowan's house, Mal knew that something was wrong. In fact it was partly intuition that had made him overcome his diffidence and go to the house.

He wanted to apologise – that had been his main reason. In all honesty he felt he had been less to blame for the bitter argument than Rowan, but he knew that her fear and pride would not allow her to speak first, even if she wanted to.

The nearer he drew to his destination, the more ill at ease he felt. He couldn't begin to analyse the feeling that gnawed at the most vital part of his mind; but there was something afoot, something in the air, and he didn't like it. He was afraid for Rowan, afraid that she was in danger.

The moaning of the wind disturbed him as he made his way along the dark lane towards the house. It sounded primeval and threatening, bringing home sharply his sense of vulnerability and increasing his unease. Shivering, he hurried on, until he came in sight of the house itself.

It was unlit, a dark, humped silhouette, and when he reached the gate Mal saw that the front door stood wide open.

Alarmed, he ran up the path and ducked into the hall, calling out, '*Rowan? Rowan, are you there?*'

No one answered him. Fumbling, he found the light switch, and as the hall flooded with brilliance he checked his watch. Just after twelve. It was possible that she had gone to bed, but surely, no matter what her state of mind, she wouldn't have left the door open? A sudden thought occurred to him, and he turned to peer back into the windswept night. Her car was not in its usual place, and Mal's heart began to beat more quickly. Where on earth could she have gone, at this hour? Certainly she hadn't taken it into her head to visit *him*; not a single car had passed him on the road.

He stepped into the house, closing the door behind him. Dead leaves had blown in, littering the floor; they crunched dryly under his feet as he approached the stairs and looked up.

'*Rowan?*'

Nothing. Mal went into the living-room, turned on the overhead light and looked slowly around. The fire was out, and Rowan's handbag was on the floor beside an armchair. Then he noticed the half-empty wine bottle and the fallen glass which lay in the centre of a dark stain.

Wherever she had gone, she had left suddenly and on impulse, and Mal's disquiet turned into something more alarming. Remembering the Crown of Horn, he searched for it, but it was not to be found. That was significant, although he could not explain why.

Taking a grip on his fears, Mal decided that the only thing to do was to check the house thoroughly to make quite certain that Rowan was not in fact asleep somewhere. But even before his eyes confirmed it, he knew that he would not find her. There was a silence to the house's atmosphere that told him it was empty.

At last he opened the front door again. And there, on the threshold, he stopped.

The gale was still howling, but above the noise of it he could hear another sound – something he had never encountered before, and which made his skin crawl with an icy, horrified disbelief. Carried from the hills, and echoing eerily on the wind, it was the baying of a pack of hounds in full cry.

Mal's eyes widened as he listened to the weird, faraway sound, and he remembered the story Rowan had told him about the dogs howling in the dead of night.

Suddenly he knew where she had gone, and why. And he knew, too, that he had to find her, before – He couldn't stop to think any further, but ran, turning back towards the village and racing against the gale with all the speed he could muster. There *had* to be some way to get to her!

It was pure instinct that made him turn towards the petrol station in the village centre, but when he saw the light under the workshop door behind the pumps, Mal's head swam with relief. He hammered on the locked door, and a few seconds later the surprised face of Bill Warden, the garage owner, looked out at him.

'Mal – what's up?' Bill stood back to let him into the workshop, where he had been tinkering with an old Riley.

Mal got his breath back. The enclosed cosiness of the shop, warmed by a paraffin heater, was an unsettling contrast to the turbulent world outside. This was where Bill spent a good deal of his time, working all hours into the night simply for the love of it. Tonight, Bill's odd hours were more of a blessing than he could ever know.

'I'm sorry to crash in on you like this,' he said, when the air was back in his lungs. 'But I've got an emergency on my hands. I need transport.'

Bill wiped oily hands on his overalls. His eyes were curious, but he realised that this was no time to ask unnecessary questions. 'What sort of transport?' he asked.

'Anything, so long as it can keep going for five miles.'

'No problem. You can take my MG, provided I get it back in one piece. Are you insured?'

'What?' Mal's face fell. 'Christ, no, I'm not.'

Bill looked shrewdly at him. 'This really is something important, isn't it?'

'Vitally. I haven't got time to explain now, but – '

'Forget it. You can tell me the whole story later. Look, where have you got to get to, did you say?'

'A place about five miles from here, out towards Countisbury.'

'Okay. Give me half a minute to lock this place up, and I'll drive you.'

Mal didn't waste time arguing politely. He said simply, 'Thanks – I can't tell you how much I appreciate it.'

'What the hell. I could do with a break, anyway. Here, take the keys. It's parked on the other side of the forecourt, and if you can get it warmed up I'll be with you in a sec.'

Mal ran over to the small sports car and unlocked it. By the time Bill hurried across to join him the engine was ticking over throatily. As Bill slid into the driver's seat and slipped the car into gear, he said suddenly, 'Bill, have you heard anything odd tonight?'

'Odd?' Bill looked over his shoulder, reversing. 'No. Like what? You did say the Countisbury road, didn't you?'

'Yes. I mean like dogs – a pack of them, baying.'

The MG glided out on to the road and Bill accelerated hard, without any regard for the speed limit. As they snarled into a bend, he said, 'Dogs? No, I didn't hear 'em. Why?'

'It doesn't matter.' Mal stared ahead through the small

windscreen, watching trees and hedgerows flashing by in the sweep of the headlights. Bill shrugged, but didn't push him for any more information, for which Mal was thankful. How could he have explained what he had heard, to someone for whom the whole idea of the ghostly hounds would have appeared ludicrous? It was possible that Bill had been too engrossed in his work to have been disturbed by the noise, but Mal felt in his bones that their cries had been for his ears alone.

Bill drove fast and accurately, taking blind bends like a rally driver, and in a good deal less than ten minutes Mal saw the belt of trees that marked the location he wanted.

He said, 'This is it.'

The MG slowed down, and as it came to a halt the lights suddenly showed another car, a Mini, parked by the side of the road. The driver's door was open, but there was no one in sight, and Mal drew in his breath sharply as he recognised the registration number.

Bill cut the engine. 'What now?'

'I – I'm not quite sure, but I've got to meet someone here, and that's their car.' Mal improvised, desperately hoping that Bill wouldn't start asking questions at this stage.

Bill, however, only shrugged again and said, 'Well, I don't mind hanging on, if it's any help.'

'No thanks. I'll be okay from here on. I'll get a lift back.'

'Okay, if you're sure.' As Mal climbed out, Bill grinned at him. 'But I'll want to hear the full story over a drink!'

'That's a promise! Thanks again, Bill – I'm really grateful.'

The MG turned and pulled away with a burst of wheelspin. The noise of its engine faded and mingled with the moan of the wind as Mal faced the gale and went towards the field that lay beyond the trees. Somewhere, in this wild wind and darkness, was Rowan. He had to find her, somehow, however impossible it might seem.

The trees hissed like snakes, and the wind screamed, its force unchecked as it rushed in from the sea. Mal felt as though the gale were in his very nerves, attuning them to their highest pitch.

He couldn't begin to guess at where or how it would end,

but he knew that all the threads of the pattern were at last drawing together.

As if to lend weight to that thought, the distant voices of the hounds came echoing to his ears. For a moment he stood still, leaning into the wind as he tried to judge where that unearthly sound came from. Then he darted into the belt of trees and ran swiftly, urgently, along the track that led towards the field.

Rowan felt as though her heart were about to burst shatteringly from her ribs, sending her into eternal blackness. She couldn't tell how long she had been running, but it seemed to her an eternity. She fought her way through clawing branches that impeded every step, tearing her legs on the snatching coils of brambles, and plunged into the hideous dark of the forest, while behind her the hounds of the Wild Hunt gave their howling cries, and the pounding hooves of the great horse thundered in her ears. Her senses were aflame and she no longer knew the difference between what was real and what was a terrible illusion. Shapes and shadows that leapt at her might have been trees or demons, and over it all rang the high, wild laughter of the Hunt's supernatural Master.

She too cried out as she ran, screaming sounds that were no longer words, the chaos of panic erupting through her mind. Her brain was in the throes of a mad nightmare, in the midst of an elemental world that offered her no sanctuary, and as she raced on her tortured consciousness became a part of that world until she could not tell whether she still existed in her own time, or whether she had been pitched headlong into another, older aeon.

Sometimes it seemed that she was herself, running upright, stumbling, falling, struggling to her feet and running again. And sometimes it seemed that, like Duir, she was no longer human, but had taken the form of a white hind that bounded through bracken and bramble and forest in a desperate bid to outrun the pursuers who would bring her down and tear her apart.

When she came to the stream, she could not even see it until the moment when her feet splashed into icy water and she fell to her knees. The shock brought back her senses momentarily, and, shuddering, she looked up through her matted hair.

As she did so, every sound that rang and dinned in her head ceased with a suddenness that was violent. There were no yelping hounds, no thundering horse, no screaming fury of the gale, no wild laughter. Only an intense and shocking silence, and a stillness so profound that time itself might have stopped.

Rowan's vision of the scene swam and wavered, then, gradually, started to right itself. She had broken out of the trees into a narrow valley, a gorge that snaked between two towering hills. There was a bridge, a small stone bridge, spanning the stream just a few yards away, and beyond it a rough track, deserted under the light of the moon. Stars spangled overhead and the ragged clouds were gone. She could hear sounds again, tiny, ordinary sounds – the chuckle of the water that flowed cheerfully around her as she knelt on the stream-bed, the secretive little whisperings of leaves disturbed by the wind that was no more than the gentlest of night-breezes. Nothing more. No Hunt, no hounds.

Rowan drew in a breath, and it rattled in her raw, wind-burned throat. The water was freezing her hands and feet, and when she tried to stand she found she couldn't, the strength was no longer in her. By agonisingly slow and painful degrees she twisted her body around until she was sitting in two inches of water, and, on all fours, she began to crawl towards the bank.

'*Rowan . . .*'

The voice came out of the dimness so unexpectedly that she cried out and flinched. And then, as she looked towards the stone bridge, every nerve in her body crawled with horror.

Duir stood upon the bridge. In the weird light he looked like a ghost, all colour drained from him by the moon. Rowan heard a sobbing gasp, but did not realise that it had come from her own lips, and she could only stare at him, incapable of moving.

He took a step forward, and then he was running towards

her, splashing into the stream, arms outstretched as if to snatch her and carry her away. Rowan's control snapped like an overtaut wire, and she screamed, flailing out with her hands as he reached her, as she felt his heat and his strength overtake her. She beat at him with her fists, struggling desperately, but the last of her strength was gone, and she was lifted upwards, to meet a wave of blackness that rushed at her out of the sky and plunged her into unconsciousness.

The Mini stood forlornly by the side of the road, and to Mal it was the most welcome sight he had ever seen. Breathing heavily, he struggled across to it with his burden and gently eased Rowan's unconscious form on to the passenger seat. She slumped against the door, water dripping from her clothes to the floor, and Mal climbed in beside her.

He thought that perhaps he would never know why she had reacted as she did when he found her. The shock of coming upon her so unexpectedly, sprawling in a stream at the edge of the forest, had been eclipsed only by the second shock – the sudden inexplicable silence that had fallen at that same moment. And, now that the world had returned to some semblance of sanity and reaction was setting in, the events of the past hour were beginning to blur into an incredible dream in his mind.

It *had* been like a dream, or, more accurately, a nightmare. An instinct that he could not give any name to had driven him on once he reached the field, compelling his footsteps in a direction that took him into the deep, dense forest between the moorland and the sea. Had he stopped to think for one moment he would have known that his chances of finding Rowan were remote, but instead he had run, searching the black, crowded woodland, certain that the sixth sense which had brought him here would also lead him to her. He had known, as he went, that he was moving in a wide circle that would eventually bring him back to the place where he had started, but still he had followed his intuition. And all the time he could hear the hounds – sometimes far away in the distance, sometimes so close that he thought he must at any moment come face to face with them – and, as their howling cries sounded around him, he had never been able to tell if what he heard was real, or if they existed only in his fevered mind.

And then he had found her, and the racket of the wind and the baying dogs had ceased as though they had never been, as though, with their use outlived, they had simply flickered out of existence, leaving only the quiet empty night.

What Rowan's eyes had seen when she first looked at him, Mal could not judge, although he had his suspicions. But when she collapsed in his arms as he pulled her from the icy water, he had known that – for both of them – the quest was over. Whatever nameless force had moved them like pieces on a chessboard was satisfied, and the game was complete.

Or almost complete. Mal glanced at Rowan's still figure. Her left hand was draped across her lap, and on the third finger he saw, as he had expected, the glint of gold. Could that one small ring have triggered off such a sequence of incredible events? He sighed, aware that that was a question to which he would never have a certain answer. Then he started the Mini's engine and, as the lights sprang on and sliced brilliantly through the darkness, he turned the car around and drove away from the field and the trees and the empty forest.

The fire in the living-room burned brightly, sending shadows dancing across the walls and warming Rowan's face and hands as she sat before it swathed in the folds of a blanket. In the kitchen, Mal was making tea. She could hear the hiss of the kettle, the rattle of cups as he moved about. Homely sounds.

She raised her head and gazed around the room, taking it in as though seeing it for the first time. It was so calm now, so quiet, as though the house itself were at peace. She thought of all those who had lived here before her, those ancestors who had taken their place among the Exmoor hills and who had found their final rest there. And something stirred in her, a feeling that she was reaching out, from her own time and her own life, to join hands with those people of the past, forming another link in the chain that had run unbroken through the centuries. She had come to Exmoor a stranger and an outsider, living in their world but not truly a part of it. Now it was as though this place – not simply the house, but the moorland itself– had taken her into its protecting embrace, welcomed her and made her one with itself. Its very essence was in her soul; she had truly come home.

Rowan turned as Mal came in, and the small moment of the spell was broken. He set down the tray he carried and stirred up the fire, sending a scatter of sparks darting up the chimney like fireflies.

They sat together, watching the moving pattern of the flames. At last Rowan broke the quiet.

'I thought you were Duir,' she said. 'I really thought – '

'I know.'

'And then when I came round in the car, and realised . . .' Her head turned, and she smiled gently. 'I still don't know what to say, Mal. It was all like a dream, and I don't know if it really happened at all. Do you think it did?'

'How can I answer?' He reached out to take her hand and squeeze it, and, for the first time, she made no attempt to draw away. 'Maybe it's best if we tell ourselves it was a dream. And now we've both woken from it.'

He felt her fingers give his hand an answering squeeze, and it warmed him as no fire could have done.

'Things have changed, haven't they?' he asked gently.

Rowan paused. Just for a moment she thought of Neil, but it was like thinking of a stranger, someone she had met only briefly and who had never truly touched her life.

'Yes,' she said, 'they've changed now.'

He touched her face, turning her head until she was looking fully at him. There was a trace of uncertainty in her eyes, but when she smiled it vanished. And when he leaned forward to kiss her, she met his lips with gentle acquiescence, her eyes closing as she laid her hands first on his shoulders, tentatively, then on his back, her arms closing around him.

Deep down inside her a flame came to life that she had thought she would never feel again, but this time it was a real flame, a true emotion. And she knew that, as it had done for Maud Fairfax, as it had done for all those other grand-daughters of the past, it would burn strongly and steadily, with nothing to quench it.

Yes, she had come home.

When they drew apart, she withdrew her hands and laid them on his, looking down at them. On her finger the Crown of Horn still gleamed, and she laughed softly.

'I wonder if Gran knows . . . ?'

'She does, I'm sure of it. I think she'll be glad that the third task had been completed.'

'Yes, I think she will, too.' And Duir and Niainn would share that feeling, Rowan thought. Human or legendary, reality or illusion, they would be glad. She turned her hand so that the ring glittered in the firelight, then she began slowly to slip it off. 'I'll put it somewhere for safe keeping.'

'No.' Mal's fingers closed over hers, preventing her. 'No. Leave it there. It's in its rightful place now. And that's where it's going to stay.'

There was no need for words. Her head rested on his shoulder, and his hand stroked her hair as they gazed into the flickering fire. A warm peacefulness, perhaps tinged with the faintest fragrance of roses, settled on the quiet room.